PRAISE FOR STINA LINDENBLATT

My Song For You

"Romantic angst powers this fast-paced novel, and readers will return to the series to learn more about the enigmatic side characters whose own stories are waiting to be told."
—*Publishers Weekly*

"The author has an amazing and deep connection with her characters.... I loved every single page."—*Extreme Damage Blog*

"From the first to the last page—greatness unfolded."—*Ellie Is Uhm ... A Bookworm*

"Filled with romance, misunderstandings, lies and a whole lot of heat ... [*My Song for You*] has everything to satisfy the romance itch in all of us."—*Twin Spin*

"Six stars—Stina Lindenblatt has a skill to write heroes with some depth like few can."—*Collectors of Book Boyfriends & Girlfriends*

"This is a sweet contemporary romance that will pull at your heart and bring tears to your eyes. But inevitably it will make you smile!"—*TBQ's Book Palace*

"Oooh, a secret baby story with a twist . . . and I liked that twist. I also really liked that this was somewhat of a friends-to-lovers story. . . A really good, entertaining read and I enjoyed it a lot. I'd definitely recommend it."—*Smitten with Reading*

This One Moment

"A well-written story that kept me entertained from start to finish."—*Harlequin Junkie*

"I loved this book; this is romance at its best, this is that perfect ending we all read romance for, this is an absolutely beautifully told love story."—*Guilty Pleasures Book Reviews*

"Very satisfying . . . Stina Lindenblatt is a new author to me and a very good one I may add. . . . I will sure keep an eye on her in the future. She is really worth it!"—*Collector of Book Boyfriends & Girlfriends*

"The story is amazing and the suspense is thrilling."—*Just One More Chapter*

"Filled with emotion, intensity, a lot of sexual tension and the perfect amount of heat."—*About That Story*

I Need You Tonight

"Ms. Lindenblatt has penned another remarkable read for this series. . . . Full of exquisite heat and passion, and the ending brought happy tears to my eyes. . . . I would highly recommend *I Need You Tonight*."—*Book Magic*

"*I Need You Tonight* is one of those books that you go into thinking one thing and end up getting your mind blown because you were not expecting the emotion that this made you feel. Honestly, this had to have been the best book of the series because of that."—*Life of a Crazy Mom*

"[Stina Lindenblatt's] writing shows superb talent and care for both the storyline and her characters. This is not a book you want to pass the chance at reading."—*Ellie Is Uhm . . . A Bookworm*

"There are so many, many things that I loved about this story. . . . I hadn't realized I'd been missing and I was craving the Pushing Limits boys until this one came along. And it came with a bang!"—*Collectors of Book Boyfriends & Girlfriends*

ALSO BY STINA LINDENBLATT

Contemporary Romances

Pushing Limits Series

This One Moment

I Need You Tonight

Carson Brothers Series

One More Chance

One More Secret

One More Betrayal

Lost in You Series

Tell Me When

Let Me Know

Romantic Comedy Novels

By The Bay Series

Decidedly Off Limits

Decidedly with Baby

Decidedly with Love

Decidedly with Mistletoe

Decidedly by Chance

Decidedly with Luck

Decidedly with Wishes

Visit stinalindenblattauthor.com for more books

MY SONG FOR YOU

STINA LINDENBLATT

*To the songwriters and musicians
who create lyrics and melodies
that help us through our heartbreaks
and bring happiness to our lives.*

MY SONG FOR YOU

1

JARED

Loneliness was a bitch. True, that wasn't the most convincing statement to say when surrounded by a group of screaming girls in a sports bar, eager to touch any part of your body they could get their hands on. And try telling that to a horny twentysomething guy. This place was a smorgasbord of groupies interested in a quick lay.

Not that I was complaining.

So far I loved what I did for a living. I loved the fans, and I loved hanging out with the guys in the band, even during our last grueling tour. But that didn't stop the nagging feeling that despite the music, the fans, and the band, despite how hard we had worked and how much we had sacrificed to get this far, something was missing.

But hell if I knew what it was.

"Oh my God," the girl in a super-tight white tank top shrieked, jumping up and down on the polished floor. Her huge tits bounced like overinflated beach balls. "I can't believe it's you. You're like my favorite guitarist of all time."

I flashed her the smile that always left girls sighing. Mason, the drummer for Pushing Limits, claimed the smile guaranteed

I'd get laid. I wasn't so sure about that. "Well, thanks. You just made my day." I had already used the same tired line five times in the past fifteen minutes. But as long as the girls at the radio-station-sponsored event didn't compare notes, they'd be fine.

Flipping my lucky guitar pick between my fingers and across the back of my hand, I glanced at Nolan with his mob of fans. His girlfriend, Hailey, was standing to the side, talking to Kirk's sister. Neither of them paid attention to the eager fans pawing at the individual members of the band. It wasn't like the two women hadn't seen it before. Although I had to admit I was impressed at how Hailey took it all in stride. Not all girlfriends were like that.

A kiss on my cheek dragged me back to my own group of screaming fans. The girl with beach-ball tits grinned at the smartphone in her hand. Had she just taken a fucking selfie of her kissing me?

"Okay, everyone," Rebecca, one of the radio personalities, said through the speakers. It was early afternoon and the brightly lit sports bar had been rented for the event, which meant the TVs weren't on, much to Kirk's annoyance. I chuckled. His occasional glares aimed at the TVs meant one thing: he was missing out on a hockey game featuring his favorite team, the L.A. Kings.

"May the games begin," Rebecca continued once she had everyone's attention. "And ladies, no mauling our special guests. You wouldn't want to scare them off, right?"

"Boo!" Mason's loud voice exploded through the stale, beer-scented air. His lazy grin, bright against his brown skin, was visible above his groupies' heads. He wasn't the only one disappointed at her suggestion. The girls crowded around him would've been more than happy to continue groping the bulky drummer—and the feeling was mutual when it came to Mas. I wouldn't have been surprised if he already had some of their phone numbers.

"Is everyone still in their assigned group?" Michael, the other radio personality, asked. His question was met with a chorus of yeses, shrieks, and hollers. "The first event is the beanbag toss. The winning team is the one with the most bags in their bucket at the end of three minutes." He and Rebecca had us line up behind the throw line in the middle of the room. In total, fifty participants, with the girls easily outnumbering the guys, had won the chance to join us today.

The two radio interns herded Nolan, Mason, Kirk, Aaron, and me to the front of our respective lines and handed us each our first beanbag. I returned my guitar pick to my back jeans pocket. And the game commenced.

Cheers and groans filled the air as each person at the throw line quickly tossed their beanbag into their team's bucket. I might have not been brilliant when it came to basketball, but I could hold my own. The beanbag landed smartly in the white bucket. I moved to the back of the line.

The next person, a brunette in a tight black dress and stilettos, hurled her beanbag at the bucket as if the damn thing was burning her hand. She missed our bucket and almost scored a point for Aaron's team.

Before I knew it, all nine girls and the one guy in my group had finished their turns, and I was up again. Like last time, I nailed the bucket, but it wasn't enough. A quick glance at the guys' buckets warned me my team wasn't doing too hot.

A hand from behind me squeezed my ass. "My turn," the I-want-to-fuck-you-all-night-long brunette said.

I gave her both a brief nod and the grin that was reserved for groupies—the one that said any other time, I might've been interested—and walked to the end of the line again. The empty feeling trailed alongside, and I glanced at Nolan and Hailey. Both were lost in their own little world, despite the fans screaming and cheering around them. They smiled softly at each other in the way I was all too familiar with after being their roommate for a short time, ever since Hailey moved to L.A. to be with Nolan. Usually the look meant he was about to become one very happy guy—as my thin apartment walls could attest to.

The ass-grabber joined me, and her gaze tore the jeans and T-shirt off my body. She leaned in, her breath against my ear. "I'd be all for you playing me like a guitar afterward."

I barked a laugh. And here I thought guys were the real winners when it came to lame pickup lines. "Thanks, but . . . but I have somewhere to be after this."

She flashed me a pout. "Maybe afterward?"

"Maybe some other time."

She brightened, failing to see the lie for what it was, and slipped her fingers in my pocket. I had no idea if she was giving me her phone number, but she took the moment to cop a feel. And from the way she smiled at me, she liked what she felt.

I stepped back and grabbed a beanbag from the bucket at the front of our line. But as I tossed it at the intended target, the brunette brushed her hand against my ass, again, and the bag missed its mark by a foot.

The loud blast of a whistle ended the game. I didn't need to count the number of beanbags to know we'd lost. Not that I really cared.

"We won!" Mas hooted.

"Wait till they've counted them, dumbass," Kirk said next to him. He gave the drummer a brief glance before returning his attention to Rebecca, who was counting the beanbags. A former hockey player, our bassist was as competitive as they came.

"I don't need to wait, douchebag. My group is just that awesome." Mason unleashed his grin on them again, and I swore some of his fans came in their panties, if their glazed expressions were any indication.

"Maybe so, but up against my athletic prowess," Kirk said, "you're toast."

Mason smirked. "Bring it on, puck boy."

Rebecca jotted on her clipboard, then counted the beanbags in Aaron's bucket.

"Do you have a girlfriend, Jared?" asked a girl who could best be described as jailbait. The rest of my team waited for the answer with bated breath.

I shook my head. "Not right now."

"So you aren't dating Tiffany Grainger anymore?" the girl with giant tits asked.

"No. We're just friends." I almost snorted at the "friends" part. I didn't think we had ever been friends. Just on-again, off-again whatevers.

"That's too bad. You guys were perfect together."

I shrugged. "With our work schedules as they are, it was too difficult to spend time together."

The only other guy in my group chuckled. "Must be a tough life, dating a supermodel."

He didn't realize how right he was, even if he had meant it another way.

"And the winner of the beanbag toss is . . ." Michael paused for dramatic effect. "Kirk Helmson's team."

Kirk's group cheered, the girls jumping up and down like hyped-up cheerleaders. One actually did do a cartwheel, but her technique was far from impressive.

"I demand a recount," Mason yelled. His fans giggled. The rest of us laughed.

"Man up, Mas," Kirk replied. "My team won and you know it."

Mason folded his arms, chin raised. "You just watch. My team will destroy yours in the next game." Mock defiance gleamed in his eyes.

"Bring it on, drummer boy."

Welcome to what it had been like touring with them for the past year. They were always trying to outdo each other in whatever competition they had going. The rest of us had long since learned to ignore them . . . and maybe place the occasional side bet.

"Good to know nothing has changed between those two," Nolan said to me as we waited for the next game to be set up. "I'd hate to lose our entertainment for the next tour."

"You mean you'd hate to lose out on winning more money from me." He and Aaron, our keyboardist, beat me hands down when it came to our little side bets. The little side bets that neither Mason nor Kirk knew about.

"Damn straight."

"So, Hailey," I said, "you're coming with us on our promo blitz, right?" Maybe then I'd have a chance of doing better in our betting game. She would unintentionally distract her boyfriend and he would screw up his bet. Or that was my plan, at least.

"I hope so. Depends on if I can get the time off. Plus we're expecting . . . a new family member."

Holy fuck! That was the last thing I'd expected. They had only been together for a few months, but who was I to judge? If anyone should know how easy it was to get a girl pregnant, it was me.

"Well, um, congratulations." I hugged Hailey and gave Nolan a one-armed hug. Fortunately, the fans were too busy listening to the sideshow entertainment between Mason and the radio personalities to notice our conversation.

Nolan burst out laughing. "She's not pregnant. We're adopting a puppy."

Hailey grinned. "Sorry. Couldn't resist."

"Not funny," I grumbled, doing my best not to let them know how I really felt. Joking about pregnancy was never a funny matter.

Shoving away the pain and betrayal from my past, I smiled, the move genuine. "So, when are you getting the new addition?"

"Today," Hailey said.

From the look on my best friend's face, you'd have thought Nolan was four years old and it was Christmas.

Rebecca announced the next game—darts—and we returned to our respective teams. I spent the next hour flirting with the fans, signing autographs, and finding out what they loved about our songs and about the band. This was one of the things I enjoyed most about what I did: interacting with the fans. The real fans. Not the groupies who were hoping to add us to their I-slept-with-a-celebrity tally. They usually couldn't tell us what they loved about our music. We were just hot bodies as far as they were concerned.

"And the grand prize," Rebecca announced, "goes to Kirk Helmson's team."

Cheers broke out among the teams, including Mason's.

"Hey, bro," Mas said with a laugh, "you finally won the Steward Cup."

Kirk snorted. "You mean Stanley Cup."

"Sure, whatev."

Kirk collected the tiny metal trophy on behalf of his team and congratulated everyone as if they really had won the most coveted prize in the NHL.

"You guys want to meet up for drinks later?" Aaron asked after we had packed up our instruments to leave. As part of the event, we had agreed to play a couple of our songs off the debut album. The president of the record label had been quite clear: under no condition were we to play anything from the upcoming album. And basically whatever he said, we did. No questions asked.

"Count me in," I said. Kirk and Mason also agreed to meet up at our favorite bar.

On my way to my apartment, I stopped at a grocery store and wandered up and down the aisles, grabbing whatever appealed to me and didn't require much thought. Cooking wasn't one of my favorite pastimes.

As I pushed my shopping cart down the cereal aisle, I spotted a woman I'd never thought I'd see again—a woman I had known back when we were kids. Only I didn't remember her looking quite so hot back then, with her long copper hair in a messy ponytail. The woman who was my ex-girlfriend-from-high-school's little sister.

The woman signing with her hands . . . to a four-year-old boy.

2

CALLIE

Oh my God. The three freaked-out words echoed in my head at the sight of Jared Leigh walking toward me in the cereal aisle. If he had been any other rock star, dread wouldn't have dragged me down like a cinder block in water.

If he had been any guy other than the one who used to see me as nothing more than his girlfriend's annoying little sister, I would've totally been fangirling, and the Oh my God would've been screams of joy in my head.

"Mommy," my four-year-old nephew said, pointing to a box of sugary cereal, "I have that one?" He signed the words as he spoke, using the American Sign Language he was learning in preschool, and gave me the same dimpled smile his father used to give me. The same dimpled smile that caused my heart to temporarily cease functioning whenever Jared flashed it.

"May I have that one?" I corrected.

"Yes, that one." Logan pointed to the cereal again and unleashed his dimpled weapons once more.

"No, say the full sentence," I gently reminded him. "Say 'Can I have that one, please?'"

"Can I have that one, please?" Without waiting for my reply, he grabbed his favorite brand and dropped it in the cart. Then he gave me a look, daring me to say no after all the work I'd made him go through just to get the cereal he wanted.

Even though I shouldn't have, I laughed. It was hard to argue when he had a point. My constantly correcting him like a grammar-crazed schoolteacher was a family-sized pain in the ass, but his preschool program, his audiologist, and his speech pathologist had all been adamant about it. In order to help Logan learn to hear with his cochlear implant and learn to speak, we had to go through these painstaking exercises.

"Hey, Callie?" Jared said. I startled. Somehow, with the grammar lesson going on, I'd temporarily forgotten he was here. In the same aisle as me. While I was with the son he didn't know existed.

Jared looked at Logan, and my heart stalled in my chest. Shit. Shit. Shit. I bit down the urge to toss Logan over my shoulder and run out of the store. Run away from the conversation with Jared I longed to avoid, much like you'd want to avoid being trapped in a room filled with pissed-off venomous snakes.

"Hi." I also signed it, a habit whenever I was around Logan.

"Hi," Logan repeated.

He cocked his head to the side, studying the tall man in front of him, who had the same wavy brown hair as his own. But Logan's hair was longish and messy. Jared's was short on the sides and longer on top and was artfully styled away from his face. He also had facial stubble that made him look even sexier. In the past five years, since I'd last seen him in person, his hotness factor had climbed exponentially. Unfortunately for my poor idiotic heart and me.

Jared smiled at Logan and crouched to his level. "Hey, buddy. You know what? That's my favorite cereal too."

Of course it was. Go figure.

"It is?" Logan also signed the words as he spoke.

Jared glanced up at me, eyebrows raised in confusion.

"Logan is deaf," I explained, "but he has a cochlear implant."

"So he can hear?"

"Not perfectly. And there are sounds he can't handle. Like music." Which was heartbreaking when you considered that his father was a talented guitarist.

"Then why the sign language?"

I narrowed my eyes at him. "Are you judging my decisions on how my son should be educated?" I might have stressed "my son" more forcefully than I'd meant to. Legally he wasn't my son. I was only his guardian.

Jared slowly shook his head. "Sorry. I didn't mean for it to sound that way."

I let out a long breath. "I'm sorry too. Let's just say it's a sensitive topic. He goes to a preschool that encourages total communication. So American Sign Language, lip reading, and speech."

"Mommy, I have a dog?" Logan asked, already bored by the current subject. He was lucky. He wasn't the one who had spent weeks studying the pros and cons of the implant and the different types of education for him, listening to arguments from both sides of the fence, spending many sleepless nights wondering which was the right choice.

He was just the one who had to deal with the repercussions of my decisions.

"May I have a dog?" I corrected.

A huge grin broke out on Logan's face. "Yes! We getting a dog."

Ugh! Head, meet brick wall.

"No, Logan. The correct phrase is 'Mommy, can I have a

dog?' And no, we can't have a dog. Our apartment won't allow animals." I didn't bother to correct his other sentence.

His responding pout was enough to break hearts within a hundred-mile radius.

"I'm sorry." And I was. I would do anything for him, if I could.

"Do you like dogs?" Jared asked, still crouching in front of his son. And I tried not to freak out more than I already was. In a city of more than three million people, the last thing I'd expected was to bump into Jared. Ever.

Logan nodded.

"My friends are adopting a puppy. I'm sure they won't mind if you want to meet it. Would you like that?"

The dimples came out full force. "Can I, Mommy?"

"Um . . . I'm not sure. We'll see." Brilliant move, Callie. How many times today are you planning to break his heart?

Jared held out his hand to Logan. "By the way, I'm Jared. Your mom and I grew up together. We used to be neighbors." Well, technically, there had been a house between us, but close enough.

"My name is Logan." He shook his father's hand while alarms screeched in my head.

"Nice to meet you, Logan."

"Nice to meet you," the four-year-old intoned back. "I like you."

"I like you too."

Logan grinned again. "I love soccer."

The corners of my mouth twitched. Following a four-year-old's train of thought could be an adventure in itself. "He saw your band perform last year at the soccer charity event." The event had been a fundraiser for a soccer program for disabled kids. Logan played soccer with hearing kids his age, but when we heard about the event and how there would be soccer-related activities, he had begged me to take him.

"I thought he couldn't hear music," Jared said.

"He can hear music, but the sound is horribly distorted. We turned the implant off while you guys played." This wasn't always the situation for someone with an implant, but like everything else, the results differed from person to person.

"How come you didn't come over to say hi?"

Very good question. "I just figured you were busy with your fans." In reality, I had been careful to make sure Jared wasn't aware we were at the event. For the same reasons I would've done anything to avoid seeing him here now.

"We have a party today," Logan said. "You come?"

The alarms went off again, drowned out by the need to be the ideal mom to a deaf boy with a cochlear implant.

"The correct sentence is 'We are having a party today. Would you like to come?'" I said to Logan.

"Sounds good to me," Jared replied. "What time and where?" He flashed his dimples, and my heart temporarily stuttered to a stop. Father and son were definitely going to kill me if given a chance.

"No, no. I was just telling Logan so he could repeat the correct sentence. It's the only way he'll learn."

"But Jared will come, right?" Logan looked at Jared with those puppy-dog eyes no mere human could say no to, ignoring me and that he was supposed to repeat the sentence correctly.

I inwardly sighed and gave up the exercise for now. I had something more urgent to deal with. "I'm sure Jared has more important things to do than come to Mrs. Rogers's birthday party." To Jared, I said, "She's our neighbor. She looks after Logan while I'm at work. It's not a big deal. Just Mrs. Rogers, Logan, and me." Nothing like those big celebrity parties he was used to. The parties he attended with his on-again, off-again supermodel girlfriend.

"She's nice," Logan said, referring to Mrs. Rogers. "You like her."

Jared unfolded himself to his full height. He was a good few inches taller than me, and I wasn't short by any stretch of the imagination. "Well, if you like her, then I know I will. Tell me the when and where and I'll be there."

"That won't be necessary," I bit out. "I'm sure you're busy." With groupies. With your band. With anything that doesn't involve me and your son.

"As it is, I'm available. I just finished up with a band event for a local radio station."

"It's going to be boring, Jared. It's not one of your rock-star parties. You won't have fun at all. It's just gonna be pizza and birthday cake."

His mouth did that annoying trick of sliding up to one side. Damn sexy smile. "Rock-star parties are overrated. And I could go for some pizza and birthday cake."

"And balloons," Logan added. "Don't forget balloons." He didn't bother to sign that, and I didn't push it. As much as I didn't want him to forget he was part of the deaf community, some days it was easier just pretending that plan didn't exist.

"I won't forget," I said. "I promise." To Jared I added, "I can guarantee you'll be bored. I'm sure there's a party you'd much rather hang out at. Maybe with a few celebrities." I nodded with finality. Problem solved.

That damn sexy smile was still there. As were the damn sexy dimples. The guy wasn't playing fair. He checked something on his phone. "Nope, no rock-star parties with celebrities on today's calendar. So I'm definitely free."

My traitorous nephew whooped at that news.

"Seriously, why do you want to do this?" I asked, somehow not stomping my foot at how stubborn he was being. Father was definitely like son. Logan could be pretty stubborn too.

"Because I haven't seen you in something like five years. I thought we could catch up. Maybe give me a break from all these crazy rock-star parties I've been attending." He winked at me.

I had no idea what it was about that wink, but combined with the dimples, it was lethal. If I hadn't been in full-out panic mode, my panties would have dampened with need.

Okay, maybe there was a little dampening going on, but he didn't need to know that. A dampening you could blame on the long drought—aka my lack of a sex life.

"What's the sign for balloon?" Jared asked Logan.

Despite my current freak-out mode, I couldn't help but smile. I'd always believed Jared would've someday been a great father. My sister, Alexis, Logan's biological mother, had disagreed. Even before Jared formed Pushing Limits with Nolan Kincaid, Alexis predicted he would one day make it big. So far it looked like her prediction was coming true. There was already speculation that their second album, which was due out soon, would outdo their debut album on the charts.

But Alexis had been positive that once Jared hit it big, he would end up regretting Logan. She'd feared that his son would be nothing more than an inconvenience to him, especially since Logan had been the result of a one-time fling years after they had broken up. They hadn't been in love. They weren't even friends at that point. She had wanted so much more for Logan, more than what she'd felt Jared could give him, regardless of whether his band hit it big or not. She wanted her son to grow up loved and appreciated. She wanted her son to grow up as part of a loving family, complete with the white picket fence and a father with a white-collar job. She wanted the same thing for her son that we had growing up.

That might've been all true, but the man standing before me wasn't acting like Logan was an inconvenience. Quite the opposite. But would he still feel that way if he found out the truth? Or would Alexis's predictions come true? Pushing Limits was a favorite when it came to the media, and not always in a good way. My dead sister's fears were justified when it came to what the media would do if they discovered Jared had a son. A son who was now deaf.

Logan would never get to be just a normal kid if that happened.

Logan proudly demonstrated the sign for balloon, which involved miming inflating one. Jared repeated it and was rewarded with a grin from the four-year-old. Warmth filled me at the bonding between father and son. I doused it with icy water. I had to end things between them before Logan got hurt. And I knew he would be. There was no way to avoid it.

The other part of me argued that I was making a big deal out of nothing. It would only be for the one time. Jared was busy and would be leaving soon on another tour. After the party, we'd probably never see him again.

While the yea and the nay were battling it out in my head, Jared raised an eyebrow at me. "So do I get an invite to the party? Or am I not cool enough to hang out with you guys tonight?"

He had asked me, but Logan decided to answer for me instead. "You're invited." Then he looked at me with those eyes that were impossible to say no to. "Right, Mommy?"

Just this one time, I reminded myself. Jared will come over, we'll catch up on whatever I can tell him, and then I can go back to pretending he doesn't exist in my life.

I told him where we lived. "Mrs. Rogers is coming over at five p.m."

He told us he would see us then and left, suddenly leaving me to inwardly freak out again. I'd just made a huge mistake and it had nothing to do with Logan.

Instead, it had everything to do with the girl who Jared had once seen as his girlfriend's annoying little sister, the little sister who'd wanted to tag along with the guy she idolized. The little sister who one day grew up and realized that the guy who was four years older than her really was an amazing guy. The real Jared, not the one the fans thought they knew. The Jared who I had been crushing on since I turned seventeen.

The little sister who couldn't risk the crush becoming something more.

But by the time I realized it would be a mistake for Jared to come over, he was gone—and I had no way to cancel on him.

3

———

JARED

The last time I saw Callie was five years ago, just before my world was turned upside down. Her sister, Alexis, was two years older than me, and had been my girlfriend when I was seventeen. Well, more accurately, she was the hot babe I'd enjoyed equally hot sex with on a regular basis. We'd dated for a few months, but then realized we were more interested in having sex together than having a relationship. Not that Callie knew that. At the time she had been a cute but awkward thirteen-year-old who I had always known would one day be beautiful.

No, Callie had been like no other girl . . . and she was still like no other girl, but in a whole new way. She might've been wearing baggy jeans and an oversized white T-shirt with paint splattered on it, but the awkward thirteen-year-old had clearly grown into the woman I had predicted she would be. A beautiful, curvy, sexy woman.

Logan's dark hair must've belonged to his father. A father who wasn't coming to the party. Callie hadn't been wearing a ring, so she wasn't married nor was she engaged. Maybe she had a boyfriend but he was too busy to attend tonight.

On the way home from the grocery store, I bought flowers for the mysterious Mrs. Rogers. I also found a dog-shaped helium balloon that was perfect for Logan. At home, I tossed the phone numbers that had been shoved into my jeans pocket during the radio event, then showered.

Afterward I sent Mason a text.

> Me: Will be late meeting up with you. Have something I have to do first.

I still wanted to hang out with the guys, but I was curious what Callie was up to these days—other than being a mother. The girl I remembered was a talented artist and had dreamed of one day working at Pixar, the animation studio.

My curiosity, though, extended only to Callie. The last thing I cared to hear about was the woman who had aborted my child two days after telling me she was pregnant, no matter what I wanted. Yes, at that point all Alexis and I had been to each other was a hot and satisfying fuck. A one-time thing. Nothing more. We had bumped into each other one day, and it hadn't taken long before we were reminiscing about the backseat of my car . . . only the reminiscing took place in my apartment.

The restlessness that had struck while I was at the radio event returned. It had been hovering around me for the past year while touring. Back then it had been easy to ignore. But now, ever since I'd returned to L.A., it was harder to pretend the restlessness didn't exist. It was like a mosquito bite. The more you tried to ignore it, the more it itched to the point of driving you completely insane.

But unlike with a mosquito bite, there was nothing I could put on this itch to soothe it. I just needed something to distract me.

Callie's apartment was in a part of L.A. where rents were higher than most twenty-two-year-olds could afford. It was definitely in a nicer part of the city than where I lived. Maybe Logan's father was in the picture after all, or she was living with a boyfriend. It seemed an ideal neighborhood to raise a child. The streets were clean, as were the houses and low-rise apartment buildings. The surrounding gardens were green and well maintained. People took pride in living here.

I found Callie's building and parked my car in a visitor space. I gathered my gifts and walked to the front entrance. Inside, the place smelled clean and safe. Callie buzzed me in a moment later and I rode the elevator to the third floor, then walked down the hall to her apartment.

I knocked on the door, and a few seconds later it opened. Callie flashed me a small, uncertain smile and let me in. She had changed out of her T-shirt and jeans and was now in a red sundress, the color faded.

"Did you have any trouble finding the building?" she asked, voice slightly shaky. She glanced up at the balloon and smirked. "I take it that's not for me." The smirk slipped away, and her teeth pressed into her lower lip. Some girls did that when they were nervous. Callie did it whenever she was worried.

"No," I said with a laugh. "I remembered how terrified you were of them."

She rolled her eyes. "I wasn't terrified of balloons."

I leveled my gaze at her, enjoying this as much as I had enjoyed teasing her when she was a kid. "Really?"

"Hey, I couldn't help that I didn't like the loud bang when they popped."

I snickered. "Is that why you always shrieked like a large hairy monster was after you?"

"Says the guy who freaked out when a caterpillar fell down the back of his T-shirt."

"Hey, in my defense, I had just watched a TV special on

venomous caterpillars. I thought it was one of those. Nice place, by the way."

"Thanks. We like it." She led me down the hallway, past an open door into what had to be Logan's room. The pictures on the hallway wall ranged from when he was a baby to more recent ones. No one else was in them. Only the baby picture looked to have been taken by a professional. The rest were snapshots that had been enlarged to fit the frames.

Like the apartment building itself, the furniture was nicer than I would've expected for a twenty-two-year-old. The couch was beige, with a few stains on the puffy cushions, but despite that, it was obviously of quality. As were the dark wooden end tables with the simple yet masculine lamps, and the coffee table on the rug, which had rectangles in various shades of brown. Everything was expensive—and oddly familiar.

More pictures of Logan, of Callie's family, and of Callie with Logan were scattered around the room, both on the walls and on the dark-wood bookshelf. No pictures of a boyfriend were visible. Maybe he was camera-shy . . . or was the photographer. Or he didn't exist.

The other pictures on the walls were ones I recognized as the style Callie would've created. They were the kinds of drawings and digital art you'd expect to find in a kid's picture book, the colors bold.

Before I could ask her about her dreams of working at Pixar, an energetic Logan catapulted from the couch and rushed over to me.

"Is that mine?" he asked, pointing at the dog balloon.

"Is that for me?" Callie corrected.

"Is that for me?" Logan grinned at the oversized balloon.

"I was gonna give it to Mrs. Rogers," I said, "but do you think she would like the flowers more?"

Callie laughed, the sound of it more beautiful than I

remembered. "I don't know. I think Logan loves flowers even more than balloons."

"No, I don't," Logan said with a pout. "Balloons better."

I expected Callie to correct his sentence, but she didn't this time. She laughed again. "You're right. Balloons are much better."

Logan took the balloon from me and grabbed my hand. "I show you my room." He led me away, but not before I caught Callie worrying her lip again.

The bedding in his room was bright green, as was the rug covering the light gray carpet. An oversized soccer-ball-shaped cushion lay on the floor. On the wall behind the head of the bed, a soccer goal had been painted with trees in the distance and a blue sky behind it. Scattered on the floor was an assortment of toys.

"Do you like it?" Logan asked, clearly proud of his room.

"It's very nice. Did your mom paint that?"

He nodded. "Mommy's an artist."

"I know. She's a very talented artist."

"Thanks," Callie said behind me, voice so soft I almost missed it.

She was standing in the doorway, her eyes fixed on the painted walls but her gaze far away. It was as if she was somewhere else. Another time. Another place.

"Weren't you planning to eventually work at Pixar?" I asked.

Her gaze flicked to Logan and the sad smile said it all. She had planned to work there, but then she'd had Logan and everything changed.

Unlike Alexis, Callie hadn't aborted her baby, even if he had put an end to her dreams.

Logan was so busy with the balloon, he missed the look on his mom's face. When he glanced up at her, she was all smiles again for him.

"I decided being a graphic designer was a better career choice. More job opportunities."

That was probably true, but I suspected that before Logan came along, it wouldn't have made a difference. She would've found a way to survive until her big chance came. She'd never been into expensive things. None of that mattered to her, as long as she was happy. Which was why her choice of furniture was not what I would've expected.

"So you work for a company?" I knew zero about graphic design.

"Maybe one day, or I can work freelance. Right now I'm working on my degree and doing freelance work on the side. Mostly covers for a few romance authors, designs for their website banners. Swag. Stuff like that. Nothing major, though."

The enthusiasm she used to have whenever she talked about her dreams was missing. It sounded like her career choice was a chore. It was just a job for her, nothing more.

"Where're you studying?"

"The Academy of Art University."

"Isn't that in San Francisco?"

Her eyes widened in surprise that I remembered. "Yes, but I was able to switch over to graphic design and take the program online."

"Switch?"

Her eyes widened even more. "I should finish getting ready for the party. Mrs. Rogers will be over soon." She didn't give me a chance to say anything else. She was already out the bedroom door.

Logan showed me around his room, signing the names for the various items.

"What's the sign for dog?" I pointed to his balloon.

He attempted to snap his fingers then patted his leg. I repeated the action and was rewarded with one of his contagious grins. He continued showing me his stuff, and I practiced the signs he showed me. I had no idea why I was bothering. It wasn't like I needed to know them, or like I would even remember them beyond today. But it was fun watching his reaction when I got a sign right and when I purposely screwed it up just to see him giggle.

As Logan showed me his favorite picture book, a loud knock came from the front door. He didn't even glance up at the noise.

A moment later, a woman in her early sixties entered the bedroom. She was dressed in a light blue blouse and navy pants, her gray hair skimming her shoulders. Logan tossed his book aside and hurled his small body across the room to her. She barely had enough time to react before his arms wrapped around her legs.

She laughed and hugged him back. "Hi, Logan. I see you have a visitor." Her gaze swept over me, but not in the same way groupies and fans checked me out. I'd seen this look before, back when my parents had interrogated my sister's old boyfriends before deciding if the guys were worthy enough to date her.

Apparently I met the woman's standards. She nodded to some unspoken question in her head and smiled at me.

"Jared, this is Mrs. Rogers," Callie said from the doorway.

"You can call me Sharon," the woman said.

"Jared's an old friend of mine from when we were kids." Callie bit her lip again and suddenly looked like she longed to be anywhere but here, with me. I'd been getting the same vibe from her since bumping into her at the store.

Sharon's face brightened as she looked between Callie and me. "Oh, is that so?"

Before I could figure out what she meant, Logan blurted out, "Look at balloon he gave me."

Sharon bent down to Logan's level. "Did Jared give you this balloon?"

He nodded. "And his friend has dog. I want dog."

"His friend has a dog." She emphasized the "a." "I didn't know you wanted a dog." Again she emphasized the "a." I could easily see her as a teacher in another lifetime.

"Yes, I do. And he has flowers."

"I see that. They're pretty flowers. I bet your mom likes them."

"They're for you," Callie blurted out in a way that came off as comical.

"How sweet. I haven't had a gentleman give me flowers in years." She winked at me. I chuckled and handed her the bouquet. They were my mom's favorite spring flowers, so I'd figured Sharon might like them too.

We returned to the living room. Callie and Logan had been busy decorating for the party. Clusters of silver and purple helium balloons were tied to the backs of the chairs set around the elegant dinner table. The pair had also painted a birthday banner, with Logan's handprints scattered over it.

The table itself hadn't been ignored either. Purple and silver streamers curled around every available space. The Callie I remembered loved birthdays, and it looked like nothing had changed since she had grown up.

And for the first time in who knows how long, I realized how much I'd missed her. How much I missed her curiosity, her determination, her generosity. The last time I'd seen her was when I had been visiting my family for our weekly dinners. She'd been walking along the sidewalk near her house with a group of seventeen-year-old girls. All giggled when they saw me, except for Callie, who had turned bright red.

"So what do you do, Jared?" Sharon asked as we sat. Logan was next to Sharon. I took the only other available spot, next to Callie.

"I'm a musician."

"He plays drums in a rock band," Logan said.

"Actually, it's guitar." I'd tried playing Mason's drums once. After he'd stopped howling with laughter, he told me to not quit my day job and to leave drumming to the professionals. I hadn't thought I was that bad, but the guys' expressions had suggested otherwise.

Sharon nodded, the corners of her lips curling down slightly. "Are you any good?"

"He's brilliant." Callie's face reddened, and she busied herself with serving the pizza.

An odd sensation in my chest stirred at her words. She wasn't the first person who had told me something along those lines when it came to my guitar playing. Groupies and fans said it all the time. But somehow hearing her say it felt different. Like her opinion meant more to me than anyone else's did, including the critics.

Shit, what was I even thinking? Callie was just an old childhood friend.

A friend with a young child, a complication I didn't need.

An incredibly sexy friend whom I suddenly wanted to get to know better, and not in the same way it had been between her sister and me. I wanted to get to know more about the woman she'd become.

4

CALLIE

"He's brilliant." Even back when he was first learning to play the guitar and hit more wrong notes than right ones, I'd loved listening to Jared. His excitement for the instrument, which his parents had given him for his fourteenth birthday, had been contagious. I was his first groupie and the president of his fan club. A very exclusive fan club, with me as the only member.

Later, after he started dating my sister, I'd remained his biggest fan. Luckily for me, he hadn't minded me sitting in his room while he strummed on his baby. It was always just him and me, the only time I got Jared to myself.

A memory revisited of when I'd been seventeen and he'd straddled me from behind to reposition my fingers on the strings in the correct chords. His body had been pressed against mine, his subtle scent doing all kinds of crazy things to me. I had been close to tossing the guitar onto the bed and kissing him. That was the first time I'd realized my attraction toward him, an attraction I'd never told anyone about.

My body heated at the memory. Needing a distraction, I grabbed pizza from the box and placed the slice on Logan's

Winnie-the-Pooh plate. And because my body hadn't gotten the hint yet, I gave everyone else a slice of cheese pizza too—anything to hide how unbalanced I felt with Jared's unexpected return into my life.

It's only temporary, I reminded myself. He'll go on tour soon and forget all about us.

Logan was watching Jared in the way kids do when they worship someone, as if he somehow sensed the stranger sitting across from him was his father. But that was ridiculous. There was no way he could know. Right?

Jared made a funny comment and laughed. His dimples came to life, and his mirror image's dimples also came to life. Sharon looked between the two males, and for a second I could've sworn something passed in her eyes that wasn't good news for me.

I brushed it off. I was being paranoid. There were millions of guys with dimples. And I was sure a large percentage were dark-haired. Okay, the odds that I just happened to be friends with several dark-haired guys with dimples were low, but Sharon didn't know that.

The quick glance she gave me was far from reassuring, but that was all right. She wasn't the one I had to worry about. Fortunately, Jared would never piece things together. As far as he was concerned, I was Logan's biological mother and he knew he'd never had sex with me.

My secret was safe.

I shoved the slice of pizza in my mouth and watched Logan laugh so hard at what Jared had said that he almost fell off his chair. For the first time since the accident that stole my sister and parents from me, a fissure formed in my bruised heart. Ever since their deaths more than three years ago, I'd been strong, doing my best not to fall apart under the newfound responsibilities piled on me, and doing my best for Logan. When my boyfriend—the guy I had loved and believed was the one—dumped me because the last thing he wanted was a kid, especially someone else's, I didn't allow myself to fall apart. When Logan developed meningitis and lost his hearing, I didn't allow myself to fall apart. And when I had to make the decision by myself as to whether or not Logan should have the cochlear surgery, I didn't allow myself to fall apart.

No matter how difficult it had been to remain strong through all of this, I had done so for Logan.

But now, with the adoring way he looked at Jared, you could've sliced me across the stomach with a dull knife and tossed me to a great white shark, and it would've hurt a lot less.

I would do anything for Logan, but I couldn't give him the one thing he needed. I couldn't tell Jared and him the truth and risk destroying Logan.

I blinked back the tears threatening to form. Logan would never have a father. If I had learned one single fact during the past three years, it was that other guys weren't much different from my ex. They weren't interested in dating a woman with a child. Add the challenge of the child being deaf—cochlear implant or not—and any interest they might have had in me plummeted to zero.

I pushed the painful memories away, did my best to temporarily patch up the crack in my heart, and joined the party. I laughed at Jared's jokes and listened to Sharon tell Jared about some of Logan's escapades. I avoided redirecting the conversation when she did that, even though I didn't want her to involve Jared in his son's life more than necessary. To do so would've added to her suspicions.

"Open my present first," Logan said, his excitement barely contained as he handed Sharon the gift he had wrapped himself. A ton of clear tape held the happy-face, potato-print wrapping paper together. The package would've looked a lot better if we had at least put the gift in a box, but I couldn't find one in the apartment and Logan had been too impatient to wait.

Sharon turned the package around in her hands, her expression thoughtful. "I can't imagine what it is. Is it a soccer ball?"

Logan giggled. "No. Soccer ball round."

"That's right, Logan," she said. "A soccer ball is round." The gift was flat. "Is it a lion?"

Logan giggled again. "Lion is big." He also signed it.

"What sound does a lion make?" Sharon asked, ever the teacher.

"Rawr."

"Do you want a pet lion?" Jared asked, signing the word "lion."

Logan shook his head. "No lions. Lions eat dogs." He pointed at the gift in Sharon's hand and practically clambered onto the table in anticipation. "Open it."

She began unwrapping the gift, taking care not to rip the homemade paper. If she didn't open it soon, Logan would do it for her.

Finally the paper was removed intact.

"I buy it," Logan said as Sharon examined the picture frame and the picture of the three of us at the playground. If you didn't know better, you would've believed we were a family, with Sharon as Logan's grandmother.

Her eyes glossed up. "Thank you. I love it." She wrapped her arms around Logan and hugged him hard.

I also gave her a light blue cardigan and a Starbucks gift card. She thanked me for them, but her gaze kept jumping longingly to the picture frame.

"Who wants birthday cake?" I asked.

"Me," Logan cried out, bouncing on his chair.

We laughed, and I headed to the kitchen to retrieve the cake. It wasn't large enough for sixty-five candles, so I'd stuck into the white frosting six red candles on one half and five white ones on the other side. I lit them, and Jared and I sang "Happy Birthday."

Logan threw in a random word here and there, but they were spoken, not sung. Once we were finished, he cheered and clapped while Sharon blew out the candles.

"Did you make wish?" Logan asked.

She grinned. "I did."

I served the cake. Before I had a chance to hand Jared his plate, Logan had devoured half of his own slice.

"I take it you like cake?" Jared said, chuckling, and my heart tightened at the memory of eating birthday cake with him when we were kids. I learned the hard way that you did not want to get in the way of Jared and his cake. But in the end I couldn't complain, even if one time he'd smeared it on my face and clothes in revenge.

"He's not the only one." Mischief flared inside me. Before I had a chance to think twice about what I was doing, I plunged my fork into his chocolate cake and removed a huge chunk of it. A healthy dose of pink and white frosting joined it.

I lifted the fork to my mouth and closed my lips around it. With a satisfied "mmmm," I slide the fork slowly out, eyes closed. The cake was good, but from the noise I was making, you would've thought I had just tasted an award-winning confection.

I glanced at Jared, prepared to smirk at him. His sexy brown eyes met mine, but now they were dark . . . with lust.

5

JARED

Callie slowly dragged the fork from between her lips and made a sound that instantly brought back memories of the videos Mason enjoyed watching on tour.

And immediately my cock responded. I couldn't remember the last time I'd fucked. All I could remember was that it had been with Tiffany months ago, when she and I were in New York City at the same time.

Shit. If Mason knew that, he would revoke my man card and call me a pussy for not getting any pussy.

"So, Logan," I said to distract myself from the thoughts about Callie that I had no right thinking—even if she was no longer thirteen years old and I was no longer considered too old for her. "Do you have any big plans tomorrow?"

Logan's face brightened. "I want to go to Disneyland. Ben's daddy is taking him to Disneyland."

The thud of a knocked-over glass startled us both. Her face pale, Callie frantically mopped up the spilled milk with paper napkins. Sharon scrambled from her seat and returned a moment later with a dishcloth. She began cleaning up the mess.

"Sorry," Callie said. "I wasn't paying attention to what I was doing."

"It's all right," Sharon replied. "It's only a little milk." And it was. But from Callie's reaction, you'd have thought she'd spilled an entire cow's worth.

"Who's Ben?" I asked Logan, curious if the mention of him and his father was what had upset Callie.

"My friend," he said.

"They're in the same preschool program." Callie picked up the sodden napkins and disappeared into the kitchen.

"His father sounds great," I said. "My dad used to take me and my sister to Disneyland too."

Logan went on to list all the other cool activities Ben's father did with his son: fishing, teaching him to play baseball, taking him on trips. As he spoke, his voice was heavy with wistfulness. He wasn't exactly jealous of his friend, but he was in awe of everything Ben got to do with his dad.

A dad that Logan didn't have.

Or maybe it was more than that. "I bet you've done some cool stuff with your mom," I ventured, attempting to steer the conversation away from his lack of a father.

He nodded. "She plays soccer with me and takes me to the park. And she and Mrs. Rogers took me to zoo once." He grinned. "I like the animals and ice cream."

"That sounds like a lot of fun."

"They were fun. But Mommy too busy. She works all the time."

He was just being an honest four-year-old. He wasn't trying to hurt anyone, but I knew Callie. If she'd heard him, and I was positive she had, his words would've cut to the marrow of her bones.

I wasn't the only one who didn't know what to say. Sharon

watched Logan, the smile on her face gone. Callie still hadn't returned.

Sharon's gaze jumped from me to Logan and back again. A thought was forming in her head, but I had no idea what it was. I had long ago quit trying to figure out women, and that included my mom and sister.

Callie walked out of the kitchen, a big smile plastered on her face. "How about I take you to Disneyland next weekend?" She hugged her son and kissed the top of his head. "I have Sunday off."

For the first time since bumping into her this afternoon, I noticed the exhaustion on her face. I mentally cursed the asshole who had done this to her. Did he even pay child support? Maybe he hadn't wanted to be part of his child's life, but it did take two to make a baby. I might not have been great in biology, but that much I did remember.

Logan cheered his mom's decision. He jumped off his chair, grabbed the string of his dog balloon, and ran to his room. The balloon dragged through the air after him, like a dog reluctant to go for a walk. Callie's plastered-on smile eased slightly to something more genuine.

"Thank you for the party," Sharon said. "I'll see you Monday." To me she added, "It was nice meeting you, Jared."

I waited until the apartment door clicked shut before asking if Callie was okay.

She picked up Logan's Pooh plate. "I'm fine. Why wouldn't I be?"

"Really? Are you forgetting we've known each other since we were kids?"

She didn't even pause in gathering the dirty dishes to answer. "We haven't seen each other in, what, five years? Maybe I've changed."

"Where's Logan's father?" I said in a low voice.

Callie's hand jerked with Sharon's plate, narrowly missing

an empty glass. "It doesn't matter where he is." Without looking at me, she returned to the kitchen.

I followed her. "What do you mean it doesn't matter?"

Her entire body stiffened. "Just that. He's not part of Logan's life and he never will be." The venom in her voice was deadly. Ouch. I was almost relieved for the asshole that he wasn't here.

I didn't say anything at first. I just watched her fill the sink with soapy water and scrub a plate clean. She continued scrubbing it long after every molecule of dirt had been banished.

She was obviously mad, but it was less clear at whom she was pissed: Logan's father or me.

I stepped behind her and threaded my fingers with hers, stopping her incessant scrubbing. Her hand trembled in mine. I fought back the urge to wrap my arms around her and do something idiotic to temporarily distract her, like run my lips along the soft skin of her neck.

I glanced away . . . to the fridge, barely visible behind a sea of Logan's artwork. All the pictures had been drawn with crayons and either contained awkward-looking stick people or colorful animals with disproportionate bodies and limbs. "Does he know about Logan?"

"It doesn't matter." The words were whispered. I couldn't be certain if they were directed at me or at herself.

"Sure it does. Why wouldn't it?"

Even though she wasn't facing me, there was no missing her flinch at my question. "Because the last thing he wanted or needed was a child."

A part of me relaxed at her words and I released her hand. She hadn't said that the last thing he had wanted or needed was another child. It meant whoever the father was didn't already have a child. He wasn't a family man, but it didn't mean he didn't have a wife.

"Is he married?"

Callie groaned and turned to face me. "You honestly think I'd be stupid enough to become involved with a married man?"

"No, I don't think you're stupid. Maybe you didn't know he was married at the time."

She let out a shaky breath and returned to washing the dishes. "No, he isn't married. And honestly, Logan and I are doing fine. Better than fine."

"Do you have a boyfriend?"

She laughed, the sound slightly off-kilter. "I have a four-year-old child, waitress forty hours a week in a diner, study graphic design part-time, attend an American Sign Language class for parents who have a deaf child, and do odd graphic design projects for a handful of clients. That doesn't exactly leave me time to have a boyfriend. Heck, it doesn't even give me enough time to date, period."

"I guess not." The reality of what she was dealing with made me want to punch the sperm donor's lights out for his part in Callie's having to give up her dreams. Not once as a kid had she mentioned that she dreamed of being a waitress in a diner when she grew up. "Which diner do you work at?"

"Blue Star. It's close to here and my boss allows me to work the early shift so that I'm home more for Logan." This might've been true, but she didn't seem happy about it.

I wanted to ask about her family, since surely they were helping her out. Her parents were those kind of people—just like my parents were. They would've rearranged the planets for her if that was what needed to be done. But I didn't want to risk her bringing up Alexis. I didn't want to risk her mentioning what my ex-girlfriend was up to. Alexis and I might not have been anything more than a great fuck, but that didn't mean I wanted to hear about her life. Maybe I would eventually . . . but not tonight.

Callie yawned. "I need to get Logan to bed now, then work on an assignment that's due soon. So . . ."

"Yeah, I should go," I said, even though it wasn't what I wanted. What I really wanted was to hold her, kiss her, tell her that everything would be all right, but who was I to say that? What did I know about anything?

She walked me to the apartment door, but before I left, I made a detour into Logan's room to say goodbye to the little guy.

"Are you going to Disneyland with us?" he asked, smiling with the same dimples that my father and I had, which made me wonder even more about his biological father. No one in Callie's family had dimples. Logan's had to come from his dad.

"Sweetie, Jared is super-busy with his band. But you and I will have a lot of fun, just the two of us."

The dimples on his face vanished and he nodded. I nearly told him I would come, just to see his smile again, but I had no idea if I could join them. I didn't want to make a promise I couldn't keep. And something about Callie's attitude made me question if she even wanted me to join them.

I left Logan's room. At the apartment door, I paused. I knew I should walk away and leave Callie and her son to live their lives while I lived mine, but for some reason I couldn't. During the past few hours the restlessness had gone into short-term hibernation. I had no idea why. Maybe I missed her friendship more than I realized. All I knew was that I itched to spend more time with her, with the girl who once had tried to tag along with Alexis and me because Alexis had told her that we were going bowling. "Bowling" had been her code word for driving to our favorite spot and screwing in my car.

Except now Callie was no longer a girl. She was a woman who had my blood heating in a way no other woman had before—not even her sister.

"I'll check with the band and see if I'm free next weekend. If I am, I'd be happy to go to Disneyland with you guys."

"That's not a good idea."

"Why's that?"

"Because I don't want Logan getting too attached to you. He likes you and I can't risk him liking you more than he should."

I should've accepted what she said, since he was her son, after all. He had nothing to do with me. "Other than your father, does he have any males in his life? Any positive influences?"

A flash of pain crossed her face, but it was gone as quickly as it had come. "He's fine, Jared. And it's better this way. Better than constantly dealing with guys letting him down and eventually walking out of his life." The real reason she didn't date.

"And you think I'm gonna let him down?"

She averted her gaze. "Goodnight, Jared."

6

CALLIE

The apartment door shut behind Jared. I leaned back against it for several minutes, staring at the picture of Logan when he was a baby.

And you think I'm gonna let him down?

That was exactly what I believed would happen. It wouldn't be Jared's fault. It was just the nature of his lifestyle.

The best thing for everyone concerned was to prevent Logan from becoming even more attached to Jared. Asking Jared to join us for the birthday party had been a huge mistake. A mistake I wouldn't repeat, for Logan's sake.

And for the sake of my own heart.

Logan was busy with his toys when I entered his room. "Bedtime," I said, and started corralling the animals from his preschooler-friendly farm set that were scattered on the floor.

"Not tired," he said and signed, but he didn't have a chance to say the final word before a yawn cut it short.

I laughed. "No, you don't sound tired at all." I deposited the animals in the plastic barn and helped him into his Spider-Man PJs, which were getting too small for him. "We need to get you some new ones."

He shook his head and signed, "No."

"Don't you want PJs that fit better? You're a big boy now." I sighed. We'd had this same discussion every night for the past week.

"No new ones. Liked these ones."

"But I bet you'll find new pajamas that you like even more."

He crossed his arms and pouted. End of discussion. I pushed away the voice pointing out that maybe he wouldn't be so stubborn if he had a father or a positive male role model he looked up to. But it wasn't as if I could go to the mall and pick him up either of those the way I could buy a new set of pajamas.

I helped him brush his teeth and read him a story. "Good night. I love you," I said afterward. I hugged him, and a memory snuck in of my mother doing the same when she put me to bed as a child. I hugged him tighter, but it wasn't just him I was hugging—it was my mother.

I kissed Logan's cheek. "See you tomorrow." I removed the audio processor from the side of his head, hidden under his hair, and placed it in the drying box on his nightstand.

After tucking him into bed, I turned off his light. The green nightlight glowed softly against the painted walls. I closed the door partway, leaving a narrow gap between it and the doorframe. Logan preferred it that way.

As I turned toward the living room, a knock on the door intruded on my thoughts about Jared. Just as well. My thoughts shouldn't have been on him anyway.

For a second my stupid brain entertained the idea that maybe it was him. But the knocker wasn't Jared; it was Sharon.

"Hi," I said, doing my best not to sound disappointed.

"I saw your friend leave and wanted to talk to you."

My stomach did a belly flop. Nothing good ever came from the words I wanted to talk to you.

Or maybe I was overreacting. Maybe she just believed Jared

wasn't a good role model to have around Logan because he was a musician in a rock band. Visions of groupies, wild parties, and drugs had danced around in her head. Who could blame her?

I opened the door wider. "Sure. Logan's in bed now." He wouldn't hear anything. I could play a Pushing Limits album at full volume and he wouldn't know it was on—unlike my neighbors. "Would you like a drink?" Milk. Wine. Something a lot stronger?

Too bad I didn't have anything stronger than apple juice. There was no point. I was a social drinker. I didn't drink at home alone, and since most nights I was alone . . .

"I'll have some water, thanks."

In the kitchen, I filled a glass of water for her and grabbed a diet soda from the fridge. Since I expected to be up late tonight working on an assignment for one of my classes, the caffeine would be much appreciated.

With drinks in hand, we sat at my parents' old mahogany dinner table, which I had inherited. It still looked festive, with balloons floating above our heads and the matching purple and silver streamers on the table. But I had a feeling the last thing I was about to do was celebrate after what Sharon had to tell me.

"Thanks again for the presents, Callie," she said. "They meant a lot to me. You and Logan are like family to me. Correction—you and Logan are family to me." She took a sip of her drink, then released a long slow breath, her gaze on the contents of her glass. "I've never told you what happened to my daughter and grandson, have I?"

I shook my head.

She placed her glass on the coaster in front of her. Sandwiched between the two layers of glass was a picture of Logan grinning at the camera. Above it, family was printed in carefree lettering. The opposite of how I felt.

"Mathew was Logan's age when it happened. He and his mom, my daughter, were in a boating accident and drowned."

A dull ache took up residence in my chest. "I'm so sorry. I had no idea."

"It happened seven years ago. Several years after my husband died of a heart attack."

I opened my mouth, but the words weren't there. Really, though, what could I say that hadn't already been said?

She gave my hand a light squeeze. "You and Logan saved me. When you two moved in, I'd been struggling with depression. I saw you and him as my second chance at the family I'd lost. Especially when I realized you were just as alone as I was."

I nodded because that much was true. Until Sharon had reached out to me, I had been alone. Alone and scared. My friends from high school had moved on. My friends back in San Francisco had no idea what I was going through. They couldn't help me. There was no one for me to turn to . . . until Sharon had stepped into my life.

I owed her everything for that.

"Logan and I consider you our family too." I hugged her.

"Can I ask you something?"

I swallow hard against the growing lump in my throat, fearing where this was headed. "Sure."

"Why don't you date? You're a beautiful and smart girl, Callie, but you never go out. You don't even go out with friends."

I swallowed again. "I can't."

"Because of Logan? You know I'll be more than happy to babysit him so you can go out at least once in a while."

"I know," I whispered before finding my voice again. "But I don't really have anyone to go out with. And I love spending my free time with Logan. Plus I don't want to be a waitress forever." I wanted to have a career Logan could be proud of. I wanted him to see that if you desired something hard enough, you could achieve it—even when the odds stacked against you were taller than the Empire State Building.

I stubbornly turned my back on the voice whispering how that wasn't completely true. Being a graphic designer wasn't my passion. That wasn't the future I had dreamed of from the moment I'd watched my first Pixar movie.

"You won't be a waitress forever, but don't you think Logan wants to see you happy?"

"I am happy." I gave her the biggest smile I could muster.

Sharon made a noncommittal grunt. "Right. In the three years I've known you, you haven't gone out on a single date. Why is that?"

"I don't like dating."

"You don't like dating . . . or is it because of something else?"

I felt my forehead scrunched into a frown. "I don't know what you mean."

"Does it have to do with Jared?"

Ice filled my veins at her words and rapidly spread throughout my body. "Jared? He's just a friend. We knew each other growing up and he used to date my sister, but I haven't seen him in years."

"How come?" Sharon sipped her water.

"I moved to San Francisco to pursue my art degree in animation." The words slipped out before I realized what I was saying. Too bad I wasn't able to snatch them from the air before Sharon registered what I'd said.

"Animation? So not graphic arts?"

Shit. "I started out in animation, but then realized I needed a career with a more solid future." For Logan's sake.

Sharon locked her gaze on mine, as if preparing to read my soul with the next question. "Did you and Jared remain friends while you were away?"

I squirmed. "No. We had our own lives. He was working hard at his music and I was busy with my studies." While this might have all been true, my silence when it came to Jared had also been partly out of fear . . . fear that I would have inadvertently blurted out the truth about Logan. I hadn't always agreed with Alexis's choice to keep Jared from knowing about his son, but I had loved my sister and would've done anything she'd asked.

"And today was the first time you've seen him since then?" Sharon asked.

I squirmed again, suddenly feeling like I was being interrogated—on the train tracks, and unable to stop the train rapidly heading in my direction.

"Well, not really. He's in a popular rock band. I've seen him on their music videos." I might have checked him out online, but nothing that would be considered stalking . . . much. "The band's debut album did well on the charts, and they're supposed to have a new album out soon. I wouldn't be surprised if it does even better than the last one. The band's super-talented."

Sharon smiled as the words gushed from my mouth. I slammed my lips shut before anything else tumbled out unrestrained.

"So he's on the road a lot?"

"Yes. They toured for about a year with the first album, opening for different bands."

"Not a great job to have if you're a father, I would suspect."

I shrugged. "None of them have kids. Only the lead singer has a serious girlfriend." That had been big news a few months ago.

"Really? So Logan isn't Jared's son?"

I shook my head a little too fast to be convincing. "Jared and I were just friends. We've never had sex. I mean, we haven't had sex together. I'm sure he's had sex before, what with all those groupies who hang out around the band." Palm, meet face.

Sharon's eyebrows rose. Not in surprise—more like she

didn't believe me and was calling me out on my clumsy attempt to hid the truth. But I wasn't lying. As much as I had occasionally fantasized about kissing Jared and having sex with him, fantasy and reality resided at different ends of the universe.

"I could have sworn they were father and son," she said. "The similarities between them are astounding. Same wavy brown hair. Same dimples. Same face. The only difference is the eyes. Logan has your eyes." The color Alexis and I had inherited from our mother.

I bit my lip, but then released it. I wasn't good at lying. Not once since becoming Logan's mother had I worried about anyone figuring out the truth. Without the side-by-side comparison of Logan and Jared, it would've been nearly impossible to randomly piece it together.

But if Sharon had figured it out, what about Jared? Had he spotted the similarities between himself and Logan, but because he knew he and I had never slept together, he never considered for a second that Logan was his?

I shook my head. "It's just a fluke."

She studied me for a long moment, then her gaze darted to the photo on the wall with Alexis in it. My rapidly beating heart climbed into my throat. I tried to swallow it back down.

"Logan isn't your son, is he?" Sharon said, then looked back at me.

"I don't know what you're talking about. Of course he's mine." The sharp lump in my throat made it hard to speak. The last word came out cracked.

But was he mine? Yes, I was his legal guardian, but I wasn't officially his mother. I had never bothered to adopt Logan because there hadn't been a reason to. As far as I was concerned, Logan was my son.

The smile on Sharon's face was sad and full of understanding, but what she understood was anyone's guess.

"Callie, I was a teacher and a very good one, I might add.

My favorite subject was math, and something about your story doesn't add up." When I didn't say anything, she continued. "You went to San Francisco, but it wasn't you who became pregnant, was it? You and your sister share the same blue eyes. The same blue eyes Logan also has." My hesitation was all she needed. "My guess is that Jared has no idea Logan is his son."

My shoulders sagged. I was too exhausted to keep up with the lies. "My . . . my sister didn't want him to know. She predicted he would one day become famous, and she didn't want their child to be dragged into his lifestyle."

"Don't you think he has the right to know?"

"It wasn't what my sister wanted, and I promised her I would never tell him."

"What happened to her?" The words were soft, like Sharon had an idea but was afraid to go there. For my sake.

"She, Logan, and my parents were driving up to San Francisco to visit me. Logan was a baby at the time. A cement truck ran a red light." I paused, the words like thistles, leaving my throat raw and scratched. "Only Logan survived," I whispered, and coughed to clear my throat. It only aggravated the pain further. "He was called a miracle baby because when the firefighters first saw the wreck, they thought there was no way anyone could've survived it."

I pulled my feet onto the chair and wrapped my arms around my legs, keeping myself together for Logan's sake.

I let out a long breath. "Logan is all I have left after I lost everything." Including the future I had dreamed about for so long.

"And you're afraid you'll lose him if you tell Jared the truth?"

I nodded. "If he finds out Logan is his son, I could lose Logan and eventually another woman will replace me as his mother. Or Jared might decide it's too difficult raising a son, especially a son who's deaf. What will that do to Logan?

Besides, Jared isn't like most fathers who go away for short business trips. His touring means he'll be gone for months instead of a few days." No matter from which angle I looked at it, no one would win if Jared found out the truth—least of all me and Logan. "No, it's best that Jared never finds out." My voice rang with certainty. If only my heart wasn't so unsure about my decision.

"But what about Logan? Doesn't he deserve to have a father? If you deprive him of his biological father and you won't date, what does that mean for him? It would be great for him to have a man in his life who can be a positive role model."

I shook my head. "What he needs is not to be hurt. And it's not like guys my age want to settle down with someone who has a child."

"How do you know?"

I let out a laugh, the taste bitter on my lips. "Because once guys see I have a child, they can't run away fast enough. And I'm not interested in dating a divorced man with kids. Those are the only guys interested in a woman like me." My voice cracked at the memory of my ex-boyfriend's final words after he found out I was Logan's legal guardian and that I refused to put him up for adoption.

Besides, it wasn't like I required a man in my life. I was a strong, independent woman.

A strong, independent woman who couldn't stop thinking about the guy she had idolized as a kid—and his heart-melting brown eyes and dimples.

7

JARED

The waitress leaned around me and placed my beer on the table. Her tits, squeezed into a black lace-up corset, brushed against my shoulder. "Is there anything else I can get you?"

I told her I was good, as did the rest of the guys—minus Nolan. Now that he had a serious girlfriend, he tended to hang out with us less than he had before. Why join us when you had a beautiful girl who was more than happy to make you come 24/7?

"What took you so long to get here?" Mason asked me, his booming voice easily heard over the loud rock music.

"I met up with someone I haven't seen in a while," I said.

"Who?"

"No one you know."

A lecherous grin slid onto his face. "Was she at least hot?"

I rolled my eyes. "Who said anything about it being a she?"

"Because it's the rule that if you're gonna blow us off, it better be for a hot set of tits."

Kirk snorted into his beer. "Since when was that a rule?"

"Shit, man," Mason said, "where have you ladies been? It's

like the unspoken rule everyone knows about."

"Riiiiight," Kirk, Aaron, and I said at the same time. I doubt even Nolan was aware of this so-called rule.

"So, are you in violation of the rule or not?" Mason pushed.

"What if I am?"

"Well, according to the rule book—"

"Which none of us have seen," Aaron pointed out.

"—the violator buys the next round of beer." Mason crossed his arms, smug in knowing that neither Aaron nor Kirk would argue against the fictitious rule at this particular moment.

"I think it's a good rule," Aaron said. Kirk nodded. Traitors.

"What happens if I'm not in violation of this so-called rule? Does the mere fact you're challenging me mean if the person is a woman, you're buying me the next round?"

"With great tits," Mason clarified.

"So, if his mom has a great set of tits," Kirk said, "that counts?"

"Oh, God," I groaned. "Do not drag my mom into this."

"No, that doesn't count," Mason said.

Kirk smirked. "Good to know."

"I'm adding to the rule. If the woman is a relative—great tits or not—she doesn't count." Mason narrowed his gaze on me. "So, dude, are you buying us the next round or not?"

I laughed. "You haven't answered my question. If the person is a woman with great tits, are you buying me the next round?"

"Definitely."

"Hey, drummer boy, how will you know if she has great tits?" Kirk was enjoying this conversation a little too much. "I didn't see Jared walk in with anyone. Did you?"

We all looked at Mason. He scrunched his lips together in thought. I didn't want to tell them about Callie. I didn't want him to even think about her that way.

Hell, I was trying not to think about her that way.

Good luck with that. But Callie had been right when she

pointed out that her son didn't need guys entering his life, only to let him down. And my becoming involved with Callie, even just as a friend, would do nothing more than complicate my life and his. None of us needed that.

Least of all me.

"Hi. Aren't you the drummer of Pushing Limits?" a woman with golden brown skin asked. Her straight black hair, with streaks of red and gold, hung down her back. Her purple dress clung to her curvy body.

"I sure am." Mason grabbed hold of her hips and pulled her onto his lap. She shrieked at the sudden movement but made no attempt to extricate herself. Instead, her arms went around his neck and she beamed at him.

I could've sworn she was an angel sent from heaven to save me from Mason's line of questioning. Not that I believed in stuff like that. But either way, angel or not, I owed her a drink.

"Congratulations," Kirk said, "she just saved your ass."

"I think you're right." I knew Kirk wouldn't push for an answer about whom I'd been meeting with. Other than Nolan, who until recently had been keeping a big secret for the past five years, Kirk was the most private member of the band. Which meant he respected everyone else's privacy.

I drank some beer and surveyed the area, lit by the dancing spotlights. The club was busy, but that was hardly unexpected for a Saturday night. I didn't have to look to know there was a huge line to get in. The club wasn't exclusive, but it was still popular with celebrities and non-celebrities alike. Which meant celebrity sightings didn't draw the same level of curiosity, unlike in some places. But that didn't mean the female persuasion weren't paying attention to us. We were four good-looking guys (five when Nolan was with us). Even before the band started getting radio time, girls were all over us—which often made me wonder if we would've done just as well if our looks hadn't been considered part of the package.

A girl about Callie's age slid in next to me on the booth seat. Aaron was on the dance floor. Mason was who knew where, doing who knew what, although I had my suspicions. Kirk was standing next to the booth, talking to two large guys. I had caught part of their conversation at one point. Unlike the rest of the band, his conversations weren't about music. With Kirk, it was often about hockey. In his past life, before becoming a bassist, he'd been headed to play hockey professionally. Even the band had no idea what caused him to switch from hockey to music.

"Hi." The girl pressed her body against my side, shoulder to shoulder, hip to hip. "You're my favorite guitarist of all time."

Like I'd never heard that line before. I gave her my best smile, one that usually had girls sighing. And this girl was no different. "Thank you."

"Is Tiffany here?"

"Not that I know of."

She glanced around, as if expecting the supermodel to emerge from the shadows.

"Do you wanna dance?" I asked, suddenly in the mood to do just that.

"That's . . . that's okay to do?"

"Why wouldn't it be okay?"

For a second it looked like she would answer, but then she changed her mind and slid out of the booth. I joined her and we headed to the dance floor.

"What's your name?" I asked. Not that I cared, but it was the polite thing to do.

"Maria."

As Maria and I moved in time to the music, our bodies pressed together due to the crowded space, only one thought filled my mind: Callie. The two girls were nothing alike. Maria's dark hair lay straight and long. Her body was that of a dancer, long and lean, and her olive coloring was also the opposite of

Callie's fair skin, with an adorable smattering of freckles across her nose. Maria was sexy as hell and she knew it. The way she moved her body screamed confidence.

Callie was sexy too, but her sexiness wasn't blatant, like Maria's. She had an innocence about her that was even more appealing.

I shoved the thought away. Because not only did I not need to think about Callie, I'd rather not think about what her innocence meant when it came to other men. If I found her attractive, so would other guys. Maybe one day she would find someone who'd do right by her and her son, and she'd let him into her heart.

For some reason, the thought chilled me from the inside. It was ridiculous, really. Logan was a great kid. He deserved to have a father, someone loving and understanding like my old man, but as long as Callie was afraid of Logan being hurt, she would never take that risk. Her son would always come first for her, to the point of her sacrificing everything else.

Not your problem, I reminded myself, and focused on Maria instead.

We danced for two more songs. Her hands were all over me, making it clear what she wanted. Only I wasn't too sure what I wanted. Other than another beer.

And then another.

Followed by yet another.

At one point Marisa—or Maria, or whatever her name was —went to the bathroom. No sooner had she left than two girls took her place. I pulled one onto my lap; the other sat next to me. Both explored me with their hands and their lips. Neither seemed bothered by the other girl's actions.

Marisa or Mary never returned. The waitress brought me another beer. It wasn't enough to block out my memories of Callie. If anything, the beer made them clearer.

8

JARED

Many things in this world are considered to be the epitome of cruelty. But when the blinding sunlight glares at you through the window because you were too drunk last night to close the fucking curtains, that easily ranks up there on the top of the list.

I groaned and snapped my eyes shut. I vaguely remembered Kirk calling it a night. I vaguely remembered him shoving me into a cab with him. I vaguely remembered stumbling up the stairs to my apartment, because I had insisted on walking up them instead of riding the elevator. And I vaguely remembered someone helping me climb said steps.

But as far as the night went, that was all I could remember, other than a few flashes here and there of dancing, talking to girls, kissing.

I also remembered a couple of other things, but I suspected they had more to do with how much I had drunk last night than reality. Things that my subconscious craved to do to Callie. Erotic things she might not have appreciated if she knew I was thinking about her that way.

Smooth fingertips trailed along my exposed abs and dipped

under the sheets covering my hips. Maybe I hadn't dreamt about fucking Callie last night after all. Maybe she really was here.

I cracked open my eyelids and peered at the blurry vision next to me. Even without blinking my eyesight clear, I could tell the girl in my dreams wasn't the one lying next to me.

"Morning," she said, her voice pack-a-day rough.

I blinked her into focus. "Um, hi?"

"How are you feeling?" She smiled sweetly. Shit, why didn't I remember having sex with her? Even in my dreams, I had imagined Callie's soft scent. This girl's perfume was much heavier. It wasn't bad, but it wasn't Callie's scent.

"Thirsty," I replied.

"I'll get you some water."

Before I could say anything, she bounced out of bed in nothing but a black satin thong and bra. I lifted the sheet to discover she wasn't the only one in her underwear. I still had my boxer briefs on. I let out a relieved breath. If I was drunk enough not to remember fucking her, I would've been too drunk to pull my underwear back on afterward.

She returned with a glass of water and a bottle of Tylenol. "This should help." She passed me the glass and handed me two pills.

"Thanks." I tossed back the painkiller and downed the entire glass of water. Luckily my stomach didn't protest. By the time I was finished, she was under the sheet, her bra no longer on her.

She didn't waste time sneaking her hand under the covers. It brushed against my dick. I jerked away, putting several feet between us.

Her lips curved into a seductive smile and she scooted closer. "I thought now that you're sober, we can finish what we started."

"What exactly is that?" "Sober" was the last word I would've used to describe my current state.

She moved her hand to my nipple and pinched it. "What do you think?" she purred.

Her previous words echoed in my head: We can finish what we started.

"So we never actually fucked last night?"

"No, you were too … um … out of it." Translation: I couldn't get it up.

She slid her hand down my chest again. I grabbed her wrist. "Sorry, I have plans."

That much was true, even if I did want to go back to sleep and wake up once this hangover was over. My family was expecting me in a few hours. Sure, we had plenty of time for what she had planned, but I wasn't interested in going there.

That wasn't to say I wasn't into sex with groupies. Like the other guys in the band, I had taken advantage of what was offered. Not a lot, mind you. I wasn't a manwhore like Mas. Maybe another time, back before I'd bumped into Callie, I might've been interested. Now I couldn't get excited about the prospect of screwing around with this woman.

A glimpse of the dream from last night repaid me a visit. I shoved it away, telling myself the dream had nothing to do with my decision.

The girl, whose name was a complete blank to me, pouted. Now I vaguely remembered seeing her red-coated lips last night; the color had since faded. Her dark eye makeup was still in place, although now it was smudged. She didn't look bad, but she did look like she was about to do the walk of shame— even if she had nothing to be ashamed of.

She stroked her fingers against my chest. "I can make it worth your while."

I released her hand and shifted away from her. "I'm sure you can, but I really do have to be somewhere important." I gave her an apologetic smile and waited while she gathered her clothes. I had tons of questions about last night but decided to save them for Kirk. She had already answered the big one I'd had. The rest could wait.

I offered to call her a cab. She shook her head and called a friend instead. She did, though, ask for my autograph. After everything, that was the least I could do.

Even though she insisted she was fine waiting on her own, I escorted her downstairs and waited with her.

"You know, you don't have to do this," she said as we stood inside the lobby, watching through the glass wall.

"What? Wait until your friend arrives? Sure I do. My mother raised a gentleman." Although I was sure Mom would've had a different opinion of what I'd been last night.

"Your mom sounds like a great woman."

"She is."

We didn't have to wait long before her friend's black Ford Escort pulled up in front of the building. The girl quickly kissed my cheek. Before I could say anything, she was out the door and climbing into the front passenger seat of her friend's car.

I returned to my apartment and drank enough water to help rehydrate me, but not enough to cause me to puke. Then I had a long hot shower to remove the stench of beer that I was positive seeped from my pores.

By the time I left for my parents' place, I looked a lot better than I had when I first woke up. That's not to say I felt a hundred percent, but it was enough to keep Mom from guessing about my night. As supportive as she and Dad were about my career choice, I knew my playing in a rock band still worried them. They'd heard the stories about all the booze, drugs, and women that came with the territory. It was hard to miss when those three things had led to the demise of so many other bands.

At their house, I parked in the driveway and walked up the flagstone path. Unlike Callie's parents, who'd moved closer to Callie's father's new job shortly after Alexis aborted our child, my parents had never had the desire to move. This place held many great memories. I swear, if my father ever had to move for his job, Mom would've found a way to take the house with her.

The front door swung open and my father stepped to the side to let me in. "So, you up for this?"

I grinned at him. Fortunately, my head didn't hurt so much now. "You better believe it."

"Good. Lunch is almost ready, then it's just you, me, and the gazebo." He said it in a low, conspiratorial voice. I chuckled. I had no doubts whatsoever Mom already knew what we were up to. And if she didn't, she would find out soon. There was no way could we hide from her that we were building a gazebo. Not unless he had convinced her we were building another tree house, but if there was one thing Mom wasn't, it was naive.

In the kitchen, Mom was busy laying out the food. A large vase of white tulips sat in the middle of the glass-top table. "Lunch is ready." She hugged me, and we all took our usual places. "How's the band doing?"

"Everyone's doing great. We had the radio station event yesterday." I filled them in on the day, minus the part about groupies groping me. There were just some details my parents didn't need to know.

"I can't believe you're touring again so soon," she said. "It feels like you just got back."

"I know but it's part of the job. Plus it's great to be out there and playing to the fans. That's what it's all about." Never mind the part where some of those said fans loved to fling their bras and panties at us.

"I know. It's just . . . well, how are you ever going to have a family if you're always on tour?"

"What, Emma isn't enough for you?" Emma had recently

discovered the fine art of walking, and kept Mom on the run whenever she babysat my niece.

"I want more than one grandchild."

"I'll be sure to tell Kristen." I winked at her.

Mom gave me her standard this-discussion-is-far-from-over look, and I laughed. Dad also laughed. We both knew Mom just wanted me to be happy and would support whatever I decided to do. Even more so if it resulted in grandchildren.

"So, what's going on with you and . . . Tiffany these days?" she asked.

"Nothing that will give you grandchildren—I can guarantee that." I bit into my BLT sandwich.

"But you're still seeing her?"

I shrugged. "We're not currently dating. I agreed to be her date to an upcoming event in L.A., but that's just as a friend."

Needing to change the current line of questioning, I blurted out, "Hey, you'll never guess who I bumped into yesterday. Callie Talbert."

"How's she and her family doing? I can't remember the last time I spoke to her mom. Not for a few years at least."

"Good, I think. Callie has a son now."

Mom's eyes widened. "She's married?" She quickly recovered and laughed softly. "Of course she's married. Just because she was a tomboy as a kid doesn't mean she didn't become a woman."

"She's not married."

"Engaged?"

I shook my head.

"But the child's father is still in the picture, right?"

Brilliant move, asshead. I had meant to distract Mom from her line of questioning about me providing her with more grandchildren. I hadn't meant to freak her out about Callie and Logan and their well-being.

"I don't think so."

"Is there any guy in the picture to take care of them?"

I shook my head even though it would've been a better idea if I had lied and told her that there was. Or, better yet, if I had just kept my mouth shut to begin with. "But you don't have to worry about her. She's doing fine."

"How could she be fine looking after a child on her own? The boy needs a father."

"I'm sure her own father is doing a great job."

"Jared's right," Dad said. "Gary and Violet aren't the type of parents who wouldn't step in and help out. They'll be a great role model for the child until Callie can find the right man for her and her son."

Reluctantly Mom agreed. Dad had a point. "So you and Callie are friends again?"

"I wouldn't say that. I haven't decided if I'll see her again . . . as a friend." I hastily added the last part before Mom got any ideas. "We're both busy with our own lives, and we're different people than we were back when we were kids."

"It wouldn't have anything to do with her being a single mom, would it?" Mom said, her gaze piercing my soul. I loved my mother, but she had a way of wringing the truth out of you with just that look.

"No, I really am busy with the band." And there was also that matter of Callie not wanting me to be part of her and Logan's life.

"What are the touring plans this time?" Dad asked, and I could've hugged him for the change in topic.

I spent the next few minutes explaining everything the band's manager had told us so far about the next couple of months. We still didn't know, though, which band we were opening for. The label was being very hush-hush about it.

Mom didn't bring up Callie or Logan again, maybe realizing I really was too busy for them. And maybe realizing that being in a band wasn't conducive to having a family—not that I planned on becoming a family with Callie and Logan.

After lunch, Dad and I disappeared into the backyard and began constructing the gazebo. It was hard work, but both of us were in good shape, which made the job a little easier. Any talking between us was kept to a minimum, our attention focused solely on building the large wooden structure. I didn't have a chance to let my mind drift to Callie.

By the time we finished several hours later, we were covered in sweat and our muscles ached.

"What do you think?" Dad asked as we stood in front of the gazebo, studying it.

"Looks good." I wasn't just saying that. Like everything we worked on together, we had taken our time to ensure it was perfect. My father and grandfather had taught me the value of working hard and not settling for less—a lesson I put to good use when it came to writing songs.

We were still examining the structure when my sister and brother-in-law joined us. Kristen was lugging three bright green cushions with daisies embroidered on them. Craig had a bottle of beer in each hand and handed them to Dad and me. The hangover from this morning had long since been sweated away, and the cold beer couldn't have been more welcome.

"Wow, it looks amazing," Kristen said, after arranging the last of the oversized cushions. Between the large, dark-wood coffee table and Kristen's decorating know-how, the gazebo resembled one straight from a home-style magazine. She was right. It did look amazing.

Mom walked out of the house, carrying Emma. The smile on Mom's face made all the hard work worth it. "What do you think?" she asked her granddaughter.

Emma hugged the bear I'd given her a few months ago and flashed me my favorite grin, complete with the dimples Kristen and I had inherited from Dad.

"Hey, pipsqueak." I ruffled the fine dark hair on her head. I was rewarded with my favorite giggle.

After excusing myself, I disappeared into the bathroom and showered. I'd missed a lot of things while on tour, but the weekly Sunday dinners with my family ranked at the top of the list.

I returned a short time later and placed a gift bag next to where Emma sat, sandwiched between her mom and grandmother on the gazebo bench. "This is for you."

My sister sighed. "You don't have to spoil her, you know."

"Sure I do. I'm her uncle. It's in the job contract." I helped Emma remove her gift from the bright-colored bag.

With a little encouragement, she ripped off the tissue paper the salesclerk had wrapped it in, revealing the toy guitar. She then patiently waited while I removed it from the box. The way the toy was packaged, you'd had thought it held important FBI secrets. Eventually I freed it and demonstrated how to use it. Designed for a toddler, it was nothing like my guitars, but it did make musical sounds when played—loud musical sounds that Emma enjoyed making every time she pressed the buttons.

Kristen laughed. "So instead of having your own kids, you're going to turn mine into mini-Jareds?"

"Damn straight." I purposely avoided looking at Mom. As much as she longed for grandchildren from both Kristen and me, I just didn't see that happening. At least not anytime soon.

9

CALLIE

Wednesday, during the lunch rush, I placed the order of fries and the cheeseburger in front of the bald-headed customer. His shirtsleeves were rolled up, revealing a tattoo on the inside of each forearm.

"I like your tattoos. What do they mean?" I smiled at him and his friend. At least I hoped it resembled a smile. My energy level was at an all-time low. Just curving the corners of my mouth up asked a lot.

"This one"—he pointed to the tattoo consisting of four overlapping circles with a fifth circle in the middle—"is the Celtic fivefold. Each of the outer circles represents an element or energy: earth, fire, water, and air. The middle circle unites them, with the goal to achieve balance between them all. Much like we attempt to balance everything in our lives."

Maybe I could get it tattooed on me, to help me balance my life and my energy levels.

Inwardly I sighed. If only it were that simple.

He indicated to the elaborate cross on his other arm. A circle, with the same intricate design, was tattooed around the center of the cross, with plainer, much thicker circles beyond it.

"This one has several meanings, such as hope, balance, transition. Some people believe the vertical crossbar represents the past and the future. The center is the present, the point of transition between the two. The outer circles could represent the moon and the sun. When the sun sets in the west, it's saying goodbye to what has been done. The rising sun is a harbinger of newness or possible change."

"Wow, that's so cool." Until now, I hadn't realized how much meaning existed behind Celtic designs. Not that I had given it much thought either.

He chuckled. "I'll agree with you there. Celtic culture is a passion of mine."

"I can see why. Can I get you anything else?"

"No, sweetheart, we're good for now."

While I'd been busy talking to them, the hostess had seated a group of college-age girls at the next table. Their clothes were trendy and high-priced, their skirts short. I glanced at my ugly brown uniform that was two sizes too big and did nothing to help my tips. I'd been working here for the past three years and I was still waiting for them to get my size.

"Hi," I said, a little too brightly. It sounded to me as fake as it felt. "Are you ready to order your drinks?"

The girls looked me over, their disgust at my outfit clear. It wasn't like they were forced to wear it, so I figured they'd get over it soon enough. What my uniform lacked in fashion sense, the food more than made up for.

"I'll have a Diet Coke," the girl with long dark hair said. Her friends ordered the same.

I returned with their drink order.

"You mean *the* Jared Leigh?" a girl at their table asked as I parked her drink in front of her. I startled at the name. "What was he like?"

"Amazing. He does this thing with his tongue that's to die

for. I actually thought I was going to die when he made me come."

I set the glass down but accidentally placed it on the fork's edge. The glass tipped over, spilling Diet Coke and ice on the table.

"Sorry," I said, grabbing the available napkins.

"Are you going out with him again?" her friend asked, more interested in the dark-haired girl's sex life than the stream of soda headed toward her.

"Maybe."

I quickly mopped up the mess and left to get a damp cloth and another drink. I deposited the new glass on the table, taking care not to spill the contents this time. She just nodded in thanks, too engrossed in her friend's sexual escapades to give me or the drink much thought.

"You're so lucky," another girl said as I continued cleaning up the mess. "I can't believe I went to a lame hockey game with my boyfriend. I could've gone with you on Saturday and met the band. Did you get their autographs?"

Jared's "friend" removed a piece of paper from her purse. I recognized his signature. Not his real one—the one he used to sign for fans. None of the other guys had signed it. "I didn't have a chance to get the rest of their signatures. I got Jared's before Amy picked me up at his apartment."

So after he'd come over and helped Logan and me celebrate Sharon's birthday, he'd gone out and gotten laid. Nice.

I took their orders, a pleasant smile painted on my face, even when the dark-haired girl demanded all kinds of changes to her order. As if tormenting me with information about what Jared had done with her last Saturday night hadn't been enough.

I busied myself with my job and avoided the girls' table as much as possible. I wasn't too keen to overhear any more details about her more-than-satisfying night with Jared. Even when I brought them their food, I did my best to escape as fast as humanly possible.

"Is there anything else you need?" I asked, after picking up the last of their empty plates. I might as well have asked a brick wall. None of them were paying attention to me. They were busy staring toward the main entrance.

"Oh my God, Courtney," one girl said, her voice hushed yet overly excited, "he must be crazy about you. Why else would he be here?"

"Did you tell him you were gonna be here?" another girl asked.

Without meaning to, I turned to the door. Jared stood there, surveying the area. I gasped and hightailed it to the kitchen. If I was lucky, he and his new girlfriend (or whatever she was to him) would leave before I had to check if the table needed anything else.

I emerged from the kitchen with the order for another table, which was thankfully nowhere near the girls' table. Like an ostrich hiding its head in the sand, I avoided glancing in their direction. If I didn't look at him, he wouldn't notice me. Okay, maybe that was a foolish fantasy, but at least it was worth a try.

"Are you going on your break soon?" Beckie asked me. Just a year younger than me, she had also left college before finishing her degree, but for different reasons.

"Yeah, unless you want to go first."

"No, I'm still good. Besides, you look like you need it more."

The break was only fifteen minutes, but if the gods of senseless lust were feeling benevolent toward me, by the time I returned, Jared and his girlfriend would've left.

I grabbed a glass of Diet Coke and headed out back. The diner had a small staff room, but calling it "small" was being generous. Right now, the last thing I needed was to be caged in. I needed to run. Run far and run fast. But since there wasn't enough time for me to do that, pacing in the alley would have to do.

As alleys went, this one wasn't too bad, as long as you didn't wander too close to the garbage. A small metal table and two matching chairs sat near the back door. They had once been white, but most of the paint had since chipped away.

After I took a sip of my drink, I parked it on the table and started pacing. My feet were tired, but that was just a minor inconvenience. Nothing I couldn't overlook.

A slight breeze swept through the alley. The sky darkened as a thick cloud drifted in front of the sun.

As I walked toward the back of the building across from the diner, the diner door squeaked open. Groaning inwardly at the loss of privacy, I turned around to see who else was taking their break.

But it wasn't one of my co-workers.

A raindrop hit my arm.

"What are you doing back here?" I asked Jared. *Why aren't you with your girlfriend? You know, the one who's ready to write sonnets about your tongue's magical abilities.*

"I came to talk to you."

"Why would you want to talk to me?" A few more raindrops splashed against me and the asphalt.

"Because we used to be friends, and I can't see why we can't still be friends."

Somehow I held back the derisive snort. Maybe if my heart didn't behave foolishly at the sight of him, things could've been very different. Maybe if Logan wasn't his son, Jared and I could've been friends. But as it was, I couldn't take the risk.

I shook my head. "I don't have time for friends. Other than my job and my education, I only have time for Logan."

Lines formed across Jared's forehead. "What do you mean you don't have time for friends?"

"Just what I said." I reached for my drink. The clouds

decided now was a great time to release their load. Neither Jared nor I moved. As a kid, I used to love running outside in the rain and splashing in the puddles, even when I didn't have my rubber boots on.

I couldn't remember the last time I'd done that.

The lines on Jared's face deepened. "Do you have friends?"

"Of course I do."

"Like who?"

"Seriously? You're gonna ask my friends' names just 'cause you don't believe me when I say I have friends?" I did what I could to sound indignant, when in reality he had nailed the truth. In high school and college I'd had a number of friends I'd hung out with. Now the number of friends I had could be counted on two hands, if you included Beckie, Sharon, and my co-workers, none of whom I had time to do anything with. Beckie and Sharon were the only ones I shared with about my life, and even then I kept it to a minimum.

Raindrops dripped down my face, but I still didn't move.

"It's not that I don't believe you," he said. "It's just I don't get why you don't want to be friends with me."

"And I don't get why you're so desperate to be friends. In case you've forgotten, I have a child. I'm not like your single friends who have time to party and pick up women." I cringed at how petty that sounded. "We have very different lifestyles, Jared. I don't know why you think mine will fit neatly with yours." I grabbed my drink from the table. "I have to get back to work." Where his girlfriend was waiting for him.

I opened the door and entered the building. He didn't say anything, but I could sense him following me. I ducked into the staff room and quickly changed into a dry uniform. Since I couldn't delay it any longer, I approached the table where Jared's latest girlfriend and her friends were, and picked up their empty dessert plates.

From the looks of it, he hadn't returned to the table. Before I could turn to leave, his girlfriend jumped out of her seat and stepped around me. She wrapped her arms around Jared's neck, her body pressed against his damp clothing.

"Where did you go?" she asked. "You didn't even stop to say hi."

He didn't?

He opened his mouth to respond but didn't get that far. Her mouth slammed into his. It was like watching a horror movie when you knew something bad was going to happen but you couldn't look away. All you could do was watch the carnage. Except in this case, the only one to die an excruciating death was me.

Jared grabbed hold of her arms, but instead of pulling her closer, he pushed her away. Not hard, but with enough force to separate them, and that included their mouths.

"I missed you," she said, loud enough for everyone at the table to hear. She smiled, but it was tentative at best.

10

CALLIE

I bolted to the kitchen, unable to escape fast enough. And yes, I might have stayed in there slightly longer than necessary.

When I finally emerged with the desserts I'd been pretending to wait for, Jared was gone. The girls left soon after.

"Callie," Alice said, "Josephine called in sick. Beckie's covering her shift tonight until the rush is over, but she can't help me tomorrow. I need you to pull a double shift."

I itched to tell her no, that my child came first, but I couldn't. I needed this job and I owed her. It was the least I could do after I had taken so much time off when Logan was hospitalized with meningitis. And let's not forget the multitude of medical, physical therapy, and audiology appointments, plus the numerous school meetings that I had missed work for during the past year.

"Okay." I hoped Sharon could look after Logan; if not, I was screwed.

Beckie waved goodbye to me, a secretive smile on her face. "Have a good night."

"You too." I hurried out of the diner and came to a sudden

stop. Jared was standing on the wet sidewalk, watching the door. I glanced back in time to catch Beckie grinning. "What are you doing here?" I asked him. The sidewalk was empty of his girlfriend and her friends.

He nodded at the diner. "One of the waitresses told me when you get off. I thought I'd walk you home."

"That's not necessary. This is a safe neighborhood and it's daylight. Nothing's gonna happen to me. Besides, wouldn't you rather be with your girlfriend?"

"What girlfriend?"

"The one who was kissing you."

"She's not my girlfriend."

"Really? Because apparently she's very intimate with your tongue and all the great things it did to her girlie parts."

He slowly shook his head. "I have no idea what you're talking about."

I choked back a laugh. Did I seriously need to spell it out? "You went down on her."

He frowned. "She told you that?"

"Well, not me directly. I was lucky enough to be serving drinks to the table when she bragged to her friends about your gifted tongue. Trust me, it wasn't something I wanted to hear." I began walking down the busy street. The rain had taken a break at some point while I'd been working. Too bad. Maybe it could've washed from my brain the image of him going down on her.

Jared caught up with me. "I never went down on her or had sex with her."

"Are you sure about that?" I shrugged, doing my best to make him think I didn't care one way or another. "Maybe you just forgot her."

"No, I haven't forgotten her. Whatever she told her friends was a lie. Nothing like that happened."

Something about his reaction made me believe him.

Besides, he didn't have a reason to lie to me. We weren't dating. He wasn't cheating on me. "I guess you get that a lot. I mean groupies who say they've slept with you just to impress their friends."

"Maybe. But that's the first I've heard of it happening."

"So you've never had sex with a groupie?"

"I wouldn't go as far as saying never. I'm not a monk. Never claimed to be."

"Okay." I turned down a side road that quickly became a residential street. On either side of the road, large leafy trees provided a canopy against the sky.

We kept walking, not saying much. It reminded me of when we used to hang out together. It wasn't awkward at all. Just the opposite. Besides, what was there to say that I hadn't already said the other night?

I was just relieved he hadn't asked about my family. I couldn't go there with him. Not now. Maybe one day, when their deaths weren't still fresh wounds on my soul.

It also meant I avoided asking about his. I knew that if I did, he would reciprocate.

"So it must be cool seeing all those different places while touring," I said.

"Not really. Usually we don't see much of anything. We drive to the next city, maybe do radio interviews while the roadies set up the stage, meet some of our fans, perform, get back on the bus, and drive to the next location."

"That sounds kind of . . ." I left the sentence hanging as I searched for the right adjective, one that sounded more upbeat than the word that first came to mind.

"Boring? Yeah, it is. But it's worth it to see the fans and see how much they appreciate the music. I mean, we get that they do, based on our album sales, but that's nothing compared to seeing them live and seeing their enthusiasm when we play." His face beamed as he spoke, and it was easy to see how much his job meant to him. He lived for it.

And that made me smile. At least one of us had been able to follow their dreams.

"What are the guys in the band like?" I'd heard rumors, but they were based on the media, and I wasn't sure how much was based on reality.

"They're great guys. Mason can be a bit of a handful at times, and he enjoys pulling pranks on the unsuspecting, but overall he means well. He's had some problems in the past, but he's keeping that part of himself in check."

"What kind of pranks?"

"One time he put rubber snakes in a drum case for a roadie to find. Unfortunately, Paul was terrified of snakes after a rattler bit him as a kid."

My hand flew to my mouth. "Oh my God! Was he okay?"

"He did get over it eventually. And there was that time when Mason told our tour bus driver that Kirk was taking a nap. It took us two hours to realize that we had left him in Tucson. He had actually told Mas that he was going for a run."

The laugh bubbling inside me broke free. "Poor Kirk."

"He eventually got over it too."

"So you're telling me you aren't ready to kill your band-mates yet?"

He laughed. "Definitely not. I can always rely on those guys to watch my back, like I'd do for them. They're like the brothers I never had. . . . Which reminds me. My mom says hi and was wondering how your parents are doing."

The not-yet-healed wound tore wide open, and I swallowed back the pain and the tears. I opened my mouth to answer, but the prickly lump in my throat prevented the words from form-ing. "They're dead," I finally whispered. "They died in a car accident a few years ago." I kept my eyes on the path ahead of me, willing my legs to keep moving.

"I'm so sorry, Callie. Why didn't you tell me?"

"Because I'd rather not talk about it." The words came out rough, weary.

Jared stopped and gently grabbed my arm, forcing me to also stop. "Hey, you know I'm here for you, right? We were once friends. If you need to talk, I'm here for you."

But that was where he was wrong. Everything had changed.

I gave him a soft smile and started walking again. "You remember when I failed my fourth-grade math test?" I asked a minute later. "I was really upset and wanted to run away and join Cirque du Soleil?"

"Are you gonna tell me that you recently did join them? Because the Callie I remember wasn't very talented when it came to cartwheels." He flashed me a teasing smile, and my heart lightened at how easy he was making this for me.

I shoved his arm playfully. "I wasn't that bad." At his raised eyebrows, I added, "Okay, I admit I wasn't great at them. I guess that's why you tried to convince me that I was better off running away and joining Bon Jovi on tour. You even tried to convince me to take you with me."

"You didn't expect me to let you meet the band without me, did you?"

"Have you met them?"

We reached the entrance of my apartment building and I paused at the door.

"Not yet. Maybe one day. So far we haven't been in the same place at the same time for it to happen."

I grabbed the handle of the glass door. "Well, thanks, Jared. I guess I'll see you around." I didn't really mean it. It just seemed like the right thing to say to someone, even if you were planning to never see them again. As much as I would've loved to see him again, I knew I couldn't.

"Hey, don't I get to at least say hi to Logan?"

"Why would you want to do that?" I asked, panic seeping in like rain through a broken window.

"Because he's a cool kid. Why wouldn't I want to say hi to him?"

"Because we've already had this discussion. I don't want you to hurt him."

"How is saying hi hurting him?"

The elderly woman from the apartment a few floors above mine walked past. Jared said hi to her and opened the door to let her in.

"Thank you," she said, and entered the building.

Jared turned back to me and missed the woman appraise his very nice ass. She grinned at me and nodded her approval. I snickered. She did have a point.

"You see?" he said with a smirk, having no idea why I was laughing. "I said hi to her and she didn't get hurt."

I rolled my eyes. "That's not the same thing."

"So explain to me why my saying hi to Logan is going to hurt him."

That was the thing . . . I couldn't.

"All right," I said on a heavy breath. "You can come up to say hi." I wanted to add, "But then you have to leave", but I was too tired to come up with a logical reason he couldn't stay longer than that.

We entered the building. I unlocked the inside door and let him in. As we approached the elevator, the door slid opened. The elderly woman who had appreciated Jared's ass stepped in first, and we followed. I pressed my lips together as we rode up to my floor, doing my best not to laugh as she checked out his backside again.

On my floor, I unlocked my apartment door to the sound of coughing from inside, and it felt as though I'd been hooked up to an IV and freezing liquid was rapidly infusing into my bloodstream. It took me a second to realize it wasn't a child coughing. I quickly opened the door and entered. Jared followed, clicking the door shut behind him.

I didn't have to wait long before Logan came charging from his bedroom. Sharon followed soon after, moving at a much slower pace. The cold chill returned full blast. This morning she had looked like she was coming down with a cold, but now she looked a hundred times worse. All I could do was stare at her as Logan wrapped his skinny arms around my legs.

I hugged him and kissed the top of his head, ignoring for the moment everything else. The exhaustion. Sharon being sick. The extended shift tomorrow. My feelings for Jared.

Sharon started coughing again. "Sorry," she said once the coughing fit finally subsided.

"Are you okay?" Unconsciously I tightened my hold on Logan, as if that would be enough to shield him from getting another serious illness.

He squirmed, and I reluctantly let go. "Why don't you go into your room and I'll be there in a minute?" I said and signed.

"Jared play with me?"

"Can Jared play with me?" I corrected.

"I can do that," Jared said. "Why don't you show me your toys?"

I mouthed, "Thanks." He gave me his standard you're-welcome nod. Logan grabbed his hand and led him into his bedroom.

"Are you okay?" I asked Sharon again, my mouth suddenly dry. Maybe it was due to my paranoia after everything Logan had been through, but I had a feeling she was far from okay.

"It's probably nothing more than a cold. But just to make sure"—her gaze darted to Logan's room—"I have an appointment with my physician in an hour."

"How are you getting there?" She didn't own a car.

"The bus."

"I'll drive you."

She shook her head. "I don't know how long I'll be, and the doctor's waiting room is the worst place you could take Logan."

"You can't take the bus. You're too sick."

"And I can't have you drag Logan to that office and risk him getting sick too. I've done my best to minimize the chance of him catching whatever I've got, but you won't be able to do the same there."

She was right, but I was also right.

Jared stepped out of Logan's room. "I can stay with Logan while you take Sharon."

"You can't do that," I blurted out.

"Why not?"

"Because . . . um . . ."

"It's a great idea," Sharon said, her voice a little brighter.

I flashed her a look that I hoped conveyed more to her than it did to Jared. While I didn't doubt for a second she was sick, she was up to something.

But I also didn't have a choice when it came to Jared looking after Logan. Sharon was right. I couldn't bring him with us, but I couldn't let her take the bus.

I let out a hard breath. "All right, but are you sure about this?" I asked him. "You don't exactly have experience looking after kids."

"We'll be fine. In case you're forgetting, I used to be one." That was hardly reassuring. "Plus I have a niece. So I'm not totally inept when it comes to kids."

I told them I'd be right back and entered Logan's room. "I have to take Mrs. Rogers to the doctor's. Are you okay if Jared stays with you till I get back?"

"Jared plays with me, yes?"

"Yes, Jared is going to play with you."

He grinned, and I could've sworn in that moment I'd never seen him look as happy as he did at that news. A pang in my heart warned me this was a bad idea, but I really didn't have a choice.

AT THE SOUND OF THE MAN A FEW SEATS DOWN COUGHING WITH that phlegmy noisy that always made my stomach churn, I subtly turned my body away from him and flipped the magazine page. A familiar model stared back at me, her makeup and glossy black hair making me feel grossly inadequate. Not that her micro-mini and sequined halter top helped much either. But even if she'd been wearing the same baggy jeans and long-sleeved T-shirt as me, she would have looked sexy.

She would have looked nothing like me.

But while Tiffany Grainger might've been a supermodel and might've had guys drooling over her, I had one thing she didn't—Logan. Sure, she never had to worry about a guy turning his back on her because she had a child. But she also didn't know how it felt to have a child love her like she was the most important thing in his world.

Too bad Logan was the only male who would ever look at me that way.

I closed the magazine and searched for one that wouldn't remind me just how lonely I really was. Which meant no magazines with articles on finding Mr. Right or how to give Mr. Right an orgasm he'd never forget.

As I was deliberating whether it would be better to read the home-decorating magazine or the five-month-old issue of Sports Illustrated, Sharon walked over to me.

I stood up. "What did she say?"

"I have pneumonia."

"Pneumonia?" I squeaked. "Will you be okay?" Of course, you idiot, she'll be okay. She has pneumonia, not the plague.

"I'll be fine. She prescribed antibiotics and told me to rest until I'm feeling better." She cringed at what that meant.

I gave her my most reassuring smile. Or at least I tried to. "Don't worry. Logan will be fine. I'll figure something out."

I was completely, utterly screwed.

11

JARED

When I was a little boy, I was a major book nerd. I couldn't get enough picture books. Twice a week, Mom would take Kristen and me to the library so I could borrow new ones. A picture book had inspired me to want to learn to play the guitar.

Next to Logan on the couch, I pointed to the cat in his picture book. "What's the sign for cat?"

He and I had been playing this game for the past ten minutes. I'd point to an animal on the page and he'd show me the sign for it. My sister had explained the importance of reading to young kids, but try telling that to her daughter. She hadn't inherited my book-nerd gene. Emma never stayed still long enough to listen. Logan was the opposite. This was the third time I'd read him the story since Callie had left to take Sharon to her doctor's appointment.

Logan pinched his thumb and index finger together and brushed them against his cheek.

"Is that like the cat's whiskers?"

He nodded. "Cat whiskers."

"Do you like cats?"

"I want dog."

"Can you say 'I want a dog'?" I felt like an idiot correcting him, but figured Callie would've done it if she were here. Besides, Logan didn't seem bothered by having to repeat the sentence. He was used to it.

"You want a dog too? Can I see it?"

I laughed. "No, I'm not getting a dog. My apartment building won't allow it. And who would look after it while I'm on tour?"

He grinned. "Me!"

I laughed again. "I don't think your mom will go for that, but would you like to visit my friends' puppy?"

Logan jumped off the couch, grabbed hold of my hand, and attempted to tug me up. "Let's go."

"Not now. I have to ask them first if it's all right with them."

The front door clicked open, and I glanced toward the hallway. Logan sat back down next to me, flipped the page, and waited for me to read the words. It was like he hadn't even heard the door open.

A minute later, Callie entered the living room. "Hi."

"Mommy!" Logan didn't sign the word this time. He catapulted himself off the seat and raced over to his mom. Callie barely had time to squat before her son launched himself into her arms.

"I missed you," she said, hugging him.

"I missed you. Did you miss Jared?"

"Of course. Did you have pizza?" There was no missing how quickly she changed the topic.

Logan nodded. She tickled his tummy, and he giggled. She smiled at him, but something was off about it.

I pushed myself off the couch. "How's Sharon doing?"

"She has pneumonia." Callie did her best to fix the fading smile on her face. It didn't work. "So I have to find someone to look after you tomorrow while I work," she said to Logan.

He pouted. "Where Mrs. Rogers going?"

"She's not going anywhere, but she's sick and can't look after you for a few days."

Logan hugged my legs. "Jared look after me and take me to see puppy."

"Sweetie, it was nice that he helped out so I could take Mrs. Rogers to the doctor, but he has to work too."

"Other than practicing with the band in the afternoon, I'm pretty free tomorrow. I can bring him with me. The guys won't mind."

Callie rapidly shook her head, eyes wide. "No. That won't work. He has preschool tomorrow morning and . . . and he doesn't like listening to music. It doesn't sound good with his implant."

"What time does preschool start and finish?"

"Eight thirty till eleven."

"I can drive him to preschool and pick him up." I turned to Logan. "Have you ever felt music before?"

He looked at his mom, uncertain if he had or not.

"Maybe," she said. "It's hard to tell. Before he got the implant, I would play music, but I didn't turn it up very loud. Thin walls."

"I bet the drum and bass vibrations feel pretty cool when Mason and Kirk play their instruments," I told him. "We can turn off your implant while the band practices and you'll be able to feel the beat." I could tell Callie was torn, as she bit her lip, so I added, "I mean, unless you have someone else who can look after him. But honestly, I don't mind. What do you say, Logan? You want to hang out with me and the band tomorrow?"

"I get to see puppy?"

"I'm not sure about tomorrow, but we can ask Nolan when we see him." That was met with an enthusiastic nod.

"Can I talk to you for a second in the kitchen?" Callie asked me. After finding a TV show for Logan to watch while we were gone, she indicated for me to join her.

"What's up?" I asked once we were in the kitchen.

"Thank you for offering to help out, but it's really not a good idea."

"So you have someone else who can do it? Or can you take time off work?"

She shook her head. "I wish I could, but someone called in sick. I'm not just working my regular shift. I have to work until eight tomorrow night."

I shrugged. "So I'll stay till you get home. It's no big deal, Callie. He's a great kid."

The panicked look from earlier reappeared on her face. She averted her gaze. "This is such a bad idea," she whispered, more to herself than for my benefit.

I stepped closer and lifted her chin, her skin soft against my callused finger. Her light perfume, which reminded me of the sweet pea flowers she loved so much as a kid, teased me. Her light blue eyes met mine. The only thing I didn't remember from our childhood was her lips. Had they always been that full? Had they always looked like they begged to be kissed?

A craving powered through me to run my thumb across her lower lip, to see if it was as soft as it looked. Her lips parted slightly. On instinct, I leaned in another inch.

The kitchen door creaked open. Callie jerked away from me as if someone had scalded her with boiling water. Logan walked into the room, oblivious to what he had almost interrupted.

"What would you like?" she asked him.

"I'm thirsty."

She rushed to the fridge, unable to get away from me fast enough, and poured apple juice into a plastic cup.

He returned to the living room with his drink, but the moment between his mother and me was over. Not that you could really call it a moment. What I had felt for her in those brief seconds was purely one-sided.

Remember, you used to date her sister. She sees you as nothing more than her big brother. And even if she didn't see me that way, she wasn't interested in dating me—for Logan's sake.

"So what time do you want me here tomorrow?" When she didn't answer, her mind somewhere else, I said, "Everything's going to be okay. He knows I'm in a band and that I tour. I'm more like an uncle to him."

Callie swallowed hard. "Six."

Fuck, that was early. I usually didn't get up until closer to eight in the morning. Sometimes even later, if I had stayed up late the night before working on a new song.

She proceeded to write down and explain his schedule and how to get to his preschool. "If you drive him anywhere, you'll need his booster seat." The entire time she talked, an odd sort of tension rolled off her. She was nervous as hell, either about the almost kiss or about leaving me in charge of her kid—I couldn't figure out which. But something made me want to wrap her up tight in my arms and tell her it was going to be okay. That I would be there for her, even if I didn't know if I could keep that promise.

"I swear, everything will be all right," I told her. But I got the distinct impression my words did nothing to alleviate her fears.

12

JARED

Thursday morning, while Logan was at preschool, I went for my daily run and hit the local workout park. So far the morning had gone well. I had survived dragging my ass out of bed early, though it had almost killed me.

On the road, as soon as the stage was packed up after the main act was finished, the tour buses would roll out and head to the next town. By then, the guys were asleep. Given how late that usually was, it wasn't surprising how we would sleep well into the morning—although I was usually the first one up, much to Nolan's annoyance. I was what he would grumpily refer to as a morning person.

Logan's preschool didn't resemble the preschools I'd seen before. It was much bigger. From what Callie had told me, the preschool specialized in working with disabled kids, everyone from toddlers to kindergarteners. The preschool also had a special program for kids who were deaf or hearing-impaired.

A few moms chatted in the small gathering area inside the building when I went to get Logan after school. It had been designated for parents to drop off and pick up their kids. Along one wall, coat hooks had been hung at little-kid height. Beneath them, outdoor shoes waited patiently in a semi-neat line.

One mom looked up and spoke to the other mothers in the group. As a single unit, they turned in my direction. Some, the ones that obviously weren't too familiar with Pushing Limits or weren't fans, just checked me out because I was a guy and because I hadn't been here before. The others had the opposite reaction: they wore the typical expression of our female fans.

"Hi," said a woman in her early twenties who was wearing yoga pants and an Oakland Raiders T-shirt. "You're Jared Leigh, right? I'm Sarina Scott. God, I love your band. You guys are amazing." She was the woman who'd set off the celebrity-alert system when I entered the room.

"Thanks."

"I didn't know you have a child."

"I don't. I'm picking up my friend's son for her."

Her blond eyebrows jerked up. "Friend?"

"Yes, Callie Talbert."

The woman tilted her head to the side, and I got the distinct feeling she was studying me. "So you're not Logan's father, then?"

"No, just an old family friend. Logan's regular caregiver is sick, so I'm taking care of him while Callie's at work."

"Are you and Callie dating?"

Two moms rolled their eyes. It sounded like one muttered, "Way to be obvious, Sarina," but I couldn't be certain.

"No. Like I said, we're old friends."

"When does Pushing Limits's next album coming out?" asked another woman who was several years old than Sarina and bouncing a baby in her arms.

"The first single comes out in four weeks, and the album releases the following week."

She gave Sarina a quick glance. "And then you'll be touring?"

I nodded.

"I seriously don't know how you do it," Sarina said. "It's no wonder so many relationships with rock stars don't last." Then she quickly added, "Not that I'm saying you can't maintain a relationship while on the road."

I laughed. "I'd hardly call myself a rock star. And you're right. It is tough." As it was, I had no idea how Nolan and Hailey planned to keep up their relationship once the band hit the road. Touring put a strain on relationships. If the length of time between visits wasn't enough of a problem, you had to trust that your significant other would remain faithful. More often than not, that tended not to happen. The last band we opened for cheated on their girlfriends and wives all the time.

But Nolan and Hailey weren't anything like those individuals. They had a strong history behind them and a friendship that had been tight for many years. I didn't doubt that if Nolan hadn't originally escaped his hometown after the shit with his old man went down, those two would've been together for the past five years instead of what did happen.

The classroom door opened, and seven kids Logan's age marched into the pickup area. Their teacher said goodbye to them, both through speech and in sign language. Some spoke and signed back. Two only signed.

One of the teachers gave me a brief nod, and I showed her my driver's license. I'd met her this morning when I dropped Logan off. Callie had already told her that I would be taking care of him for the next few days. Security was tighter here than it was on tour—for good reason.

Logan rushed over and grabbed my hand, then pulled me toward another man who was standing there with a little boy. The man had arrived soon after me but hadn't joined the group of mothers I'd been with. He'd been talking on his phone.

"This is my friend, Ben," Logan said. "This is his daddy." There was both awe and wistfulness in his voice when he said the last word. My heart clenched.

The man held his hand out to me. "Hi, I'm Tony."

I shook it. "Jared."

"I haven't seen you here before."

"I'm helping Logan's mom out. His regular caregiver is sick. Callie and I are old friends."

"Daddy, can we go to the playground with Logan?" Ben asked.

"Sure, for a short time. If it's okay with Logan's da—er, friend."

"That's fine. Logan and I are free for a while longer."

"We're gonna see his band," Logan said. "He plays guitar."

"What kind of music do you play?" Tony asked as we helped the boys change into their outdoor shoes.

"Rock."

"You do that full-time?" Curiosity marked his words, which lacked the judgmental tone I often heard when people found out what I did for a living . . . before they learned about the band's success on the charts with our last album, that is.

"You mean play in a band?" I asked.

He nodded.

"Pretty much. We're just waiting for our new album to be released, then we're back on tour again."

"Album? What's your band's name?"

I told him.

"I've heard of you guys, but I'm more into country."

By "heard of," he no doubt meant the controversies that had swirled around us on more than one occasion.

"So, you're a stay-at-home dad?" I asked as we walked outside to the playground behind the school. The temperature had already warmed up, the sun bright in the sky.

"No, I have a computer programming company, but I work

out of my home so that I can be there for my son more. I used to work for a multinational corporation, but with the long hours expected of me at the office, I was rarely home when Ben was awake." At least he was home more than I would be if I had a child and was still touring.

The boys climbed onto the swings and asked us to push them. Callie had already warned me not to push Logan too high. The swings tended to make him nauseous.

"So what's the deal with you and Callie?" Tony asked. "She seems nice."

At something in his voice, a hint of jealousy sparked in me, and I turned to him, my attention no longer on Logan. But before I could figure out what he was really asking, Logan and the swing slammed against my leg. I fell backward, and my ass landed hard on the gravel.

Without missing a beat, I replied, "She is nice," and pushed myself up, my pride more bruised than my backside.

Tony and I continued talking while the boys played. I was so used to talking to my bandmates, fans, groupies, media, and people from the record label that it felt weird talking to someone who had nothing to do with the music industry. We chatted about all kinds of things, but mostly about the boys. Tony told me all the stuff he and Ben did together, and that made me think about my own father—and what Logan was missing out on because of Callie's fear of him getting hurt.

But despite his original question about Callie, he didn't seem interested in her the same way that I was. Relief extinguished the jealousy.

Tony and Ben eventually had to go home.

"How 'bout we go visit your mom and get some lunch?" I said to Logan on the way to my car.

He jumped up and down like a cheerleader buzzed on caffeine. "Yay! Chocolate milkshake and fries."

I chuckled at his enthusiasm. "Okay. Milkshakes and fries it is."

The diner was busy when we arrived, with several people waiting ahead of us for a table. The place resembled a restaurant from the fifties, but more recently renovated. In the far corner was an old-fashioned jukebox, but I couldn't tell if it worked or was just for display. It wasn't currently playing any music. White and black tiles covered the floor, like a giant checkerboard. Bright red chairs and booth seats added a splash of color. The only things out of place were the dozen framed photos with a windy-weather theme, including a picture of a guy standing in the wind with his umbrella inside out. Some had a more comical feel, while others showcased the emotion behind the high winds in the pictures.

A woman with chin-length blond hair smiled at Logan. "Hi, honey," she said in a faded Texas drawl as she ruffled his hair. "You come for the usual?"

Logan nodded enthusiastically.

"All right. I'll get you a table in your mom's section as soon as I can." She winked at me and walked off to the kitchen, stopping briefly to speak to Callie.

Callie looked in our direction and smiled at us. Despite the exhaustion that was clearly weighing her down, her smile was bright and warm.

We didn't have to wait more than five minutes before the woman, whose name, I learned, was Alice, led us to a booth. Logan sat and I took the seat opposite him.

Alice handed me a menu and Logan a coloring page with the kids' menu at the bottom. "Callie'll be with you in a minute." She walked off, leaving me to study my menu.

"Other than fries and chocolate milkshakes, what else do you recommend?" I asked Logan. I removed my guitar pick from my pocket and flipped it between my fingers and across the back of my hand.

He shrugged and started coloring the elephant with his favorite color of crayon—green.

"Do you like burgers?" I asked.

Before he had a chance to answer, two chocolate milkshakes were placed in front of us. A tall swirl of whipped cream with a cherry sat on top of each shake.

"If I remember correctly," Callie said to me, "you used to love chocolate milkshakes."

"Still do." I just couldn't remember the last time I'd had one. You tended not to go for drinks with the guys and order milkshakes. Beers were the drink of choice when the band went out.

"I see you haven't changed much." She gestured at the guitar pick.

I'd started playing around with my picks back when I was first learning to play the guitar more seriously. Strumming the instrument somehow grounded me, but when I didn't have my guitar with me, this did the trick. It had gotten to the point where half the time I did it unconsciously.

"Do you know what else you would like?" Callie pushed back a stray strand of hair that had fallen out of her ponytail.

"I'll have a cheeseburger with bacon."

"Do you want fries or a salad with that?" She grinned, knowing full well what I thought of salad. In my opinion, the only time lettuce should be on my plate was in a burger or sandwich. Lettuce was for rabbits, not people. She left without waiting for my answer.

"Can I try?" Logan pointed at my guitar pick, and I spent the next few minutes helping him with the trick.

"Don't worry," I told him after he dropped it on the table for the tenth time. "It just takes practice." I took the pick from him and slipped it back into my pocket.

Callie returned ten minutes later, placed our plates in front of us, and set a plate of fries and a club sandwich next to Logan's. "I'll be right back."

She returned minus her tray and sat next to her son. "Alice insisted I take my lunch break while you two are here." She hugged her son. "How was preschool?"

Logan mumbled what sounded like "good" around a mouthful of fries.

I sampled a fry. "Okay, these have to be the best fries I've ever tasted. How am I only learning about them now?"

Callie laughed. It was amazing how much a person could miss hearing a laugh, especially hers. "Had a lot of experience with fries, huh?"

"You better believe it. You forget I've traveled extensively around the US and Canada. Although I must admit poutine is up there too."

Lines formed between her eyes. Who knew a frown could look so adorable? "Poutine?"

"It's fries, gravy, and cheese curds. It's really good."

She screwed up her nose. "I'll have to take your word for it."

We spent the short time she had left for her lunch break eating and talking. The tension from the past few days, since I first bumped into her, had eased slightly, though it still lurked under the surface. For a second, the urge to kiss her senseless and convince her to tell me what was really bothering her pulsated through me, but I suspected that even then she wouldn't tell me.

"Okay, buddy, are you ready to watch the band play?" I asked as Callie got up to return to work.

She kissed him on the cheek. "I have to work late tonight, but I'll be home in time to tuck you into bed."

"Aren't you gonna kiss Jared?" he asked.

She gave a nervous laugh. "Why would I do that?"

"'Cause he got hurt at the playground. You have to kiss him all better."

Her eyes widened. "Are you okay?" she asked me.

"I'll survive. I wasn't paying attention while Logan was swinging and ended up on my as—I mean, my butt."

She chuckled and began walking away.

"No, Mommy. You have to kiss him."

I held my hands out to the side. "You heard him. You're supposed to kiss me." I might have also smirked, challenging her. Why, I had no idea.

She leaned down and gently pressed her lips against my cheek. I'd expected a quick peck, like my great-aunt gave me when I was a kid. Instead, Callie's soft lips lingered for a moment before she slowly pulled back. My breath halted in my chest, heart beating louder than Mason's bass drum.

I ached to grab her back and taste her lips on mine, but she was already out of reach.

"You feel better now?" she asked.

No. "Yes."

"Good. I'll see you two tonight." And with that, she walked away—leaving me still craving to taste her for real.

13

JARED

I parked behind Kirk's jeep on the street in front of Mason's building. Mason lived in a studio loft that had once belonged to a musician. The man had sound-proofed the place, which meant it was a perfect location for us to practice.

I knocked on Mason's door. Logan and I didn't have to wait long before it opened.

Mason's gaze dropped to Logan. "Is there something you've been keeping from us?"

"Logan, this is Mason, the drummer," I said. "Logan's the son of one of my friends. She has to work and her babysitter is sick."

Mason raised an eyebrow. "So you thought you'd fucking bring him to work, like one of those spend-the-day-at-your-parent's-job events?"

"Fuckin'," Logan repeated.

Shit. "Logan, we don't use that word," I gently admonished.

That caused Mason to snicker. "If you didn't want him talking like you, why the hell bring him here?"

"Fuckin'."

I grounded my teeth together. "I'm seriously going to kill you, Mas." Right before Callie killed me.

He grinned at me. "You're welcome."

We entered the loft, Logan holding tight to my hand. Mason lived on the top floor, in one corner of the building. Large windows filled most of the space on the two exterior walls. Mason wasn't much into furniture and went for the minimalist look, which meant there was plenty of room for our instruments and amps in the center of the room. Much like Callie's parents, Mason had great taste in furniture. But unlike Callie's parents, Mason's taste ran more modern.

And yes, I'd finally pieced together why Callie's furniture looked more expensive than what I would've expected a twenty-two-year-old to own, and why it had looked familiar. She had inherited it when her parents died.

"Hey, man." Tomas gave me his standard head nod, his lips stretched into a wide grin.

"Congrats. I heard you're now drumming for Burning Wire." They were a new band that had started to generate buzz in the L.A. music scene. They weren't bad, but Tomas was much too talented for the band.

"Thanks. They're a great bunch of guys." He peered down at Logan. "Hey, buddy." He gave the four-year-old a fist bump, which Logan happily returned. Then to Mason and me he said, "I'll let you guys get to work. See ya later!"

The introduction of Logan to the rest of the guys in the band went a little more smoothly than it had with Mason. Hailey had the day off and was sitting with Nolan on the black leather couch.

"Logan, this is Nolan, our lead singer, and his girlfriend, Hailey."

"You have puppy, yes?" he asked them, his small body pressed against my legs.

"Would you like to see a picture of him?" Hailey asked.

Logan took a tentative step forward. "Yes. Please."

She removed her smartphone from her purse and handed it to him. On the screen was a fluffy, nine-week-old golden retriever puppy, snoozing on Nolan's shirtless chest. The puppy wasn't the only one sleeping on the couch. Nolan looked pretty out of it.

"His name is Rocky," she said. "He's a golden retriever."

"Why the fuck is our lead singer half-naked with a dog sleeping on him?" Mason asked. "Who the hell removed his nuts and gave him ovaries?" He laughed. I glared at him, my message clear. He abruptly stopped.

Kirk and Aaron looked from Mason to me, amused.

"My sister makes me cough up a quarter every time I swear around her kids," Aaron said.

"Not a bad idea." I pointed at Mason. "Every time you swear, you have to pay Logan a dollar."

"Why the fuck do I have to pay him a dollar when Aaron only has to pay a fucking quarter?"

"Oh, look at that, Logan," I said, doing everything in my power not to strangle our drummer. "Uncle Mason owes you two bucks. By the time practice is over, you could be a millionaire."

The guys and Hailey laughed. All the guys but Mason, that is. He reached into his back jeans pocket and pulled out his wallet, then handed Logan the money. Logan's face lit up.

"Do you wanna feel some music now?" I asked him.

"Don't you mean f—uh, hear music?" Mason said, frowning. I had no idea if that was because not being allowed to swear would kill him or because my question confused him.

"Logan's deaf."

"If he's deaf, why's he wearing a hearing aid?"

"It's not a hearing aid. It's a cochlear implant, but he doesn't like how music sounds with it. So I thought that maybe instead he could feel the vibrations through the floor while we play."

At the volume we practiced at, he was bound to feel something.

"Wanna feel music," Logan said, pointing to the drum set.

I crouched down to his level. "I want to feel the music," I corrected. Christ, I was beginning to sound like his parent. "Can you say that for me?"

"I want to feel music," he enunciated slowly. Close enough.

"I'm going to remove the processor now. All right?"

Logan nodded, and I repeated the steps Callie had showed me this morning so that the sound waves wouldn't be transmitted to his brain, to be converted into sound.

"He can't hear now?" Mason asked.

"Nope. Now he's completely deaf."

"Fuck. Fuck. Fuckity fuck. Sorry. Just needed to get those out."

Kirk slapped Mason on the back. "That's four bucks."

"How the fuck do you figure that? The kid can't fucking hear me."

"Yes, but maybe he can lip-read," Kirk said. "Besides, we didn't say Logan had to hear you in order for you to owe him. Read the fine print."

"Promise me, puck boy, that you'll never have kids." Mason removed ten bucks from his wallet and handed it to Logan. "There you go, kid. Now I've got a four-cuss credit."

Logan looked at me and grinned, having no idea why he had just earned the money. The bigger question was how I was going to explain his sudden windfall to his mother. Either way, she would be less than thrilled at how much Logan's vocabulary had grown in one afternoon.

I indicated for Logan to follow me to my guitar. I lifted the strap over my head and turned the guitar on, then indicated for Logan to sit near me on the hardwood floor. Watching his expression, I strummed a few random chords. His eyes widened and he placed his hands on the floor. I played some more, and his face lit up brighter than before.

"I wanna try something," I said to the guys. "Each of you play a couple of bars from 'Take Me Tonight,' but one at a time. I want him to feel the vibrations from the different instruments." The lyrics weren't exactly kid-friendly, but Logan couldn't hear them, so it didn't matter.

I indicated for Mason to go first. Logan bopped his head in time to the drum beat. This was followed with Kirk on the bass, Aaron on the keyboards, and finally me on the guitar again. The drums and bass got the biggest reaction from him.

"Told you drums are the best," Mason said. "You know, if it weren't for the part where he obviously likes drums better than the guitar, I'd swear he was your son."

"Idiot. I've already told you he isn't my son."

"I heard what you said, but are you sure you've never banged his mother?"

What the fuck? "Of course I haven't."

"Maybe you've just forgotten it. You were drunk or something."

"I'm positive I've never f—uh, slept with her."

"Then how come he looks a lot like you?"

Logan looked back and forth between us. Fortunately, he couldn't hear Mason.

"Just because he and I both have dark brown hair doesn't make him my son. Kirk has brown hair too."

"Yeah, but Kirk's hair isn't wavy and Kirk doesn't have dimples. You and the boy have the same dimples."

"That doesn't mean he's my son." God, sometimes I wondered whether Mason's mother had dropped him on his head shortly after he was born.

"What color is his mom's hair?" he asked.

"Red."

"What color are her eyes?"

"Blue."

"Dimples?"

Callie's smile popped into my head. "None, but that doesn't prove anything."

Mason shrugged. "Whatever you say. But I still think he looks a lot like a mini-you." He snorted. "As if one of you isn't already enough."

Logan signed something, but I had no idea what it meant. Seeing that I didn't understand, he said, "No play?"

Everyone's gaze shifted back and forth between Logan and me, but I couldn't tell if they were buying into Mason's way-off theory.

"For the last time," I said, "he's not my son. So let's drop it and play."

Mason got the hint and began playing the opening beats of our upcoming single. We all joined in soon after.

We continued playing for the next few hours. Surprisingly, Logan didn't get bored watching us. At one point he got up and bounced around like he was dancing, the way little kids do. The light steaming through the windows shone on him, like he was the real star of the show. Hailey joined him. It was the cutest thing I'd ever seen.

For a moment, I imagined that Hailey wasn't the one dancing with Logan, and that it was Callie.

A sudden longing for the girl who'd been in my thoughts a lot lately—more than she should've been—came close to knocking me onto my ass for the second time that day.

14

CALLIE

I quietly unlocked my apartment door, in case Logan was already asleep. Light spilled from his room, as did Jared's deep voice as he read from one of Logan's favorite picture books.

I closed my eyes for a moment and let his sexy voice fill me with love, desire, and a wish that everything was different between us. That instead of Jared reading to my nephew, he was reading to our son.

But I had long since learned—after Jared started dating my sister, after my parents died, after Logan got meningitis—that wishes came true only in fairy tales.

Or maybe they just didn't come true for me.

Tiptoeing so as not to disturb them, I walked to the doorway and peered in. Logan was under his covers. Jared sat next to him on the bed. The two together—father and son—made an adorable picture. And that made my heart squeeze tightly, both in joy and in sadness. How would Jared feel if he knew Logan was his son? What would he do if he found out that I had known all these years and never told him?

But I couldn't have even if I had wanted to. I couldn't break the promise I'd made to my sister. I had loved her too much to go against her wishes. She had been there for me whenever I needed her. She had taught me how to apply makeup. She had helped me with my math homework. She had encouraged me with my artwork whenever I got frustrated because something about the picture I was working on wasn't right.

Even though she had died and I was struggling to figure everything out myself, I couldn't tell Jared the truth. Maybe part of that had to do with how long it had been since I'd last talked to him. And what would I have said to him anyway? Talk about an awkward conversation. In the end, it had been easier pretending Logan's father didn't exist.

Besides, I didn't even know if he wanted a child. He hadn't when Alexis had told him she was pregnant. It was one thing to hang out with a friend's child. It was another when you were the one responsible for the child.

I also couldn't tell him, because what if Jared decided he wanted Logan in his life and won custody of his son? I couldn't risk losing yet another person that I loved.

Jared glanced up from the book. He nudged Logan. "Look who's home."

"Mommy! Jared read to us."

I climbed onto the bed with them, with Logan sandwiched between us on the twin bed. "What is he reading?" I already knew. It was one of Logan's favorite books.

"It's *Storm Is Coming!*"

"Logan's been teaching me the signs for the different animals." Jared demonstrated his new skill, signing "cow," "sheep," "duck," "dog," and "cat."

"That's really good," I said and signed. All the while, my ovaries were screaming, Daddy material alert! Damn ovaries. They must not have read the memo.

Jared read the book again, and I did my best to look at the pictures and not sneak sidelong glances at him. Did my best not to wonder if Logan would look even more like his father when he was older. I was doomed if he did. I was just surprised Jared hadn't noticed the similarities.

Jared finished the story and I tucked Logan in.

"Did you have fun today?" I asked.

Logan nodded. "Jared play guitar and I get lots of money."

"You did? Jared paid you to watch him?"

"No. When Mason say 'fuckin'.'" He smiled, proud of his newfound income.

Jared had the decency to at least look sheepish. "Sorry 'bout that. Mason isn't used to being around kids. If it makes you feel better, he mostly swore while Logan couldn't hear him, but Kirk still made him cough up the money because it was the principle of it that mattered."

There were so many choice words on the tip of my tongue, but I managed to rein them in. "Just because an adult swears," I said to Logan instead, "it doesn't mean you're allowed to. Okay?"

"Okay."

I kissed his cheek. "I'm glad you had fun today."

Jared and I said goodnight to him. I removed his audio processor and put it in the drying box, then we left his room.

"Do you want me to leave or do you want to hang out for a bit?" Jared asked in the hallway.

I had assignments due soon, not to mention I had a few projects clients were waiting for, but all I had the energy to do was to watch TV.

I grabbed us some drinks, and Jared and I settled on the couch. I curled up at one end. He sat in the middle. At one point during the show, he lifted my feet onto his lap and removed my socks.

"What are you doing?" I asked, relieved I had at least bothered to redo my nail polish last night. Not that I'd expected anyone—least of all Jared—to see my red toenails.

"You worked twelve hours, so I bet your feet are sore."

My feet. My shoulders. My entire body.

"So I'm going to massage them," he explained.

"And I'm guessing you're a pro at that?"

He smiled, and as usual his dimples almost did me in.

At his expert touch, my feet turned to liquid—not to mention a few other body parts. Each nerve fiber came alive, which said a lot after how dead my feet had been since midway through my shift. If Jared ever gave up playing the guitar and creating songs, he could make a great living giving foot massages, with me as his number one customer.

"Are your feet the only parts that are sore?" he asked, after finishing with my now very happy feet.

"Were sore. Past tense. You cured them."

"Good to hear. Anywhere else?"

"My shoulders and back are sore," I said without hesitation.

He spread his legs and patted the spot between them. This time I did hesitate. The nerves in my feet weren't the only ones that had come alive. The nerves between my legs had ventured closer to happy land. Who knew what would happen if his magic fingers touched any more of me?

"I don't bite," he pointed out.

"Nice to know." With a deep breath, which failed to do what I had aimed for, I moved between his legs.

His hands kneaded my shoulder muscles. I winced at his touch, but then let myself go as he continued working on them, releasing all the knots. The man was magic when it came to his hands.

I moaned. I couldn't help it.

Jared's hands stilled for a second. "You okay?"

"Oh, definitely." My voice came out low and husky. Now that was unexpected.

Working with a game plan different from the one my brain

had agreed to, my head moved to the side, exposing my neck. I closed my eyes.

Lips, warm and soft, hovered over the exposed skin, teasing me. I leaned back against his hard chest. I couldn't remember the last time a guy had touched me this way. It felt good, better than I remembered.

His hands drifted up along my ribs, lightly tracing them. A shiver ran though me. I was dreaming this. I was so tired from work, I must have fallen asleep on the couch. Now I was dreaming that Jared was touching me in the way I longed for.

His hands cupped my breasts and his thumbs brushed against my nipples. My very happy, perky nipples. I groaned.

Best. Dream. Ever.

The lips moved to the shell of my ear. The tip of a tongue trailed along the outside. My panties grew damp with want.

My eyes still closed, I turned my head to taste those lips. Sadly, they were just part of my active imagination, but that was okay. A girl couldn't be too fussy.

The kiss was a brief touch of the lips. Nothing more than a tease. Against my wishes, my eyes opened a crack.

Then they snapped open fully.

I scrambled off the couch, but in my haste to escape Jared— the real Jared, not the dream Jared—I tripped over his leg and landed on my ass. Nice.

"Sorry," I croaked, "I thought you were someone else." Jared was the guitarist of a popular band who spent a lot of their time touring. He didn't have room in his life for a girlfriend, especially one with a child. Which meant this was about him getting laid—like I was nothing more than another of his groupies.

That thought was a bucket of icy water between the legs.

He frowned. "Who the hell did you think I was? Logan's father?"

I laughed, the sound bitter. At least he had no idea how he

had nailed the truth square on its nose. "Of course not. I'm . . . tired." My butt smarted from the impromptu landing, slightly eclipsing the smarting of my pride at his reaction. "But you have to agree that what just happened was a mistake, right?"

He narrowed his eyes. "You're right. It was a mistake. It won't happen again."

At his cold tone, my heart tore into several pieces. But that was okay. There was only room in it for one person anyway. At least that was what I kept telling myself.

I mentally straightened the no vacancy sign on my heart and walked Jared to the front door. "Thanks for helping me today." I gave him a bright smile even though I felt anything but happy. "Miserable" was a better word for it. "It meant everything to me when you brought him to the diner. I miss him a lot when I'm working, and . . . Well, thank you."

He returned my smile, but it seemed as forced as mine felt. "You're welcome."

Everything between us had suddenly shifted, and if I could have rewound time to get a redo, I would've jumped at the chance. Only this time my body wouldn't have experienced his touch. My lips wouldn't have experienced his kiss.

And I wouldn't have been left craving more—a more I'd never get to have.

15

JARED

But you have to agree that what just happened was a mistake, right? Callie's words repeated in my head as I drove away. I'd lied when I had agreed that the kiss was a mistake.

It had felt like anything but a mistake.

The only mistake was when I lashed out at her and told her it wouldn't be repeated. The last thing I was ready to do was walk away from Callie yet again.

And I suspected it had to do with more than just wanting to be friends.

A lot more.

I drove aimlessly around L.A., my mind careening everywhere. To the conversations I'd had with Callie since first bumping into her at the store. Mason's comments at practice today. The similarities between Logan and myself that I couldn't ignore.

It wasn't until I pulled into my parents' driveway an hour later that I realized my driving hadn't been aimless after all. Deep down, I knew what I had to do.

I rang the doorbell. Mom answered it a moment later.

"Is everything all right?" She opened the door wider to let me in.

"Why wouldn't it be?"

"Because it's Thursday night. You're four days early for Sunday dinner."

I smirked. "What, that's the only time I'm allowed to visit my parents?"

"Hey, you know I'm always thrilled to see you and your sister." She hugged me. "It's just very unexpected."

So was my reason for being here.

"I was just wondering if you have any photos of me when I was four or five."

"Of course we do. It will just take some time to go through the pictures to find them."

She led me to the guest room and pulled from the bookshelf several narrow plastic boxes, each containing a couple hundred photos. "Unfortunately, your father wasn't into organizing photos until after we got the digital camera."

We both grabbed several boxes and carried them downstairs to the kitchen. We spent the next hour at the table sorting through pile after pile of photos. Since they had dates printed on the back, Mom decided this was as good a time as any to start organizing them.

"I have some bad news about Callie's parents," I finally said, after deliberating over the best way to tell her. "They died a few years ago in a car accident."

"Oh, God." Mom's hand flew to her mouth. "No wonder Violet never returned my call. How are Callie and Alexis doing?"

"I don't know about Alexis, but Callie's still hurting."

We continued searching through the photos.

"Here's one of us when we were camping during spring break." Mom turned it over and read the date. "You're about four in it."

I took it from her and studied the picture. Kristen and I, along with Mom and Dad, were standing in front of the rowboat, waiting for Dad to take us out on the lake. Both Kristen and I had fishing rods. Unlike Kristen's, mine was nothing more than a toy. We were all grinning.

The similarities between Logan and four-year-old me were startling. Both of us had the same amount of wave in our hair that caused the ends to curl up. We both had the same face shape, with the chubbiness in the cheeks that came with being four. And we both had the same dimples.

If I didn't know better, I would've sworn that Logan and I could've been brothers—with twenty-two years between us. The one thing I did know was that Logan couldn't possibly be mine. Callie and I had never had sex. That much I could guarantee.

Whoever his father was must look a lot like me. That was all there was to it.

"Can I keep this?" I asked.

"Sure. Do you want any more?" Mom handed me another photo. In it I was holding my first guitar. It had been just a toy, but back then it had felt real to me.

"I'll keep these two. Thanks." I helped Mom finish organizing the photos. "Does a birth certificate include the father's name?"

"Your father's name is on yours, if that's what you're asking," Mom said, peering at me with her usual astute eyes. With Kristen and me as her kids, she'd learned that what we said wasn't always what we meant. We'd been skilled at skirting the issue—and she had been equally talented at getting the truth from us. But for now, she was calmly waiting for me to reveal the real reason for my question.

"But is it mandatory to include it?"

"My guess is no. I'm sure that when some babies are born the mother has no idea of the father's identity."

A smile twitched at the corner of my mouth at what she was implying.

Her head tilted slightly to the side, not enough to be noticed by most, but enough for me to recognize I didn't have long to come up with a plausible lie. "Is there any particular reason why you're asking?" she said.

"Not really. The drummer from one of the bands I used to hang out with just found out he has a kid." I inwardly cringed. The lie wasn't even in the neighborhood of answering her question.

"A drummer? Or is there something I should know that you aren't telling me?" Those astute eyes homed in on me again, and I squirmed, just like I had when I was a kid and was trying to get away with something.

I formed a smirk on my face that I prayed was convincing enough. "No one has claimed I'm a dad, if that's what you're asking." I pushed away from the kitchen table. "I should be going. I have an early morning meeting tomorrow."

THE NEXT DAY, AFTER I DROPPED LOGAN OFF AT PRESCHOOL, I returned to Callie's apartment. The memory of four-year-old me in the photo wouldn't let go. I wandered around the place, unsure what I was looking for. Maybe a photo of Logan's biological father. Some proof the guy existed. And yes, I was a tad bit curious about how much he resembled me.

The search started out casual. I just scanned the photos displayed around the apartment, where anyone could stumble across them. The pictures of Callie's parents filled me with sadness. Her mother and father had been like second parents to me. There were a few things they knew about me that my own parents didn't, like who really had broken the bathroom window at my house when I was thirteen. None of Alexis's pictures looked recent, but thinking back to a conversation she and I had once had back in my senior year of high school, this didn't surprise me. At the time she'd been finishing her nursing degree and had planned to spend a few years volunteering with Doctors Without Borders or the Red Cross. Maybe she was still working overseas doing that.

When that search revealed nothing beyond pictures of Logan and Callie, and of Callie with her family, I entered her room. This was the first time I'd been in here. Like the rest of the apartment, it was furnished with what I'd guessed was her parents' old furniture—all of it dark, reddish brown wood.

A Mac computer sat on the antique-looking desk that used to be in her father's home office. It was an odd contrast of old and new. This computer was a top-of-the-line model, like the one my brother-in-law used when he worked at home. Callie was studying graphic design. It would make sense that she needed a computer like this.

Two framed pieces of artwork, which I was positive Callie had created, hung on the wall behind her bed. One was a rough cartoon sketch of two white ducks and a duckling. The parents—a heart pendant around the mother's long neck—were gazing down at their duckling, proud smiles on their faces. The duckling was inspecting a worm on the ground.

The next picture was similar, except this time it had been created on the computer with lots of bright colors. Callie really was talented, not that I'd ever doubted that. It was a shame her talent had gone to waste now that she was no longer pursuing her dream of working for Pixar.

I turned away from her artwork and checked out the framed photos lined up on her oak dresser. If pictures of Logan's father existed, they weren't here. Like before, these pictures were of her family. Some were of her old friends from high school and from when she lived in San Francisco. There wasn't a single photo of someone who could've been her old boyfriend.

The other photos were of Callie and me, taken before I began "dating" Alexis. In one, Callie was smiling, my arm around her shoulder. I was sixteen years old, Callie was twelve, and we had gone camping with our families. Alexis had opted out of the trip. Even back then Callie had been pretty. If things had been different and there hadn't been that four-year age difference, I could've easily seen myself dating her when she was older. She was sweet, funny, and generous, and she had a way of making you feel good about yourself, even when you were having the worst day ever. And with Callie, it wouldn't have been about the hot sex. It would've been something more real. Of course, if she had wanted to have hot sex at the time, I wouldn't have complained.

The final picture caused my heart to trip over itself. In it, Alexis was holding a baby, and the love in her eyes was unmistakable. She must have been twenty-three years old in it. Her blond hair had been cut to shoulder length, and the baby couldn't have been more than a few months old. The baby—a boy, if the blue blanket wrapped around him was anything to go by—had spiky brown hair. This must've been Logan.

My heart pinched that she could show so much love toward her nephew but hadn't wanted to give our own baby a chance. Unlike Logan's father, I would've been there for both her and our child.

I returned the photo and turned toward the door . . . except something held me back.

I wasn't even sure what compelled me to do it, but I opened the top drawer of the dresser, wondering if Callie kept anything important there, the way I did. Fortunately, it didn't contain Callie's underwear. Despite what I was doing, even I had my limits. Going through a woman's underwear drawer without her permission went well beyond creepy.

The drawer contained her jeans, neatly folded. I carefully pulled them out and found an envelope at the bottom labeled birth certificates. Underneath that was a large brown envelope that I ignored for the moment, homing in on what was on top.

I hesitated for several seconds, my hand hovering over the top envelope. I released a hard breath, picked the envelope up, and removed the birth certificates. The first document was Callie's. Both her mother's and father's names had been included. The second certificate had Logan's name on it, with Callie's last name listed also as his. But Callie wasn't listed as his mother—Alexis was.

My heart stopped beating as I did the mental math. There had to be a mistake. Logan couldn't be my son.

I looked at where the father's name should've been listed. Alexis hadn't declared his name. What were the odds the baby hadn't been mine after all?

Without thinking, I opened the other envelope. Inside it were legal documents. I skimmed them very quickly, realizing that they named Callie as Logan's legal guardian.

The question about the odds that Logan wasn't mine was not the only one firing around in my head. Why was Callie claiming Logan was her son? She had given up on her dream of working as an animator for Pixar, but why? And where was Alexis? Had she gotten up one morning and decided that being a mother wasn't in her plans after all? That Doctors Without Borders was more important to her?

The questions kept circulating, but one specifically kept coming back—did Callie know who the father was, or had Alexis lied to her? Or maybe Alexis didn't know who the father was. She liked sex. There could've easily been other guys. Any one of them could've been responsible for creating Logan.

I could've asked Callie, but what would I say? I was snooping in her drawers. She wouldn't appreciate that. And Callie had been lying to me about her relationship to Logan.

Who was to say she wouldn't continue to lie about the real father, assuming she knew who he was?

I returned the birth certificates to the drawer and yanked my phone from my back pocket. I needed answers, and there was only one person I could think of who could give them to me. But I no longer had Alexis's number, nor did I have any idea where she lived—or if she was even in the United States. Maybe she was working overseas as a nurse after all, and Callie was looking after Logan while she was gone. But then why was Callie lying about being his mother? And what kind of mother left her young child so that she could volunteer overseas for a few years?

I ignored the loud voice in my head pointing out that maybe Callie's parents weren't the only ones who had died in the car accident.

I sent Callie a text.

Me: What's Alexis's #? I need to talk to her.

She finally responded an hour later, confirming my worst fears.

Callie: She was in the same car accident that killed my parents. She also died.

When I was fifteen and playing football, I'd been about to hurl the ball to my teammate when one of the guys from the opposite team forgot what the "touch" in touch football meant. His shoulder made contact with my stomach, hard, causing me to land on my ass and knocking the air out of me.

That was the best way to describe how I felt after reading Callie's text. I sat down on her bed, struggling to get the air back into my lungs.

Callie's text was followed up a moment later with.

Callie: Why did you need to talk to her?

"Because I want to know if I'm Logan's goddamn father," I muttered. "The only biological parent he has left." But instead of telling her that, I typed.

Me: I'm sorry, Callie. I didn't realize. Don't worry. It's nothing important.

I waited a minute, hoping she would text me right back and admit that Logan was my son . . . but she didn't. And why would she? She had no idea that I knew Alexis was his biological mother.

My thumb hovered over the keyboard as I deliberated if I should ask her if Logan was my son. No, not yet. Before I could confront her with what I knew, there was one other person I needed to consult with first.

I skimmed through my list of contacts.

16

CALLIE

"**Y**ou're on break now," Alice said, walking past me on her way out of the diner kitchen.

"Okay." I returned to my locker and checked my phone to make sure everything was all right at home. Not that I expected there to be a problem. Logan was still at school.

Jared had sent me a text.

> Jared: What's Alexis's #? I need to talk to her.

My heart slammed to a standstill at his words and my mind spun with all kinds of reasons as to why he wanted to know—including the one involving last night's kiss. He'd kissed me and realized how much he wanted Alexis back in his life. He'd never wanted me. It was always my sister.

I deliberated all the possible answers I could give him, which included that I had no idea what her number was or where she lived. But then he would want to know what had happened to cause this apparent rift between her and me. Despite the six-year age difference between Alexis and me, I had loved my sister. I couldn't lie and pretend otherwise.

With an ache in my chest at what I had to tell him and at how he wanted her back—and how our kiss had made him realize that—I responded with the truth.

> Me: She was in the same car accident that killed my parents. She also died.

And because I obviously felt the need to torture myself some more, I added.

> Me: Why did you need to talk to her?

A moment later he replied.

> Jared: I'm sorry, Callie. I didn't realize. Don't worry. It's nothing important.

Don't worry, it's not you I want, his real meaning shouted in my head. It's your sister. It's always been your sister.

I swept the pieces of my heart into the dusty corner, then headed outside for my break.

17

JARED

Fortunately, that afternoon during band practice Mason didn't give me a hard time about the similarities between Logan and me. I might have exploded if he had. We threw ourselves into what we had to do for the next few weeks. Yes, Callie had lied to me—making her no better than her sister, if my suspicions were correct. But I couldn't let her betrayal and the news about Alexis sidetrack me from what was important to the band and me.

Hailey wasn't here this time, but Logan kept himself busy. When he wasn't watching us, he sat on the couch and played a game on my iPhone.

I tapped him on the shoulder and signed, "Time to go home."

Back at his apartment, I opened the door and the delicious smell of dinner greeted us. Callie entered the hallway and smiled at her nephew. Her yoga pants and plain green T-shirt skimmed her curves, reminding me how amazing she had felt in my hands last night.

I kicked that thought hard in the ass.

She hugged him tight. "Did you have fun with Jared?"

"Yes. I meet the puppy." He wiggled out of her arms.

"Puppy? Which puppy?"

"His friend's puppy. You come too?" His face was so hopeful, I smiled despite everything.

For the first time since I'd entered the apartment, Callie looked at me, her lush lower lip caught between her teeth. She quickly turned away, but not before I caught the hurt glistening in her eyes—because I'd inadvertently brought up the past by asking about Alexis.

"When?" Callie asked.

"Next Friday," I said in a surprisingly calm voice. "Hailey's working that day, so it'd be after she finishes work. I figured we could swing by and pick you up from the diner on the way."

For a second it looked like she was going to say no, but I wasn't the only person who hadn't built up an immunity to Logan's expression. Christ knew I had trouble saying no to it.

"All right," she said to Logan. Then to me she said, "Are . . . are you staying for dinner?"

"No. I already have plans."

She nodded as if everything was fine. As if we hadn't kissed last night. As if she hadn't been lying to me all this time. "Well, I guess we'll see you tomorrow. Thanks again." She glanced at her nephew. "Logan, say thank you to Jared for looking after you today."

"Thank you." He threw his arms around my legs and hugged me.

Fuck, what was I going to do if he really was my son?

Cameron was waiting for me in the lounge when I arrived, with two beers on the table in front of him. The place wasn't busy yet, but the L.A. Kings were playing on TV tonight (according to Kirk), so I wouldn't have been surprised if the place filled up soon.

I sat across from Cameron, relieved the nearby tables were

empty. This was one conversation I didn't need anyone accidentally overhearing.

He slid a beer toward me. "Here, you sounded like you might need this."

"You might just be right. It depends on what you have to tell me."

"So, what's up?"

That was what I had always appreciated about my old classmate—he was straightforward and always to the point.

"You practice family law, right?"

"That's right."

I gulped back some beer and sat back in my chair. The irony of the seat being red wasn't lost on me. It was Callie's favorite color. The color could also mean so many things. Sex. Danger. Anger. Power. Love. I would've been more than happy to take the first and the last one, but those options weren't available to me right now. And if my suspicions were correct, they wouldn't be after this conversation either. At least not with Callie.

"I might have a situation, and I'm not sure what to do about it." I told him about Alexis, about Logan and Callie, and about the birth certificate. The entire time I spoke, he just listened, his calm demeanor not hinting at what he thought about it all.

"Have you asked Callie if she knows who the father is?" he asked once I was finished.

"I've tried, but she avoids giving me a straight answer."

"Is there a chance Logan belongs to someone else?"

"There's a good possibility. It was a one-time thing. Anyone could be his father." But not everyone would result in a child who resembled me at the same age. I handed Cameron the photo and pointed out the similarities between Logan and me.

"If you asked Callie, do you think she would tell you?"

I thought about it for a moment. "I don't think so. I have a feeling she'll deny it. Is there a way I can find out the truth without involving her? That way, if I'm not the father, she can continue lying about being his mother and it has nothing to do with me."

"And what if it turns out you are the father? Are you ready for that kind of responsibility, Jared? From what you've described, Callie is perfectly happy caring for Logan without any assistance from you. Why not walk away and let her be?" He wasn't suggesting I do exactly that. His tone implied that I should consider all possibilities before making a move I might later regret.

"If Logan is mine, then he's my responsibility. I owe it to him."

"Are you dating Callie?"

I shook my head. "We're just friends." But could we still be friends if my suspicions were right and Logan was my son? All she had done since we'd met at the store was lie to me when it came to him. Just like Alexis had done when she said she had aborted our child.

"Your responsibility to the boy would be purely financial, then?"

"Well, no. I want to be there for him as a father too." Like my father was always there for me.

"So you're looking at shared custody with the mother?"

"I'm looking at custody, yes. But I don't know if Callie is his adoptive mother." All I'd found were documents stating that she was Logan's legal guardian.

Cameron nodded slowly. "This could get interesting. But first things first. We need to determine if you are indeed the biological father."

"How do we do that?"

"You and the boy would go to a third-party DNA collection site. I can arrange an appointment for you if you want."

"Will it hurt Logan?" That was the last thing I wanted to do to him. None of this was his fault.

"No. The technician wipes a swab on the inside of your mouth. It's easy to do and painless."

The weight of two tour buses fell from my shoulders at his words, and I nodded. "Does it matter that his biological mother is dead?"

"No. They will only compare your DNA to Logan's. The results through the lab I deal with are ninety-nine-point-nine percent accurate. If the test comes back showing that you are his father, we can use the result in court if it comes to that."

A small part of me asked what the hell was I thinking. Cameron was right. If Callie was keeping the truth from me, then why was I so eager to make my life more complicated than it needed to be? But a large part of me couldn't walk away, just as I hadn't been able to walk away when Alexis first told me she was pregnant.

"How long before we know the result?" I asked.

"Generally three to five days."

I took a deep breath and let it out slowly. My decision was still the same. "Okay. Let's do it."

18

JARED

When we were kids and still believed in Santa, time enjoyed tormenting us. The closer you got to Christmas, the slower each second ticked by—or so it seemed. By the morning of Christmas Eve, it felt like the twenty-four hour clock had added another forty-eight hours and Christmas morning would never come.

The same could be said when it came to waiting for news that could change your life. Tony said something, but I had no idea what. I'd been like this for the past four days, ever since Logan and I had gone to the lab for DNA testing on Monday. I'd been so distracted while practicing with the band, Mason had all but told me to pull up my big-girl panties and get with the program.

Or maybe he had said that. I couldn't remember.

All I was capable of was staring at Logan on the playground slide, mentally freaking out at what the test result would mean. So far I had no idea what I would do if it came back positive— or how I would feel.

I was just relieved that Logan hadn't mentioned the trip to the lab or the test to Callie. Guilt stomped through me at how not only had I kept the truth about it a secret from her, I had bribed Logan to keep quiet about it. I'd told him that he and I were just checking that we didn't have what Sharon had, then took him out for ice cream afterward. That way if he did tell Callie, she would've had no idea what we had really been up to.

My phone rang in my back pocket. As I pulled it out, my fingers were shaky, as they'd been each time it had rung in the past four days.

I checked the number and my heart slammed hard against my ribs, possibly fracturing a few of them. Cameron. I accepted the call. "Do you have the result?"

"I do."

"Hold on a second," I told him. To Tony I said, "I have to take this call. Can you watch Logan for me?"

"Sure."

I strode away from the playground equipment, far enough to talk to Cameron in private, but close enough so I could still see Logan on the kiddy-climbing wall. "Okay, give it to me."

"He's your son."

At those three simple words, it was as if the air in my lungs had been squeezed out and not a single molecule of oxygen remained. It felt like a lifetime before I was capable of taking another breath. "So what now?"

"It's up to you, but I suggest you talk to Callie first before you proceed. For starters, you need to find out the legal relationship between Callie and Logan. The answer will affect how we proceed next. But I ask you one more time, as your legal counsel and friend: Are you sure you want to proceed with this?"

Logan giggled from the platform and waved at me, a wide grin on his face. My heart, which was still slamming hard against my ribs, swelled for a second. "I'm positive."

"Okay, I'll wait for your call." We spoke for another minute or two before ending the conversation. I inhaled deeply and walked over to . . . my son. Shit. What the hell did I know about being a parent? I was just getting the hang of being an uncle to a toddler. A father to a four-year-old who happened to be deaf was completely different.

And how was I supposed to tell Logan that I was his father? I couldn't just blurt that out on the playground: Hey, guess what? I'm the asshole dad who hasn't been around in your life. I needed to talk to Callie first, and then I could tell him the truth. Somehow.

Logan rushed over. "Can we eat lunch with Mommy? Want fries and milkshake."

My insides tightened at his request. Ever since the incident with the kiss and then the damning birth certificate, I'd avoided Callie as much as possible. When I arrived at her apartment so she could go to work, she hadn't had time to talk to me before she had to rush out. And those few moments we did have had been filled with tension. I could only guess that she was still upset about the kiss.

Well, the kiss was now the least of her problems.

"Sure," I told Logan. "Why not?"

We said goodbye to Ben and Tony and drove to the diner. Alice took us to the same booth as before. Callie showed up a couple of minutes later with the chocolate milkshakes.

She gave me a hesitant smile. Even with the lies and betrayal circulating between us, the smile gave me a weird sense of hope. Added to that was the desire to taste her mouth again—only this time I craved more than a brief kiss.

I seriously needed to have "idiot resides here" tattooed on my forehead.

Like last time, Callie returned with our food and sat next to Logan. "How was preschool?" my deceptive ex-friend asked.

"It was good." Logan popped the milkshake straw in his mouth and sucked down a good portion of his drink.

"Mrs. Rogers called this morning. She's feeling better and

will look after you again starting tomorrow." She paused. "I thought maybe we could cook dinner for Jared tonight, to thank him for everything he's done for us."

My milkshake went down the wrong way and I started coughing. Sure—I donated the sperm, and you make me dinner to say thanks.

"Are you okay?" she asked with more concern than she had the right to feel.

"I'm fine. Dinner sounds great." And because I felt like being an asshole, I asked, "So what exactly happened to Alexis and your parents? How did they die?" For a second, regret kicked me hard in the chest, both for being an asshole by asking Callie the question while she was at work and because her parents and sister weren't just statistics. They were people I knew and cared about in one way or another.

Callie pressed her teeth into her lower lip again and glanced at Logan. He was too busy shoveling fries into his mouth to notice. Callie's voice came out as a pained whisper. "They were driving up to visit me when I was living in San Francisco." Her voice wavered. "A cement truck failed to stop at a red light and hit them. They . . . they didn't make it."

Even though I already knew that they had all died, just hearing how it had happened and hearing the guilt in Callie's voice, as if she was personally responsible for their deaths, was too much. It felt like someone had dropped me into the depths of the frigid ocean, and the intense water pressure was squeezing the air out of my lungs. Holy fuck. My hand slammed against my mouth. I wished again that I had known about the accident. I could've been there for her. For my son too.

She stroked her hand over Logan's hair. He smiled at her, but it was clear he had no idea what we were talking about or that it impacted him.

"So, Logan, do you have any grandparents?" I asked, despite knowing the truth.

"No," Logan said. "Just me and Mommy and Mrs. Rogers." He reached for another fry and beamed at me. Then he returned his attention to his milkshake.

To Callie I said, "Did your parents die before he was born?" I just wanted to see if she would admit the truth—or if she would compound the lies she'd already told me with more lies.

"Um . . ." Her eyes grew wide. "Yes. Yes, they did."

"When did they die?" I knew I had her. Now I wanted to see how long it would take her to figure out how much I'd pieced together.

She swallowed hard. "Just before he was born."

I ignored what she had said. To my ear, my tone sounded cool and calculating, nothing at all like the usual me—but nothing about this situation was usual. "And then to end up with Logan after Alexis died . . . that must have been tough."

When I was eleven, my sister and I had been playing catch in the living room, which was strictly forbidden. Kristen had thrown the ball at me, but her aim was way off and the ball flew into the glass vase on the bookshelf—the vase that our grandmother had given my mom shortly before Grams was diagnosed with the cancer that later claimed her life. Mom loved that vase. I had been positive my sister would suffer a heart attack from the panic at what she had done.

That was exactly how Callie now looked sitting across from me.

For a second I could have sworn she was going to bail without another word. To her credit, she just sat there, in shock. The same way I'd felt when Cameron had phoned me this morning.

At last she whispered, "You know, don't you?"

"I know enough. We can talk about it tonight."

She nodded, the movement barely perceptible, and pushed her plate away, the food barely touched.

Logan still seemed oblivious to the tension between us. He finished the last of his fries and smiled at us. "All gone."

"That's right, Logan," Callie said, eyes damp. "All gone."

19

CALLIE

Shit. Shit. Shit. I might have also thrown in a bonus "fuck" or two while I was at it during my shift. After Logan and Jared had left, I forced myself to ignore the hot mess waiting for me at home, and focused on my job.

The diner door opened, and my mouth dropped open at the sight of *her*. She walked in with a man ten years older, who was wearing a suit I was positive cost more than what I made in three months. Tiffany was wearing a red jumpsuit that was practically painted on, her cleavage on display. It looked good on her, a direct contrast to how it would've looked on me. Her shiny, perfectly straight black hair swung down her back.

I brushed behind my ear a stray strand of hair that didn't care to stay put in my ponytail. It must have suffered from an inferiority complex after seeing Tiffany's silky hair.

Alice greeted them and led them to the booth in my section that Jared and Logan had vacated not that long ago. I bet the seat where Jared had sat was still warm. Though nothing about him had been warm when he left with his son.

I finished delivering the plates to one of my tables and walked over to where Tiffany and the man were seated.

"I'm ready to settle down here," she told him. "It will make it a lot easier for working with the children's charity. I want to be more hands-on than I've been. Sending them a check once a year just doesn't do it for me. I need to do more. And I know Jared will be thrilled when I tell him. Part of our problem was that we didn't live in the same city—" Her words came to a standstill when she realized I was standing next to the table, privy to her conversation.

"Hi, I'm Callie, your waitress today. Would you like something to drink?" Somehow I said it with a level of enthusiasm I didn't feel.

"I'll have a sparkling water with a lemon wedge," Tiffany said.

The man ordered a double espresso.

When I returned with their drinks, they had switched topics. As far as I could tell, it had to do with acting. "Are you ready to order?"

Not surprisingly, Tiffany ordered a plain salad with no dressing, not even on the side. My stomach rumbled at the image in my head of her lettuce-only meal. Even rabbits ate more—but I guess rabbits didn't pose for the cover of *Vogue*.

"I wonder what she's doing here," Beckie said from behind the counter, her eyes darting briefly toward Tiffany.

Liam, a part-timer who usually worked the evening shift, grabbed a glass and began filling it with Coke from the soda fountain. "Rumor has it she moved to L.A. to focus on her acting career. And rumor also has it she's hoping to make things more permanent with her ex."

At the thought of which ex he was referring to, dread skated through me and did a triple axel. Kristi Yamaguchi would've been impressed. "You mean Jared Leigh, right?"

Beckie's jaw dropped open, and for a second all she could do was gape at me. I gave my head a barely there shake. Fortunately, she got the hint and shut her mouth.

"That's right," Liam said. "He's the lucky guy. Why go after a lowly waiter and drama student like me when you could have a rock star?" He smirked and walked off with his order.

"I thought you were dating Jared," Beckie said.

"Nope. He was just looking after Logan for the week." And possibly discovered he was Logan's father.

Inwardly I groaned and glanced at Tiffany. If she and Jared were getting back together, what did it mean for Logan? Or maybe Jared wasn't interested in having Logan in his life, because he'd be too busy with his famous girlfriend to have time for a little boy.

As much as I wished the end of my shift stayed away for as long as possible, time was not rooting for me. In fact, I could've sworn it picked up speed just to spite me, forcing me to face Jared that much sooner.

On the way home, I took a detour. Little old women with walkers moved faster than I did as I plodded home. I told myself the detour was so I could buy a special dessert for Jared and Logan. A way to say "I love you" without saying the actual words.

Although from the way Jared had looked at me in the diner, "love" wasn't in his vocabulary when it came to me. "Throttle" would've been a better word.

Once home, I went straight to my bedroom and parked my purse on the floor next to the desk. I could hear Logan's favorite TV show through the wall. *Shit. I can't do this.*

I closed my eyes, willing time to turn back three weeks. Instead of going to the grocery store when I did—the day I bumped into Jared—I'd wait until the next day. I would've willed time to go back to the day before Alexis and my parents died, so that they would still be alive, but that might've been a little greedy. Best to aim small.

I reopened my eyes and walked into the living room.

Clearly I hadn't willed hard enough (or however it worked). Jared was on the couch, watching TV with his son.

He gave me the standard chin nod and went back to the show. Unlike in the past, the smile of greeting was absent. My heart free-fell from its location in my chest, conveniently knocking my ovaries out cold. But that was okay. I didn't require them anyway.

"Mommy!" Logan scrambled from the couch, which suddenly looked as worn as I felt, and flung his small body at me. I gathered him in my arms and held him tight. His body was warm against the chill that now filled the room. I kissed his cheek and let him go so he could return to his show.

I entered the kitchen and placed the Black Forest cake in the fridge. *Breathe in. Breathe out.* Simple, really. As long as I remembered to do those two things, I would be fine.

Jared remained in the living room with Logan while I cooked dinner. Normally he would've joined me and we would've talked about our day and about those years before our lives had moved in different directions.

This time, instead of laughter, silence crowded the space.

I focused on making dinner and keeping myself together, for Logan's sake. During dinner, while we ate, I did my best to smile even though I was dying on the inside.

And the Academy Award goes to . . .

Once we were finished, I cleared away the dinner dishes and returned with the dessert.

"Yay," Logan cheered.

I cut him a small slice and handed him the plate. "Do you want to go to the park after dinner?" I asked him. "You can bring your soccer ball."

"Are you and Jared playing with me?"

"I don't know about Jared, but I definitely am."

Jared smiled at his son. "Me too."

We finished our cake and headed to the nearby field, Logan

proudly carrying his ball. Growing up, neither Jared nor I had played soccer. Beach volleyball, yes. Soccer, no. So I was surprised at how skilled he'd become.

"When did you learn to dribble a ball like that?" I asked.

"Nolan played soccer as a kid. The band and the roadies used to play whenever we had downtime before the shows. Nolan taught the guys in the band a thing or two because he got tired of always losing to the roadies." He chuckled.

That was the only time he laughed while talking to me. He cheered Logan on and goofed around with him, but as far as he was concerned, I was the leper he wanted to keep his distance from.

By the time we had finished playing, Logan was too tired to walk home.

"You want a piggyback ride?" Jared asked him.

"What's a piggyback ride?" Logan looked around, as if searching for piggies.

Jared flashed me a look that could have easily been translated as *What kind of fucking parent are you to have deprived my son of a piggyback ride?*

I simply shrugged. I was hardly going to admit that I'd been paranoid about dropping Logan, so I had never attempted it.

I helped Logan onto Jared's back and we walked home. With each step that I took, the bigger the knot in my insides became, to the point where I didn't think I'd ever be able to untie it.

Once Logan was in bed and Jared had read him a bedtime story, I tucked him in and kissed him good night. And for the first time since he was diagnosed, I was glad Logan was deaf. At least then he wouldn't hear what Jared and I were saying—and, I hoped, neither would the neighbors.

I was standing by the living room window, staring out but seeing nothing, when Jared entered. His reflection moving in the window jarred me out of my trance.

"So when the fuck were you planning to tell me that Logan is my son?"

I dropped my head forward. The cool glass pressed against my forehead but did nothing for the headache I sensed coming.

"That's what I thought. . . . Fuck. I trusted you, Callie. I thought you were different than your sister. Did you know that she lied to me too? A few days after she told me she was pregnant, she told me she'd aborted the baby. All this time I had a son and had no idea."

My eyes widened. Alexis had lied to Jared—and to me? But why? "I didn't know," I said. "I only knew that she had decided to raise the baby on her own. She said it would've been different if you two had been in love, but you weren't and it would be unfair to the baby to be placed in that kind of situation. She felt it was better for the baby to be brought up by a single mother than by two parents whose only interest in each other was purely sexual." Yes, it had been quite the conversation to have with your seventeen-year-old little sister. Maybe it had been her way of making sure I didn't follow in her footsteps.

"I don't get it," he said, voice tight. "Why did she lie to me, telling me that she'd had an abortion and then keeping the baby?"

Good question. I shrugged, my head still resting against the window. "I have no idea. Maybe she was going to include you in his life but then changed her mind. She also wanted to protect Logan, and felt the only way to do that was to keep you from being part of his life." I flinched at how horrible that sounded, even though it was the truth.

"Like fuck she did." He grabbed my arm and forced me to turn around to face him. "How the hell does keeping him from his father protect him?"

"Because she believed in you."

"Right. That's why she kept me from knowing the truth. Doesn't sound like she believed in me at all."

"That's not true," I bit out. "She knew, like I did, that you were talented and would go far with your music. We both believed that one day you would be where you are now."

"So you believed in my musical abilities, but not in my ability to be Logan's father?"

"Yes! Maybe! All she knew was that one day you would hit it big, and where would that leave the baby? You wouldn't be around much, always on the road or in the recording studio. She was afraid that you'd regret your child, and then what would happen? She would be left raising Logan on her own in the end." Except it wasn't Alexis who had been left with that responsibility. It was me.

And it was me who was now the sole bearer of Jared's hate for what my sister had done in order to protect her son. Their son.

"Is that what you thought? After knowing me all those years, is that what you thought too?"

Breathe in. Breathe out. That was all I had to do.

"No. At least not at first." I had believed that Jared would be there for his child, even if he wasn't romantically involved with my sister. In time, Alexis had convinced me otherwise.

Jared stepped closer. "What changed your mind?" The pain in his tone was undeniable. I inwardly flinched.

I didn't have an answer that I could tell him without betraying my heart, which had foolishly began falling for him since he'd become part of my life again. So I kept silent, letting him fill in the blanks as he chose.

His face darkened at my silence. "When did Alexis and your parents die?"

"Just after he turned one."

"And he thinks you're his mother?"

I bristled at this. "I am his mother."

"Legally?"

"What does that have to do with anything? I'm the only mother he remembers. He doesn't even remember Alexis." My voice cracked with guilt at my sister's name. "I've been with him since the day he regained consciousness at the hospital after the accident." My eyes misted at the memory of his tiny bruised body in the hospital crib. Until now I'd kept that memory locked away.

"Fuck. Logan was in the car accident?"

I nodded, and the sobs that had been building just under the surface broke free. After the accident I'd barely had time to cry and mourn my sister's and parents' deaths. Everything had happened so fast when it came to all the difficult decisions I'd been forced to make on my own about Logan's future.

Warm, solid arms enveloped me and held me close to an equally warm, solid body. The familiar scent of woods and spice and man also wrapped around me. It soothed me, but not enough to bottle up the more than three years of sorrow I'd been holding on to. It felt so good to be held by him that for a moment I pretended the last five years had been a bad dream.

Eventually my sobbing slowed to a hiccup and the memory of what had led me to cry against Jared's chest returned full force—including the distrust and aversion he now felt toward me because of my role in keeping Logan's paternity a secret from him.

I pulled away and attempted to dry my cheeks with my fingers. "You know what the hardest part is? Despite what you might think, Alexis was an amazing mother. Her world revolved around your son. But Logan doesn't even remember her." He did in those early days, though, and would cry himself to sleep because he wanted her and only her. Over time, as I became his sole parent, the one person he could rely on, her memory faded. "To him, the girl in the pictures was his aunt." It killed me every time he referred to her that way. "I thought it would be easier." For me or for him? I had no idea anymore.

Jared's gaze dropped to the floor for a moment. When his eyes met mine again, the storm of emotions in them terrified me. I had no idea what he was thinking, which left me feeling stripped and vulnerable. I wrapped my arms around myself, shielding me from further pain.

"Legally, what are you to my son?" he finally asked.

"I'm his guardian. My parents must have convinced Alexis to make a will." My parents had also been listed as guardians, for all the good that had done Logan.

Jared scrubbed his hand against his face. "So even then, in the event that she died, she couldn't be bothered to admit the truth and list me as his legal guardian? She was willing to risk my son's future for her idiotic charade? And what would have happened to him if you'd been in the vehicle? Who would've taken care of him then?"

"He would've been placed with children's services and put up for adoption." At his darkening expression, I added, my anger equaling his, "What, you thought it would've been better for Logan to be handed over to you? You could have been on tour then, for all she knew. Then what would you have done?"

But even my own words sounded hollow. Deep down, I knew Jared would've stepped up when he needed to, but I had allowed my sister to sway me, the way she always did. The more time that had gone by, the easier it had become not to contact Jared after my sister's death and tell him about his son. And besides, Logan was the only family I had left. I needed him as much as he needed me. I couldn't let Jared take him away from me.

"My sister and her husband would've been more than happy to take him in."

"Yes, but when Alexis wrote the will, your sister was still in college." Like I had been. "And it wasn't as though my sister was expecting to die." I swallowed hard, searching for the strength to ask my next question. "Now that you know the truth, what does it mean?" I chewed on my lip, hoping it meant nothing. That we could go back to how things were before and no one else had to know the truth, including Logan.

"I want custody of my son. I want him to know who his father is. And I want him to be part of my family, like he should have been from the beginning."

Panic hit me like a boulder speeding down a steep slope. "You can't do that," I practically yelled.

"Legally I can. I already have the DNA test result to prove he's my son. His biological mother is dead, so legally I can have full custody of him, especially since the fact that he is my son was kept from me."

"But I'm his mother."

"Legally, you're not."

"When did you become a fucking lawyer?" My legs were shaking uncontrollably at the possibility that I would lose not only the one person who loved me but the only family I had left. Before my legs could give out on me, I stumbled to the couch and sank down on it.

Breathe in. Breathe out.

Jared sat next to me and let out a hard breath. "Hey, at least now you can go back to studying animation. You no longer have to worry about Logan, and you won't have to spend your life working at the diner. Now you can finally date again and not worry about Logan getting hurt. You can finally have your life back."

"How can I not worry about my son? He's the only part of my sister I have left! Don't you get that?" I said, stubbornly refusing to quit calling Logan my son. I didn't care what Jared said—Logan was still my son. I might not have officially adopted him, but in my heart he would always be my child.

"You really don't believe I'll be a good father, do you?" Jared said, his voice reminding me of the eye of a hurricane, ready to lull you into a false sense of security before the vicious winds hit again.

"How could you be? Have you forgotten what you do for a living? Have you forgotten Logan is deaf? Are you planning to bring him on tour with you? What about his school? Are you planning to bring the necessary specialists with you to help him learn to communicate?"

"My parents and sister will help out."

But not me.

Numbness crept in at the implication behind his words. He didn't trust me because I'd kept my promise to the sister I'd loved.

"What about the media and paparazzi?" I asked. "Once they find out about him, he'll never be left alone. He'll never have the same freedom other kids have."

"That's not true. The paparazzi don't target most celebrities' kids. Most people aren't even aware those celebrities have kids."

It might've been true, but all I could see in my mind were those celebrity kids who were constantly in the limelight. With Tiffany and Jared possibly getting back together, there was no way Logan would stay free of the spotlight.

Jared pushed himself off the couch. "I've made up my mind, Callie. Your sister and then you kept me out of my son's life for whatever misguided reasons you had. I'll never get those years back, but I definitely plan to be in his life from now on."

Without giving me a backward glance, he stalked out of the living room. A few seconds later, the apartment door clicked shut.

In the end, after everything was said and done, everyone had left me. Alexis. My parents. My ex-boyfriend.

And soon Logan and Jared would be added to the list—and I would lose everything that mattered to me.

20

CALLIE

In the staff locker room the next day, I stripped my uniform off and changed into my jeans and T-shirt.

"Any big plans for tonight?" Beckie asked, even though she already knew the answer. In the years she'd known me, I never had big plans for the night. The only exception was when I'd celebrated mine or Logan's birthday with pizza and cake.

"Logan's taking Jared to visit Nolan Kincaid and his girlfriend's puppy. So I'm watching a movie till they get back." And eating a container of ice cream.

Ice cream was supposed to be great if you were dealing with a broken heart because a boyfriend dumped you or had been caught cheating on you. What about when the guy you loved discovered your son was really his, and decided that you no longer fit in his son's life the way you used to? Would ice cream fix that kind of broken heart too?

As luck would have it, I'd bought a container of triple fudge chocolate supreme the other day. I was all set for a fun-filled night.

"You really need to get out more," Beckie said. When I

opened my mouth to argue, she rushed out with, "I mean date. You need to find a great guy who makes you happy."

"I'm happy." This would've sounded more convincing if I hadn't grumbled it. "I am, really."

She shook her head. "No, what you are is overworked. You work here full-time, you take classes online, you work as a graphic designer on the side, you're taking a sign language class, and you have a son. You need more fun in your life."

"Logan and I do lots of fun things together." Just not as much as we would have liked. Even the trip to Disneyland, which I'd idiotically blurted out that he and I would do last weekend, had been postponed indefinitely. But now that Jared planned to take Logan from me, "indefinitely" had become "permanently."

From the way Beckie sadly shook her head, I had a feeling that either she disagreed with me or my interpretation of her words wasn't quite what she'd meant—or a combination of the two.

Before she had a chance to list all the fun things missing from my life, I grabbed my backpack and hightailed it from the staff room.

The door of the diner hadn't even shut behind me when an enthusiastic Logan came racing at me from nowhere and hugged me. "Hey, what are you doing here? Weren't you guys going to see the puppy?"

"We are," Logan said. "You said you come with us."

He was right, I had said that, but after everything that had happened between Jared and me last night, I figured I was uninvited.

Or maybe I had just hoped I was, because the idea of spending the afternoon with Jared sounded like the worst possible idea in the arena of bad ideas.

My mouth twitched with the urge to tell him I couldn't, but then I realized I needed to make the most of the few precious moments I had left with Logan. Soon I'd be nothing more than Auntie Callie, and I didn't know if that meant I'd still have visitation rights.

I probably should hire a lawyer to find out.

I let Logan lead me to Jared's car. The booster seat was a different model than the one in my car. He must have bought one. I looked at Jared, eyes wide.

Understanding where my thoughts were, Jared answered, voice low so that Logan would be less likely to overhear him, "I haven't told him yet."

I nodded. It was up to Jared as to when he wanted to break the news to Logan. He was on his own for that. I'd be there for Logan, of course, but that was about it.

The car ride over to Nolan and his girlfriend's home was quiet, if you could call an excited four-year-old who was about to play with a puppy quiet. The journey couldn't end soon enough for him.

At the lead singer's house, a modest two-story home in a decent neighborhood, we parked on the street and climbed out. Jared let Logan ring the doorbell, and a small barking noise greeted us.

Logan pointed at the door, a huge grin on his face. "Puppy!"

The smile on my face at seeing him this happy was as wide as his.

The door opened a moment later to reveal the hottest guy I'd ever seen. Well, second-hottest after Jared, but considering how mad I was at him, he didn't count.

"You have to excuse Rocky," Nolan said. "We're still training him." He crouched to Logan's height and held up his hand for Logan to high-five. "You ready to meet him?"

It was a good thing Logan's head was securely attached to his neck, otherwise it might've fallen off from how fast he was nodding.

Nolan opened the door wider to reveal a beautiful woman

with long dark hair in jeans and a purple Pushing Limits T-shirt. She was kneeling and trying to restrain an excited fluff-ball from charging at us. One hand was gripping his collar, the other held against his chest.

My heart melted at the sight of the puppy. It hadn't stood a chance, if truth be told.

"Hi, Logan." The woman smiled in a way that told me the two were already acquainted. "You want to pet Rocky?"

I knelt next to Logan and held out my hand, showing him how to approach a dog. The little furball sniffed and licked my knuckles. Logan giggled.

"How old is he?" I asked her.

"Nine weeks."

"He's adorable."

"Adorable and a handful," she said, "but I'm glad we have him. Now I have someone to keep me company when the guys are on tour. I'm Hailey, by the way."

"Hi. I'm Callie."

"It's nice to finally meet you. Jared said you guys have known each other since you were kids."

"That's true. How did you and Nolan meet?"

"Same deal. We were once best friends, but it wasn't until he returned home last December that things between us changed." The look she gave her boyfriend, who was talking to Jared, said it all. She was deeply in love with him, and from the look he gave her in return, the feeling was mutual.

Rocky licked Logan's hand, and he giggled in surprise. Hailey showed him how the puppy liked to be stroked. Forget Disneyland—Logan had found his new happy place.

Maybe, if he was lucky, Jared would get him a puppy.

I couldn't tell if Jared had already told Nolan and Hailey the truth about Logan. If she did know, she said nothing that would give it away.

The puppy jumped up against Logan's legs, and he laughed

again. I retrieved my smartphone from my purse and shot a few photos. At least I'd have those once he was gone.

Tears welled up. I blinked them away.

"Rocky, no jumping," Hailey said, pushing the energetic puppy back down. "How 'bout we go outside? Maybe you can get Rocky to play catch with you, Logan."

Their backyard wasn't huge, mostly just grass and some flowers and shrubbery around the outside, along the fence. But it had plenty of room for a young puppy and four-year-old boy to play in. Hailey gave Logan Rocky's favorite ball and we watched them run around. Logan's throwing arm needed a little work, but Rocky didn't care. He bounded after it and tried to pick it up in his mouth.

While they played, Hailey and I talked. Any other time, under different circumstances, it was easy to see that she and I could've been good friends. But now that the situation between Jared and me had changed, it would never happen. Her boyfriend was Jared's best friend and bandmate, which meant she had to be on Jared's side—even if she wasn't.

A hand rested against my lower back, and I startled. "I have a feeling he'll now expect me to get him a puppy," Jared said, his mouth close to my ear. A shiver of desire shuddered through my body. Stupid, traitorous body.

"I suspect you're right," I replied in as cheerful a voice as I could muster, given the situation between us. "Then he'll have someone to keep him company while you're touring."

The hand on my back jerked away, as if Jared had just realized he'd accidentally placed it there. "It's not like I'm leaving him alone in the apartment."

Yeah, but you'd be leaving him with your family instead of the only mother he's ever known. The words hovered at the tip of my tongue, but I needed to keep things civil between us. "I'm sorry. That's not what I meant. It's just Hailey said she's happy to have Rocky to keep her company while the band's away touring."

Hailey returned from retrieving the ball from a bush. "Nolan said you guys are going to Disneyland tomorrow. I've always wanted to go there." She looked longingly at her boyfriend, standing next to her.

"We are?" My gaze shot to Jared. He threw the ball for Rocky and Logan to chase after.

"I'm taking Logan since he wants to go," he said.

"And when exactly were you going to ask me?" My throat closed up, shrinking to the width of a straw, making it hard to squeeze out the last words. He was already pushing me out of Logan's life.

"You can come with us if you want."

Now if only it had sounded like he actually meant it.

I focused my attention on Logan, but I could feel the quizzical gazes aimed at Jared and me.

"Do you mind if I use your bathroom?" I asked Hailey.

"No, go ahead." She told me where to find it.

I didn't really have to go. I just needed several minutes on my own to pull myself together. I didn't need Logan to witness me falling apart.

The bathroom was decorated in a soothing blend of earth tones, but it wasn't enough to help with the turbulent emotions inside me. I slid down the wall and pulled my knees to my chest.

Yesterday, after I'd told Jared what had happened to my family, I'd thought that I'd be dealing with a drought of tears for the next twelve months, after almost drowning Jared with how much I'd cried.

I was wrong.

21
___

JARED

"What's going on with you and Callie?" Nolan asked as soon as the back door shut behind him.

I slipped my lucky guitar pick from my pocket and toyed with it. Everything was going to shit and I had no idea what to do about it. "There's nothing going on. She's a friend, that's all." A friend who, until her betrayal, had felt like something more than a friend. Thoughts about her—some X-rated—had constantly paraded through my head ever since the kiss.

Even after I'd discovered the truth about Logan.

"Right. So why are you taking her son to Disneyland without discussing it with her first, and then making it clear that she isn't welcome to join you guys?"

"I told her she could come if she wanted."

Nolan's eyebrows arched up in that you've-got-to-be-fucking-kidding-me way of his. "I've dealt with blizzards warmer than how you just treated her. And again, why are you taking *her* son to Disneyland?"

I checked to make sure Logan was busy. I had no idea how I

was going to tell the four-year-old that he was my son, but this wasn't when and how I'd planned for it to happen. He was still running around the lawn, throwing the ball for Rocky, then racing after it, giggling. He wasn't the only one enjoying himself. Rocky was having as much fun with the game as Logan.

"That's the thing," I said, keeping my voice down so he couldn't hear me. "Logan isn't her son. He's mine."

For a couple of seconds Nolan and Hailey just stared me, at a loss for words. I knew the feeling.

A crow cawed from a nearby tree, eager to share some unwanted advice. It was Nolan who finally broke the silence between us. "What the hell are you talking about?"

I briefly told them about Alexis and what she had told me, and then how I'd discovered Logan's birth certificate. I also pointed out that Callie had known all this time and had kept the truth from me. "The DNA test came back. He's my son."

"Sounds like she was only trying to protect him," Hailey said, her expression suggesting she would've done the same. "You can't blame her for that. But anyone can tell that she cares deeply about you. Maybe she thought she was doing the right thing for him and for you."

I scoffed. "Callie doesn't care deeply for me. We hadn't even seen or talked to each other for five years until I bumped into her and Logan in the grocery store."

"You're wrong. I've seen how she looks at you. Even after everything that's going on between you two when it comes to Logan, she looks at you like you're the world to her."

"That's crazy. I was fooling around with her sister back when I was in high school. Callie and I were just friends. Nothing like you and Nolan. She was more like a little sister." Except now the last thing I would have considered her to be was a little sister, especially my own. Far from it.

"What's going to happen now that you know Logan's your son?" Hailey asked. "Will Callie still be his mother?"

"She's not his mother. She's his aunt."

"As far as Logan is concerned, she's his mother. What are you planning to do? Tear him away from the only mother he remembers?"

"Well . . . no. Callie can still visit him."

"As his aunt?" Nolan said. It wasn't really a question.

"Of course as his aunt," I said, a little more forcefully than I had meant to. "His biological mother is dead."

Hailey reached for Nolan's hand, her face pale. "And so is Callie's mother. And so are her father and sister. What about her grandparents or other relatives? Do any of them live in L.A.?"

"No. Her grandparents died years ago."

"So you'll take away the only family she has left. How do you think she feels about that?"

"She'll still get to see him." But even as I said it, I knew Hailey was right. Family had always been important to Callie, like mine was to me. She could have given Logan up for adoption right after his mother had died. It would've made her life simpler and she wouldn't have been forced to give up everything she had worked hard for. But she had sacrificed everything—for the only family she had left.

"How are you planning to tell Logan?" Nolan asked.

Logan was still laughing at the puppy's antics, oblivious to the conversation about him and his future.

"I have no idea, but I'll have to tell him at some point."

"I wouldn't tell him yet," Hailey said. "Spend more time with him. Be father and son. Show Callie that you'll be the kind of father Logan deserves. And once you tell him the truth, give him time to adjust before you remove him from the only home he's known . . . especially since Callie won't be a major part of his life anymore. Think about what he needs over what you want."

Hailey's words were like a knock to the head. No wonder Callie had looked so panicked. It wasn't because she'd been caught in a lie. Her life would be torn apart all over again, and this time I was the one responsible for her pain.

22

———

CALLIE

It was official. My butt was numb from sitting on the bathroom floor for so long. How long? God knows. But long enough for everyone to wonder if I had an exotic gastrointestinal disease that required a ridiculous amount of time in the bathroom.

A knock on the door interrupted my pity party for one. "Callie, are you okay?" Jared asked.

Define "okay." "Yeah. I'll be out in a minute." Or a hundred and fifty.

"Can I come in?"

"I'm busy."

"On the floor?"

And that was what happens when you had a pity party on the floor next to the door. At least if I had enjoyed it from the toilet seat, I could have easily pulled off the GI disease excuse.

Knowing he wouldn't leave until I let him in, I reached up and unlocked the door. Then I scooted out of the way.

He entered and lowered himself onto the cold tile floor next to me. "Comfy?"

"Very."

"I'm sorry I've been an ass. I guess I was in shock, but that didn't give me the right to act that way."

I sniffed. "You're right. You were an ass." And a few other names I could think of that would've shocked my mother, had she still been alive.

He let out a sharp breath, as if gathering his thoughts. "When she first told me she was pregnant, I did what any other twenty-one-year-old guy would do—I panicked. I had goals and they didn't involve a baby, at least not yet. But the truth is that even though I didn't love your sister, I would've been there for her and our child. I would have loved our child. Things would have been challenging, but I'm positive we would've figured it out.

"But then two days later she told me that she couldn't go through with it. She had aborted the baby. She hadn't even talked to me first. She told me it was her choice and I had no say in it. I was angry. I called her a selfish bitch. I said all kinds of things I shouldn't have."

I fiddled with the wet tissue in my hand, unsure what to say. Did I think my sister was a selfish bitch? Far from it. She had been the sweetest, most generous person that I knew.

"She did what she believed was best for you and your unborn child," I told him.

"Right, she did," he said. From his tone, it was clear he believed that as much as he believed in Santa.

"If she'd known the kind of father you would've been, the father I've seen you be with Logan, she would've done everything differently." If only she hadn't been so blinded by her own insecurities when it came to Jared. Things could've been so different, and she might still be alive.

The disbelief in Jared's tone settled on his face. He shifted slightly, his arm brushing mine. A hum buzzed through my body, radiating from that spot. I gasped softly, but not enough for him to realize what his touch did to me. He never needed to know that.

He pushed himself up and held his hand out to me. "We should probably go back outside, before Logan wonders what happened to us."

I barely managed to ignore the tightness in my chest as Jared pulled up me to stand. My legs were a little wobbly from sitting on the floor for so long, and I stumbled.

Jared placed his hand on my hip to steady me. His fingertips slid under the hem of my T-shirt and brushed against the skin just above the waistband of my jeans. The nerves between my legs perked up. I was surprised they remembered what to do after the past three years of my self-inflicted celibacy.

"So when are you telling him?" I asked.

"I don't know. Hailey told me I should give him time to get to know me first. Spend time doing father-and-son activities with him."

"That makes sense." I could hug her for that. "So he won't be moving in with you yet?"

"No. But if you're okay with it, I thought I'd hang out at your apartment in the evenings. We can do things together . . . and I can still read to him before he goes to bed."

So we'll be like a family? I kept that to myself. I still didn't know how I factored into this—and I was afraid to ask. "I'm sure Logan will like that."

"Plus I have years of child support to make up for. I'll talk to my lawyer and the bank and have it dealt with."

I nodded, even though it wasn't his money I longed for.

While the tension between us didn't completely vanish, it did lessen. He didn't trust me after what my sister had done to him, and I was waiting for him to rip away the only family I had left. But for Logan's sake, we had to at least try. So much was at stake—and not just my heart.

Logan was yawning when we stepped into the backyard. "It looks like Rocky wore him out," I said, grinning.

"I think it went both ways," Nolan said, referring to the puppy lying on his side, fighting to keep his eyes open.

Jared scooped Logan up. The four-year-old rested his head against his father's shoulder and his eyelids began to droop. The sight of them this way was enough to melt my insides in a good way, despite the tension that lingered.

"Logan," I said, "what do you say to Hailey and Nolan for letting you visit Rocky?"

He signed "thank you" and murmured something that could have been the same.

"You're welcome," Hailey said.

Jared drove us home and carried his sleeping son upstairs to my apartment. "Do we wake him so he can eat dinner first?"

"We could try. Otherwise he might wake up in the middle of the night hungry." Or wake up way earlier than I wished to get up tomorrow morning. I'd already learned that lesson the hard way.

He lowered Logan onto the couch while I went into the kitchen and made a grilled cheese sandwich and cut apple wedges. Logan was half awake, watching TV with Jared, when I returned with his meal. As painful as it was knowing that one day this scene would no longer be part of my life, I couldn't stop the smile that snuck onto my lips at how adorable they looked together. I still had no idea how Jared had figured out he was Logan's father, but if he had seen himself next to his son, he never would've doubted it for a second.

I placed Logan's food and milk on the table. "Dinner."

Jared carried him to the table, causing the four-year-old to giggle. I returned to the kitchen to cook dinner for Jared and myself. By the time the food was ready, Logan had finished his meal and was in the bathroom with Jared, getting ready for bed.

I joined them for a bedtime story, with Logan sandwiched between us on the bed.

"I never knew you were so talented," I said, referring to his funny animal voices.

"I'm a man with many talents." He winked at me. For some reason, my face heated at this and he chuckled.

He read Logan two more books, signing the animal names he'd learned. By the end of the second book, Logan's eyelids were beginning to droop shut again. I helped him with his implant and signed "good night" before kissing him and tucking him into bed.

Jared did the same. If someone were to peer into the window and watch us, they would've mistakenly thought we were a happy family. For a moment, I wished perception and reality were the same. But I had long ago learned that wishing was for dreamers, and my days of dreaming were long over.

I returned to the kitchen and dished out the spaghetti and meatballs. I set the plates on the dining room table, along with two sodas. "Do you want to stay and watch a movie?"

"You okay with that? You don't have to study or anything?"

Yes, I did have to study, but I wanted to hang out with Jared even more. I wasn't ready for him to leave just yet. "No, I'm fine to watch a movie."

Once Jared and I finished our meal, we picked up our drinks and sat on the couch. It felt natural, like when Jared had helped put Logan to bed.

I sat next to him, my legs curled to the side, but careful to keep several inches between us—even though I craved to curl up against him and rest my head on his shoulder.

Jared searched for a movie to watch on TV. "How about this?" he asked.

I read the movie's blurb. "You want to watch a horror movie?"

"Sure, why not?" He smirked. "You're not scared, are you?"

"Of course not," I scoffed. Which was a total lie. Horror movies had always scared me, and he knew it.

"This isn't so bad, is it?" Jared chuckled as I watched the movie from between splayed fingers.

"No, not at all. In fact, I might let Logan watch it before bedtime tomorrow."

Jared laughed again. Seriously, was he not watching the same movie as me? There was nothing funny about a deranged doll hacking up people. I thanked all things holy that Logan was a boy and didn't have any dolls. Otherwise I might've had to do some serious spring cleaning the next morning and chuck them.

"Here, I'll keep you safe." Jared wrapped his arm around me and pulled me against him.

Too bad for me I actually believed him. I lowered my hands from my face in time for the psycho doll to sink its teeth into the legs of its next victim.

I cringed and turned to stare at Jared's chest. His very nice chest under the fitted gray T-shirt he was wearing. Maybe I could watch it for the rest of the movie. You know, just to ensure some creepy doll didn't wander into the apartment and plunge a knife into it.

"Thanks, but as strong as you are"—I placed my hand on his abs, which flexed under my touch, then relaxed—"I don't think you're much protection against that." I waved in the general direction of the TV, my attention still on his hard chest and abs.

Jared laughed once more, and his stomach muscles rippled under my hand—the hand that had returned to his abs right after gesturing toward the TV.

I looked up. Instead of the you're weird expression I was expecting, his eyes were dark. My gaze dropped to his mouth, and my lips parted involuntarily as I fantasized about kissing his mouth again. Except this time I wouldn't fall off the couch. This time, if he gave me a chance, I'd kiss him back. Really kiss him back.

And then . . . his lips were on mine.

I had no idea who started it, and I didn't care. All I knew was if this was a dream, I didn't want to be awakened.

His mouth briefly touched mine for a heartbeat, then moved slightly away. Fear stroked a finger across my back and I held my breath. Any second he would realize he was making a mistake, realize that the last person he should kiss was me.

His mouth remained in place, hovering close to mine, his warm breath mixing with mine. Then the moment of deliberation was over. His lips crashed against mine again, and this time it wasn't the sweet yet brief kisses we'd experienced before. This time his tongue slipped between the seam of my lips, and I let him in.

I'd always expected that Jared would be a great kisser. How could he not be? But my expectations were nothing like reality. He tasted me, consumed me . . . made me feel like the earth was shaking under my feet. I'd found heaven—and I was ready to move in, permanently.

I let out a soft moan. Then it was as if my body had taken over my brain's job. My lips still attached to his, I shifted to his lap and straddled him. His hands settled on my hips, keeping me in place, and the pads of his fingers crept under the hem of my T-shirt, stroking my skin. A slight tremble danced over my body.

My fingers knotted in his hair, relishing the silky feel of the strands, and I ground my aching center against his hardening length. "Oh, God," I groaned. Forget the kiss—my body wanted so much more. And it seemed like Jared was on the same wavelength.

Or at least I hoped he was on the same wavelength.

"Are you gonna marry Mommy and be my daddy?" Logan's soft voice said.

Startled, I jerked away from Jared, my breath coming hard. It was only because of his hands on my hips that I miraculously didn't end up on the floor.

I scrambled off him and tried to formulate some sort of answer, but the words refused to form any coherent sentences in my head. All I was capable of was opening and closing my mouth like a zombie.

"Sometimes when two people . . . um . . . like each other, they kiss," Jared said, stumbling over his words. "But that doesn't mean they'll get married."

Logan blinked, not having heard Jared's answer. I signed it. Well, attempted to. They hadn't exactly covered this scenario in the sign language classes I was taking. And I could guarantee it wasn't part of Logan's preschool curriculum.

From the way his shoulders sagged, you'd have thought Jared had just told him Santa didn't exist. I gathered him in my arms and hugged him. Then I pulled away and signed, "Why are you awake?"

He signed back, "Thirsty."

"I'll get you some water. Okay?"

He nodded.

I took his hand and led him to the kitchen. A few minutes later, he was back in bed, eyes closed.

I left his room and walked smack into Jared in the hallway. He had been deep in thought when Logan and I had left the kitchen.

"I should go," he said. "I'll pick you two up tomorrow morning. Around eight?"

I nodded. Disappointment gnawed at me that he wasn't even staying to watch the movie. Although at this point it was safe to say we weren't watching the rest of it.

I walked him to the door. He didn't kiss me again. If anything, he couldn't escape fast enough.

I shut the door behind him, and the light inside me that had appeared when Jared first stepped back into my life dimmed.

23

CALLIE

With the exception of the one time when Alexis, my parents, and Logan had been driving to San Francisco, Logan had never left L.A. You'd have thought we were driving to a foreign country based on his excitement on the way down.

Then again, we were talking about Disneyland.

Because we couldn't play music, I sat in the backseat with Logan so it was easier for him to hear me. Fortunately, he never brought up the kissing incident again.

And neither did Jared.

In fact, Jared acted as if we hadn't kissed at all.

Pathetic. The word twisted around my heart, its barbs digging in. When would I learn? I wasn't special to Jared. He wasn't falling in love with me the way I was falling for him. I needed to get over him and move on.

If only it was as simple as that.

"Look. There's Disneyland." I pointed to the Ferris wheel and the roller coaster, needing a distraction from the pain.

"Do you remember coming here when we were kids?" Jared asked me.

"I remember you were madly in love with Cinderella." To Logan I said, "He wanted to get her autograph so badly, he dragged our families around, searching for her."

"Did you see her?" Logan asked. I couldn't tell if he was impressed or not that Jared had at one point crushed over a Disney Princess.

I giggled. "No. It was Cinderella's day off."

"Did you get any autographs?"

"Yes. But only from Winnie-the-Pooh and his friends."

Logan's face lit up at the mention of Pooh.

Jared found a parking spot on the grounds. Holding Logan's hands, we walked through Downtown Disney, with its restaurants and Disney-themed stores, to the main entrance. Because it was spring break, the lines through both security and the main park gate were long. Once we were through them both, Jared loaded Logan onto his shoulders.

"Where to first?" I asked Logan. "You want to visit Winnie-the-Pooh and go on his ride?"

"Yes, Pooh!" Logan bounced on his father's shoulders.

I smirked at Jared. "I guess you're not moving fast enough."

"What's that?" Logan asked, pointing to a white and gray building that resembled a small Louisiana plantation, complete with four white pillars extending to the roof above the second floor. A graveyard on the grounds in front and to the side of the building added to the haunted feel of the place.

"It's the Haunted Mansion," I said. I didn't get to finish what else I was going to say, because—

"Oh. My. God!" a female voice shrieked. A cluster of twenty-year-old females rushed in front of us and suddenly stopped. I swear they were bouncing as much as Logan had been on Jared's shoulders.

"Oh. My. God," the shrieker repeated. "You're Jared Leigh. Guitarist for Pushing Limits."

Her sidekicks squirmed their way between me and Jared, effectively pushing me out of the way. Nice.

I rolled my eyes and signed to Logan to check he was okay.

"Oh God, he's sooooo adorable," the shrieker said. At first I thought she was talking about Jared, because he certainly was adorable, especially with his son on his shoulders. But then I realized she meant Logan.

"You guys look like you could be brothers." She raised her smartphone to take a photo.

A bad feeling rushed me at the realization that it wasn't only Jared's face she was planning to shoot a picture of. I stepped in front of her, blocking her view of Logan.

"What the fuck?" she said.

"Language." I scowled at her.

"That's a dollar," Logan said, holding out his hand.

Jared chuckled and patted his son's leg. "Sorry, buddy, but that only applies to Mason."

"No pictures," I said, pointing to Logan. "I don't want his picture to end up on the Internet."

She rolled her eyes. "Like it isn't already up there. You post it on Facebook, right?"

What, was she studying pre-law? "No, I don't. My son's safety is my number one priority."

She mumbled something that could have been sorry.

"You're more than welcome to take photos of Jared." Because that was part of his job, even if this was his day off.

Jared removed Logan from his shoulders and posed with each girl separately. I even took a group shot of them with the girl's phone, with Logan holding my leg so he didn't inadvertently wander off.

While Jared signed their Disney books, Logan and I joined the long line for the Haunted Mansion. He had decided he wanted to go there before seeing Winnie-the-Pooh. Jared sidled up to us five minutes later.

"Are monsters in there?" Logan asked his father, eyes wide.

"No. But don't worry—if there are, your mom will protect you." Jared winked at me.

This time it was my eyes that widened, but for a different reason: Jared was still calling me Logan's mom. But then, what did I expect? He would hardly call me Logan's mom one day and then suddenly refer to me as just Callie or Aunt Callie the next. But eventually that day would come. I'd been Logan's mom for so long that once he stopped calling me that, it would feel like hot iron stakes being hammered into every inch of my body.

"You better believe it," I said. "It's in my job description to tickle all monsters until they surrender." I tickled Logan. He giggled and squirmed. Jared grinned at us, as did the much older couple behind him.

"What an adorable family," the woman murmured to her husband. My face heated and I turned away.

While we waited, Jared quizzed us on different ASL signs, inspired by the graveyard-themed decorations. Ghost. Monster. Grave. You know, all those useful terms for everyday conversation. Jared had to Google some of them. Then he invented a game where we told a story with them, each of us saying a sentence before it was the next person's turn.

"The ghost was hungry," Logan said, signing the sentence. Jared only had to sign the words he knew, which was more than I realized. The man had been practicing.

A newfound warmth directed at him bubbled inside me, but his actions shouldn't have surprised me. This was the Jared I'd always known and looked up to.

Jared leaned toward me. "Ghosts can get hungry?"

I giggled. "Apparently so."

"The ghost wandered through the house, searching for marshmallows." Jared signed "ghost" and "house."

"Ghosts eat marshmallows?" I asked, somewhat doubtful of

this unknown fact.

With a straight face, Jared replied, "Of course they do. Why do you think ghosts are white?"

"Ghosts eat lots and lots of marshmallows," Logan said, giggling.

Jared gestured at his son. "See?"

Once we entered the gathering room inside the mansion, Jared picked up Logan so he could see and hear. And so he wouldn't be scared within the crowded space.

"Whoa," Logan said, as the walls started stretching upward, and we sank into the depths of the mansion. A short time later, we were sitting in a black buggy, listening to the recorded tour. Logan sat between us, his face with a continual expression of wonderment.

The rest of the morning went the same way. We laughed and joked with Logan, but not once did Jared give me any indication of what last night had meant to him. The kiss had been an accident, like the other time. But this time we had only kissed because of the horror movie.

I kept telling myself this as we waited in line for the Winnie-the-Pooh ride and then for the Pirates of the Caribbean. It was easier believing that than to face the truth: the kiss had been purely one-sided.

But what did I expect? The man had tons of groupies. It wasn't like he'd spent the entire tour depriving the female population of those lips. If he had, riots would've occurred. That much I was positive of. Many girls had no doubt sampled those lips. I was just one of them.

We were standing near the lagoon, watching Peter Pan's ship sail by and eating soft pretzels, when a girl my age stepped up to Jared. She could've been a model for a sports magazine, with her long blond hair, tight athletic body, and tan. Think beach volleyball, but instead of a skimpy bikini, she wore jeans and a fitted cotton-candy-pink T-shirt.

She smiled sweetly at him and kissed him on the cheek.

With a sigh, I grabbed Logan's hand and walked off. I had no idea where we were going and I didn't care. I just needed to get away. As it was, Jared had already been asked, while we were wandering around the grounds, to sign the breasts of another groupie. I knew his fans were important both to him and to the success of the band, but it would've been nice to spend one day without them always being in our face. Alexis had feared that this would happen, and more than ever now, I got why she had felt that way. How many pictures had already been taken of Jared and Logan together without us knowing about them? How many would show up on the Internet soon, with everyone speculating who Logan was?

"Do you want to go on a roller coaster?" I asked him.

"Big big roller coaster?"

"No, that one's in the other park." And Logan would be too small for it. "There's one in Toon Town."

Logan dragged me forward, even though he had no idea where Toon Town was located. "Is Jared coming?" he asked.

"I'm sure he'll catch up with us." Once he'd finished socializing with the fan.

A moment later, my phone pinged and I read Jared's text, asking me where we were. I didn't respond. I had no idea why I was so pissed at what had happened. Jared didn't owe me anything. He and I had kissed, end of story.

A guy with messy blond hair and nerdy glasses, which made him look even hotter, checked me out. A shy smile slid onto his face. Logan was at the entrance of the nearby gift store, inspecting a toy, oblivious to the stranger.

The guy spoke briefly to his friends then walked toward me. It had felt like so long since a guy even noticed me, and vice versa, that my pulse fluttered in my veins. Maybe this was just the kind of distraction I needed right now.

24

JARED

One minute I was watching the Peter Pan ship in the lagoon, the next some woman's lips were pressed against my cheek. That wasn't to say this had never happened before. It was a hazard of the job. People assumed that because you were a "celebrity," fans had the right to push the boundaries when it came to acceptable behavior. If you saw a stranger on the street, you wouldn't go up and kiss them. Right?

I backed away from the mystery kisser.

"I'm a huge fan of yours," she said. "I've been learning to play on the guitar some of your songs from the first album. I'm not great at it. Nothing like you. I also sing and I'm hoping one day to land a record deal. Did I mention I also write my own songs?" She spoke so fast, I barely caught most of what she said.

"Nice to meet you." Where the fuck did Callie and Logan go? They'd been right next to me a moment ago.

"Do you have any advice about getting into the industry?" she asked. Before I could reply, she squealed. "Oh my God, I can't believe I'm actually talking to the Jared Leigh."

I scanned the crowded area for Callie and Logan while the girl continued talking nonstop. I don't think she realized I was no longer listening.

"Sorry, I have to go," I said, inching away. "It was nice meeting you."

She grabbed my arm. "Could . . . could I have your autograph? It would mean so much to me." Without waiting for a response, she whipped out a notebook from her purse and shoved it at me. "When's the band's next album coming out? I can't wait to hear it."

I took the book and pen from her. "The first single releases April fifth. The album is due out April twelfth," I said, signing her book. I handed it back to her, and before she could launch into a new line of questioning, I said "bye" and walked off.

I wove in and out of the steady stream of people milling around the grounds. Once I was far enough from the girl, I sent Callie a text. She and Logan could've been anywhere. I wasn't worried about them, but the point of today was for us to spend the day together. After our kiss last night, I found myself wanting to spend a lot more time with Callie. I just didn't know in what context I wished to spend it. Everything was complicated between us. That kiss had made it more so.

I never should have kissed her. While the kiss had felt good at the time—more than good, incredible even—Logan's unexpected interruption had been the splash of icy water I needed. Callie had lied to me with her omission about who his father really was. Was I ready to trust her fully after that?

I had no idea in which direction Callie and Logan were headed, but there weren't a huge number of rides he could go on due to his size. I stalked past Cinderella's castle. Callie still hadn't responded to my text.

And then I saw her. She was flirting with a nerdy guy wearing glasses. He laughed. She smiled . . . and I saw red, the volcano's-about-to-erupt shade of red. What the fuck was she doing with him when she was supposed to be keeping an eye on Logan?

I scanned the area but couldn't find him. I stormed over to the happy couple. He was asking for her phone number when I approached them.

"She's not interested," I practically snarled at him, then turned on Callie, my tone not softening any. "Where's Logan?"

"There!" She pointed to the gift store, which looked like it could've been a mini pastel-colored version of the Taj Mahal. An open-concept Taj Mahal, with no doors or windows . . . just a huge opening in the walls so visitors could easily walk in and out. Logan was happily checking out the toys. "And what right do you have to tell Mark that I'm not interested in going out with him?" she asked.

You remember the old cartoons where the character had steam hissing from his ears, and you knew without a doubt he was pissed? That guy had nothing on Callie.

Luckily for Mark, he was wise enough to step back, hands raised. "Look, I'm not interested in getting into a fight."

"Don't worry, he's not about to hit you," Callie said. "Given that some girl was just kissing him, the last thing he has the right to do is judge me."

"She kissed my cheek," I countered. "It's not a big deal." But as I said it, I knew I'd feel the same way if I caught a guy kissing her—cheek or no cheek.

"Right, it wasn't. Did she give you her phone number so you guys can hook up later?"

"So what if she did?"

Callie grunted. "Such a guy response. You kissed me last night, then you couldn't get out of the apartment fast enough."

Shit. Was that what this was all about? The air in my lungs left in a hard rush. "It wasn't like that."

"So what was it like?"

"It's complicated."

"Yeah I get it. I'm your ex-girlfriend's little sister . . . and you'll always view me that way." She stalked into the gift shop, not even noticing Mark had disappeared, our drama too much for him.

I stood frozen. It wasn't that I didn't want to be with Callie in that way. I did. But I also didn't want to destroy what we did have between us. Like I'd told her, everything was complicated. Wouldn't it be better that we were just friends, for Logan's sake? If things didn't work out between us, then what? What would it mean when it came to my son?

Logan was showing Callie some Toy Story figurines when I approached. He returned the box to the shelf. "Roller coaster now?" he asked.

We walked toward Toon Town. Logan was so excited about the small roller coaster, he didn't notice the tension between me and Callie. He just held on to our hands and dragged us forward.

We waited in the line and did our best to entertain the impatient four-year-old. Eventually I gave him my iPhone to play with after he grew bored of the game Callie had dreamed up to keep him busy.

My head was bent near hers, so that the people in front and behind us weren't inadvertently part of our conversation. A subtle shift of her head and my lips would've been on hers. "I'm so attracted to you, Callie. And no, I don't see you as Alexis's little sister anymore. But damn it, you lied to me, and I don't know what's going to happen going forward. I'm confused, and now I have a son to consider."

"You're confused or you're mad? You're about to make a decision that will rock my entire world. So it's okay if you don't want me in that way."

"Oh, I want you in that way. Don't misunderstand me."

Fuck, did I ever want to kiss her now and prove just how much I wanted her in that way. I was falling for her hard, which was only making things more difficult. It would've been so much easier if Callie had been the one I was involved with when Logan was conceived, I thought. And if she had been honest with me. Without her lie hanging over my head, I could have easily seen a future with us together. I could have easily seen us as a family.

But she had lied, and that changed everything.

"Whatever," she said. "You're leaving soon anyway. You won't have time for us once you're gone . . . and besides, I'm not interested in dating. Been there. Done that. Didn't bother to buy the T-shirt."

"You seriously aren't planning to date again? You going all nun?" Not to sound like a caveman, but I was all for that idea. If I wasn't going to have sex with her, I liked the idea that neither was any other man.

She rolled her eyes. "No. That implies I won't ever have sex again. I don't have a problem with having sex. It's having my heart kicked over a cliff that I have issues with."

"Why do you think that's gonna happen if you date some other guy?"

"Do you know what my ex-boyfriend said to me? The ex-boyfriend I was in love with and who I thought loved me?" She turned her face, attempting to hide the hurt there. But it was too late. I had the urge to drive up to San Francisco and introduce my fist to his face.

"What did he say?"

"His exact words were, 'Why the hell would I want someone else's reject?'" She glanced meaningfully at Logan. "I never heard from him after that. But I did hear a week later that he was seeing someone else."

She shrugged but still didn't look at me. The roller coaster had suddenly become the most fascinating sight around for her. I could have stripped naked and she wouldn't have noticed. "Turns out he wasn't the only guy to feel that way about dating a single mother. But when it's the guy who already has a kid, it's a very different standard. When you were walking around with Logan earlier today, it was like the Ovary Alert System kicked into full effect. Girls came running, and none were turned off by the fact you have a kid with you.

"But that's okay," she continued. "I'm getting used to it. People tend to leave me. My sister. My parents. My ex-boyfriend." She glanced at Logan, and while she hadn't said his name out loud, the meaning was clear. After all was said and done, she was expecting Logan to leave her . . . because of me.

I rested my hand on her upper arm. Logan was still busy with the game on my iPhone and wasn't listening to us. "I really wish we could work together for the next few weeks. See how we do together with Logan."

Those gorgeous, hopeful eyes of hers widened. "Does that mean you're willing to let me stay in his life?"

"I'm trying to work that out in my head. . . . Damn it. I even wish I could see how it would go between you and me, too. That kiss was so damn hot. Would you be willing to see where this leads us?" Would you be willing to work at regaining my trust?

"Okay, but what about when you go on the road?"

"Yeah, the road is tough and there are no guarantees. Touring puts a massive strain on relationships. You could be the one who grows bored of me never being around." The truth was that with Callie as my girlfriend, I'd never be tempted to stray. No other woman came close to her. But I couldn't handle the thought of her eventually realizing she could do better than me. "I'm willing to give it a try, though. . . . I can't stop thinking about you, Callie. And I know for certain that I was supposed to run into you that day in the grocery store and to get to know you again. So let's just see where things go with us."

"Okay," she whispered, and stepped back, ending the intimacy between us—for now. "But we should keep it just between you and me." Her gaze slid meaningfully to Logan. She didn't want to get his hopes up when we were still figuring things out ourselves. She didn't want to risk hurting him in case things didn't work out between her and me in the end.

25

JARED

"Are you sure about this?" Callie asked as I drove the three of us to my parents'. Her knee bounced even though there was no music playing in the car.

I put my hand on it. I recognized the bouncing from when we were kids. Every time she thought she was going to be busted for something she'd done, her knee had this fascinating habit of bouncing. The more nervous she was, the faster it bounced. Right now it was moving faster than a freaked-out turkey on Thanksgiving morning.

"It's going to be fine," I told her.

"Do they know?"

"No, not yet. I told them about your parents and Alexis. But I wanted to introduce him to my parents first before I said anything else. And I wanted to introduce him to Emma."

"Emma?"

"My fourteen-month-old niece."

As we pulled down the side street where Callie and I used to live, she let out a small gasp. "What happened to Mr. Lewis's porch? Someone fixed the swing. It's no longer tilted."

I chuckled at the memory of us swinging on it when we

were kids. The old house was squeezed between where she used to live and where my parents still lived. We had been sitting on it while I helped Callie with her ninth-grade math assignment. Math had never been her favorite subject. In a fit of frustration, she threw her body back on the swing. It hadn't been quite the same after that. But even though we'd offered to repair it, Mr. Lewis told us he was fine with it the way it was. "Dad and I replaced it while he was in the hospital two years ago."

"Hospital? What happened to him?"

"He broke his hip."

"Oh my God. Is he okay?"

"He's fine now. He's still making those stone carvings of his." A few of his newest forest animals had taken up residence in his garden—including a rabbit that Emma thought was real.

Craig's SUV was already parked in the driveway when we arrived at my parents' house. Callie helped Logan out of his car seat. He jumped down, clutching the palm-sized stuffed Pooh he'd gotten at Disneyland yesterday.

Biting her lip, Callie looked up at the house. She had always gotten on well with my parents, so I couldn't figure out why she was nervous. I should've been the one who was nervous. They were about to meet their grandson—the grandson they didn't know existed.

I lifted Logan so he could ring the doorbell. A moment later, the door opened. Kristen was holding Emma in her arms. "Oh, good. You're just in time." She held her daughter out to me.

"Just in time for what?"

"Your niece pooped her diaper and I thought you could use practice changing one before you have your own kids." She grinned at Callie, mischief in her eyes. "Diapers are in the bathroom."

With a sigh, I took my niece and was rewarded with an unpleasant smell. "Phew, what on earth do you feed this kid?"

All Kristen did was cackle.

"So, Logan," I said, "you wanna help me change a diaper?"

Frantically shaking his head, he grabbed hold of Callie's leg. You'd have thought, based on his reaction, that I had asked him to deal with toxic waste.

Or maybe I had.

Seriously, what did my sister feed her daughter?

Mom rushed out of the kitchen. Before anyone could say anything, she had Callie in a tight embrace . . . like Callie was her own child. A child who needed comforting after losing someone she loved. "I'm so sorry about your parents and Alexis. I wish we had known." She released my girl from the hug, worry still on Mom's face.

"I'm sorry I didn't tell you. I was just so overwhelmed at the time and in shock, I didn't think to tell you. I didn't think to tell most people."

Once again regret powered through me at how different things could've been if I had remained in contact with her after she and her family had moved away. At how different things could've been if not for the lie between us about Logan. I could have been there for her. My family could have been there for her. She wouldn't have been forced to go through everything alone.

Mom smiled at her, her love for Callie undeniable. "Well, I'm glad to have you back with us again." She then squatted in front of Logan. "And who is this big boy?"

Still clutching Callie's leg, Logan moved to hide behind it. "He gets shy around strangers," Callie explained, "but he gets over it quickly. Logan, this is Jared's mom and his sister, Kristen. They're really nice. His mom used to bake the yummiest chocolate-chip cookies when I was a kid."

At the words "chocolate-chip cookies," a huge dimpled grin

broke out on Logan's face. Mom gasped and looked at me, but at least she had the foresight not to say anything.

"I'll tell you later" was all I said.

"Would you like a cookie?" Mom asked her grandson, not missing a beat.

He nodded, and she led Logan and Callie into the kitchen with Kristen while I changed Emma's diaper.

When I returned, thanking God that Logan was already potty-trained, I introduced Emma to Logan and Callie.

"Did Uncle Jared give you a clean bum?" Kristen asked her daughter.

"She's good to go, but next time you do your own dirty work." I smirked at my sister. As I handed Emma to Mom, I added to Callie with a wink, "Don't worry—Emma got her sparkling personality from me and not my sister."

Callie giggled. "I see things haven't changed between you two."

"You'd think with him away touring all the time that I'd miss him, wouldn't you?" Kristen said, chuckling.

Mom sat at the kitchen table and deposited Emma on her lap. Logan showed his cousin his stuffed Pooh. She reached out, possibly wanting to chew on it.

"So how old are you, Logan?" Mom asked him.

Logan held up his fingers to show his age. "Four!"

"Wow, you're a big boy." Mom bounced Emma on her lap, getting a giggle out of her. Logan poked her gently in the stomach, which made her giggle more. Mom glanced at Callie. "He's hearing-impaired?"

"No, he's deaf, but he has a cochlear implant."

Craig entered the kitchen through the back door. "Sam sent me in for the chicken."

"Dada," Emma said, holding her arms up to her father. Mom passed her granddaughter off to him, like Emma was a football.

"Why don't we go outside?" Mom didn't wait for a reply. She grabbed the casserole dish with the chicken pieces from the counter and hustled us out the back door.

Outside, I placed my hand on Callie's lower back and let my thumb brush against the skin under her T-shirt, as much for support as for contact. I would have kept it there if we'd been alone. If we hadn't been in front of all these people—especially Logan—I would've kissed her deeply. I hadn't kissed her lips since Friday night, and the memory of her taste and the feel of her soft lips against mine had been playing overtime in my head.

I was royally screwed.

Even after dropping her and Logan off the previous evening following our trip to Disneyland, I hadn't gotten a chance to kiss her. The guys had been waiting for me, and Callie needed to get the very sleepy Logan to bed. All I'd had time to do was give her a quick kiss on the cheek—not the kind of kiss I was aching to give her.

And I couldn't do that now either. I could only sneak in subtle touches of her body—until I could get her alone tonight.

Logan spotted the old tree house in the backyard and scurried over to the thick trunk. In awe he gazed up at the large, finely crafted wooden structure, complete with a balcony.

"Wow, your parents still have it?" Callie said, grinning.

"They saved it in case Kristen and I gave them grandkids one day." The structure was still solid, and Dad had recoated it with stain the previous summer.

"Is it safe?"

"Absolutely."

Callie helped Logan up the steps. A moment later they disappeared inside the wooden structure.

I was about to join them when Kristen sidled up to me. "I didn't know you were dating Callie."

"We're just friends."

Kristen rolled her eyes. "You just keep telling yourself that." Snickering, she left to play catch with Emma. A few minutes later, Logan and Callie emerged from the tree house, and before I knew it, the three of us, along with Kristen, Craig, and Emma, were running around the backyard, kicking a beach ball like it was an oversized soccer ball. Mom and Dad cheered from the sidelines. Logan and Emma giggled the entire time as they attempted to kick the ball around.

And damn, it did my heart proud seeing Logan enjoying himself like this. With his family.

After we were finished eating dinner, Mom stood up and started gathering the plates. "Jared, can you help me with the dishes?" she asked, even though I already was. It was her hint that she wanted to talk to me—alone. Callie offered to help, but Mom waved her off and told her to take it easy. She already knew Callie worked full-time and took online classes part-time. It was clear to her that Callie was exhausted.

Mom and I finished gathering the dishes and carried them into the house. "Logan's the reason you came over last week to check out the old photos, isn't he?"

"Maybe I was just interested to see what I looked like when I was four." I placed my stack of dishes on the counter and leaned back against it, then toyed with my lucky guitar pick as I waited for the Q&A to begin.

"Right. So it's just a coincidence he looks a lot like you did when you were the same age? I just never realized you and Callie had been dating."

"We weren't . . . and we're still not. He's not Callie's. He was Alexis's son." I told her the entire story of what had happened. Mom didn't say anything while I spoke. She just listened, her face not betraying her thoughts.

"The poor girl," she said, after I explained how Logan had ended up deaf. "Callie had to go through all of that on her own? She never should've been thrown into that situation."

I had no clue which situation she meant: Callie being a single mom to her nephew, the meningitis and subsequent deafness, or both.

"So what are you going to do about my grandson?" She stressed the last two words, making it clear she had no intention of not being a part of his life. But this didn't come as a surprise. Mom would never turn her back on a grandchild, no matter what the situation surrounding him.

"Callie and I haven't told Logan the truth yet. I'm spending time with him first, letting him get to know me better before we finally tell him."

"But you're planning to have joint custody with Callie, right?"

"I have no idea what I plan to do." It was true. I knew my options. Cameron had discussed them with me at length.

"I can imagine there's a lot to consider. It's obvious Callie loves Logan as much as if he were her own biological son. I can imagine it would devastate her if she lost him. But you also have to consider what will happen if you marry another woman. If you and Callie have joint custody of Logan, it means he would be shipped back and forth between you two, never feeling like he truly belongs anywhere, especially if you and your wife have children of your own. And then there's the touring you need to consider. How often will you be in Logan's life while you're on the road?"

None of this was news to me. God only knew how many times over the last few days I had considered leaving the band just so I could be there for Logan. "You think I should give Callie full rights to Logan and walk away as his father?"

"Heavens, no. I just want you to make sure you're doing what's right for everyone, but especially for your son. If you decide to be his sole parent and not share custody with Callie, we would definitely take care of him while you're touring. He would be treated no differently from Emma or any other grandchild."

"Even if you'd have to drive him to the special preschool he goes to for his deafness?"

"Yes, even then." She closed the dishwasher. "Can I ask you something? If it's none of my business, just tell me so."

"Sure."

"What's going on with you and Callie?"

I cringed inwardly. "What do you mean?"

Mom peered out the kitchen window toward the gazebo where Dad and Craig sat. Logan was running around the massive tree trunk, with Emma toddling after him, while Kristen talked to Callie.

"I've seen how you look at Callie," Mom said. "You admire her, respect her. But there's also something more. I guess I just want you to be careful. She's been through a lot in the last few years. Don't add to her pain more than you have to."

The back door suddenly opened, and Callie and Logan stepped inside the kitchen.

"He needs to go to the bathroom," Callie said, walking past.

Mom grabbed the cake from the fridge and went outside, leaving me to think about what she had said.

Was I making a mistake when it came to Callie? She had been avoiding relationships in the past out of fear of being hurt. I had no intention of hurting her, but if Mom was right, it might be impossible to avoid doing just that if things didn't work out between Callie and me, at least when it came to Logan.

But as much as I knew I should walk away before things became even more complicated, I couldn't. Not when all I could think about was kissing her. Not when all I could think about was being inside her.

I was seriously fucked.

26

CALLIE

Once Logan was finished in the bathroom, he opened the back door to the yard and rushed out to the gazebo, where Jared sat with his family. Unlike Logan, I didn't rush to join them. I stood in the doorway, watching everyone. Jared's mom was exactly as I remembered: friendly, kind, generous. She would do anything for her kids—and grandchildren. I had no doubts that she, Jared's dad, and Kristen would welcome Logan into the family without question.

Logan climbed onto Jared's lap, completing the picture I didn't belong in. They were the happy family I had long since lost and would never have again.

But while sadness clung to me like a child's blanket, another emotion, one that provided a different kind of warmth, filled me. This was exactly what Logan deserved. I might not have a family, but at least Logan would finally have one to replace the family we had both lost. I couldn't have wanted more for him than that.

I went outside and sat next to Jared on the gazebo bench. His hand shifted from Logan's leg to my lower back. A tingling sensation warmed my skin at his touch. I greedily leaned into his hand.

"Who wants cake?" Jared's mom asked, pointedly looking at Logan.

He bounced on his father's lap, yelling, "Me, me, me."

Everyone laughed. The nervousness I had felt on the way here eased. Alexis had told me once that she feared his family wouldn't be so accepting of her baby. It was another reason she hadn't told Jared she had decided to keep their child. I'd argued that she was wrong, because I knew his family better than she did. *See, Alexis, I told you they'd love him as much as Mom and Dad did.*

Jared's mom finished serving the cake. "So what are you up to these days, Callie?" she asked before I could stuff a piece of homemade cake in my mouth. I had missed her cakes and cookies. The store-bought stuff wasn't the same.

"Weren't you planning to study something to do with drawing cartoons?" Kristen asked.

"Animation," I corrected. "I decided to become a graphic designer instead." I shoved a forkful of cake into my mouth. Unlike before, it felt like I was choking down a piece of chalk.

"How come?"

"More job opportunities."

"I guess that's true," Jared's mom said. "But it's sad you had to give up your art. You're so talented."

"I still do it, just not as much as I used to." I didn't have time for it with everything else going on in my life.

"I love Mommy's pictures," Logan said, now that he'd finished his slice of cake. "They look like the ones in my books."

"You mean picture books?" his grandmother asked.

He enthusiastically nodded.

"How come I haven't seen them, other than those on your walls?" Jared asked.

I shrugged. "I tend not to show them to anyone." Because

then they would know I was a failure. I had done nothing toward achieving my dreams.

"I would love to see them," his mother said, smiling. "You have to bring them with you next weekend when you come for dinner."

"I will. Thanks."

After we finished with dessert, Jared drove us home. It was already past Logan's bedtime when we arrived. As was the usual routine now, we both got him ready for bed, and Jared read him three picture books.

"So when are you going to show me the pictures that Logan mentioned?" Jared asked, after we tucked him into bed and left his room.

"You really want to see them?" The tension between us was thick. I was practically bursting at the seams to touch him, but I was also curious to see what he would think about my artwork. Nervous but curious.

"Of course. I agree with my mom. You're a talented artist, Callie. I'd hate for you to give that up."

Easy for him to say. Would things with the band still have been as they were for him if Alexis hadn't lied about the abortion? Would he still have had time to write songs and perform? Or would he only have been able to just play around with the guitar from time to time?

"They're in my bedroom."

Jared followed me into the room. I indicated for him to sit on the bed, then retrieved the stack of printed digital artwork from my closet. I had created them after my parents and Alexis died. Logan was the only person who had seen them.

Some were pictures of kittens, puppies, chubby birds and owls, rabbits, and mice. The animals in the earlier pictures had large, sorrowful eyes. The later ones were of animal families doing fun activities together, like having a picnic or paddling a rowboat—stuff I used to do with my family. Those were Logan's favorite.

Jared leafed through the thick stack of paper. "Wow, these are amazing. Logan's right. They do look like they could be from a picture book."

"Thanks."

"Have you considered doing this professionally?"

"I don't think there's a huge demand for it." Not unless I wanted to be a starving artist. Eventually my parents' life insurance money, their savings, and the money I got when I sold their house would run out. The rent on this apartment and Logan's preschool and medical expenses weren't exactly cheap.

"I was thinking more like an illustrator for children's books," Jared said.

"I don't know...."

He studied my favorite picture. In it, a boy fox and a girl rabbit were hanging out in their tree house. The corners of Jared's mouth curled up, and for a moment all I could think about was tasting those perfect lips.

"Do you enjoy doing them?" he asked, snapping me out of my lust-filled moment.

"Yes." That was an understatement.

"More than being a graphic designer?"

I nodded. I didn't mind graphic design, but it wasn't where my heart lay. It didn't mean the same to me as music meant to Jared, or as my artwork meant to me.

"I'm not saying you have to give up your plans to be a graphic designer. Not unless you want to work in the diner for the rest of your life. But I think you should at least give being an illustrator for kids' books a chance." He placed the pictures on the bed. "You're too talented an artist to abandon your dreams," he murmured, his breath warm against the shell of my ear. "You just need to adapt them to make the most of what you have."

The tip of his tongue traced the outer edge of my ear, and I groaned. It had been three years—three very long years—since I'd last had sex. The closest thing to sex that I'd enjoyed during that time was the erotic romance novels my friends in San Francisco had introduced me to. And let me tell you now, they weren't all that satisfying. It was like showing a delicious cake, complete with mounds of whipped cream and chocolate, to someone on a diet, and telling her she couldn't have any. Not even a bite.

Jared's lips trailed a hot path along my jaw, then gently pressed against my mouth. He pulled back slightly and tenderly grabbed my lower lip between his teeth.

I moaned and parted my lips, begging for his tongue to invade my mouth. Understanding my silent pleas, he stroked his tongue against mine. Warmth spread through my body, aiming for the spot between my legs that had threatened a lifelong strike if a man didn't touch me there soon.

I threaded my fingers into his hair, keeping him close. I knew what I desired, but what about Jared? Sure, guys loved sex, but if we went there, it would only further complicate our situation.

Or would it?

Jared had wanted to see if we could make things work when it came to our relationship with Logan, and he wanted to see where that might take us. Did that include sex?

"Do you know the last time I fucked someone?" I blurted out. Really smooth, Callie.

Jared blinked. "Excuse me?"

"Three years. Not that I'm counting or anything." Because I was. "I mean, I should've been able to," I rambled on, like a train that hadn't been maintained in God knows how long. If I didn't stop now, I'd be facing a train wreck instead of great sex. "It wasn't like Logan could have heard anything." I giggled nervously. And because this train wreck wasn't happening fast enough, I had to add, "Do you have any condoms with you?"

He took a step back, possibly ready to make a break for it. "Wait a second. What are you talking about?"

"Sex."

"Yeah, I got that. But why?"

"Because I want sex." While I could still get it. "It's been a while and I figured you'd want it too, now that we're seeing where things go between us." Wasn't that part of the package deal? I really should have checked the fine print.

"Hey, what's really going on, Callie?"

Idiot. The word impaled me like a two-by-four caught up in a tornado-strength wind. Suddenly the gray carpet in front of my feet was the most fascinating item in the room.

Too bad Jared didn't agree with me. He hooked his finger under my chin and forced me to look at him. "I didn't come into your room because I want to have sex with you."

"You don't want to have sex with me?" Someone hit me with that two-by-four, please.

"That's not what I said."

"So you do want to have sex with me?"

"I didn't say that either."

"Right." I started for the doorway.

Jared blocked my escape. "Trust me, Callie, there's nothing I want more than to be inside you, but are you sure that's what you want?"

"Definitely," I whispered, the image of Jared being inside me doing weird things to my voice.

Jared cupped my cheek with his hand and leaned in to kiss me. It had only been a few minutes, but I missed those soft sexy lips. The scent that was all man, all Jared, snuggled up to me. I wanted him. I wanted him now.

His hand left my cheek and trailed down my throat to my breast, hidden under my bra and T-shirt. His thumb brushed against my nipple. I sucked in a sharp breath. The thumb then teased said nipple into a hard peak, straining against the cotton of my bra.

My entire body went on high alert, hoping this was the real thing and not a drill. I didn't know what I would do if he changed his mind. Possibly knee him in the nuts. That sounded fair.

"And yes, I do have a condom with me," Jared said against my mouth.

"Good," I whispered back.

"Maybe we should remove your pictures from the bed first."

"That might be a good idea." I quickly gathered them up, my hands shaking, and placed the stack on my desk.

From behind me, Jared wrapped his arms around my waist and pulled me against him. His hardening length pressed into the curve of my lower back. "Are you nervous?" He tenderly kissed my neck.

I shook my head. "It's just been a while." And there might've been a place, deep down, where I realized this was a mistake. I was falling in love with Jared, but he wasn't in the same place as me. For him this was just sex.

I removed my T-shirt. It landed somewhere by my feet. I reached behind me to unhook my bra.

"What are you doing?" Jared asked.

"Er, removing my clothes? Unless you want to have sex with them on." Maybe he didn't want to see my body naked. I didn't exactly have a supermodel body like his ex-girlfriend. My body came with extra padding.

I crossed my arms in front of me. I'd never been self-conscious about my body until now. Before becoming Logan's mom, I'd run daily. My body had been toned and, according to my ex, incredibly sexy. Now the only exercise I got was walking to and from the diner (if you didn't count the running around I did at work).

Jared unfolded my arms. "No, I want to see you naked." He then murmured against my ear, "But I want to be the one to get you naked." His hand skimmed up my arm and I shivered in anticipation.

The white cotton fabric against my girls loosened, and a second later my bra joined my T-shirt on the floor. My heart hammered a frantic beat in my rib cage, eager to get this party started.

Before I had a chance to take my turn in our stripping game and remove Jared's T-shirt, he took my nipple into his mouth. He alternated between sucking it and flicking it with his tongue. I moaned, this time louder than before.

Jared chuckled against my breast, and my knees came close to buckling under me at the delicious sensation.

He stood up, a satisfied smirk on his face. I grabbed the hem of his T-shirt and yanked him back toward me. He lips met mine again.

While he kissed me senseless, I inched his T-shirt up his hard abs and chest. Although Jared had never been into team sports growing up, other than tossing the ball around with his buddies, he had definitely been busy when it came to keeping in shape. With my lips against his, I couldn't tell how many packs he had on that stomach of his, but it was definitely up there in number.

"You've been working out?" I managed to say, my breath ragged.

"It's great for relieving stress," he murmured.

"So is sex."

"I know, but I tend to avoid the groupie thing. Which means I have to find another way to relieve the stress. So I run, and when I can, I hit the gym and lift weights."

His words repeated in my head as I searched for some hidden message I missed the first time. "Are you telling me you don't have sex with groupies?"

"No, but I am telling you I don't do it all that often. Groupies can cause nothing but trouble if you screw the wrong one." I couldn't tell if he knew this from experience, and I had a feeling I didn't want to know. Especially not now.

There was only one thing I was interested in doing, and he was standing in front of me.

I drew the edge of Jared's T-shirt up his body. A moment later, it joined the party of clothes on the floor. As did our jeans. Our underwear were the last items remaining on our bodies, and it was tough to miss the hard length straining against the black fabric of Jared's boxer briefs.

A shy smile crept onto my face. "Does this mean you want to have sex with me?" I glanced meaningfully at his cock.

He grunted, then his mouth was on mine again, the only answer I needed.

He walked me backward until the mattress pressed against the back of my legs. I sat down hard. His mouth still attached to mine, Jared kneeled onto the bed and guided me until I lay back, my legs dangling over the side. He removed his briefs, exposing his oh-my-goodness thick length, then pressed his cock against my core and rocked against me.

You know how when you watch fireworks and the first few are breathtaking, but they're just the warm-up to the main event? Well, even those fireworks are pretty damn fine.

I moaned. "Oh God, I want you inside me so badly."

He smiled, his eyes dark. It wasn't his usual smile, the one that set my heart off in a happy dance. It was a hungry smile that had an entirely different effect on my heart. My breathing picked up to a near pant.

He didn't say anything. He just moved off me and hooked his fingers under the waistband of my white cotton panties. With the same hungry grin he peeled them slowly down my legs, his fingers burning a path in their wake.

He dropped them somewhere on the floor and nudged my thighs wide apart. "Relax, Callie."

Easy for him to say. He wasn't the one exposed and vulnerable in so many different ways.

Guiding my legs, he bent my knees and shifted his position so his head was between my legs. His tongue reached out and repeatedly flicked my clit, taking it closer to its happy place. I fisted the sheet with both hands.

Jared continued tormenting me in all kinds of delicious ways, alternating between sucking and licking. I bucked and wiggled against his talented tongue, even with his hands on my hips. That girl in the diner a week and a half ago had been right, even if she hadn't realized just how right she was.

"You taste amazing, Callie. I could spend the whole night just feasting on you."

Usually when the hero in erotic romances said this, I would giggle because it sounded so corny in the book. I was wrong. Hearing Jared say this to me took erotic to a whole new level. I craved to do all kinds of things to him. Hot things. Things I'd only read about in my favorite books.

Things I had never attempted with my ex.

Jared slipped a finger inside me. His mouth left my clit, which was on the verge of singing hallelujah, and another finger plunged inside.

"You're so fucking hot and wet," he groaned. His skilled fingers alternated between scissoring and thrusting inside me.

"Jared," I moaned. "I'm gonna come any second."

He chuckled. "That's the general idea."

"I want you inside me. Now." I couldn't have made my voice any more pleading if I'd tried.

"We have plenty of time for that."

That's what he thinks . . . I didn't have a chance to finish that thought. An orgasm to rival all orgasms rocketed my body.

"Oh God, Jared," I screamed out. Now that was a first. I'd never been considered a screamer before.

The orgasm hit me so hard—thanks to the incredibly long drought between the last time I'd had sex and now—that it took me a long moment to regain my senses.

My eyes closed, I was vaguely aware of Jared climbing off the bed. A second later, the mattress dipped again under his weight.

I opened my eyes to discover that not only was Jared now naked, but his cock was jutting out, proud and eager. He ripped open a square foil package and rolled on the condom. Then he positioned himself between my legs and slowly pushed his tip inside me.

"God, Callie, you're so tight," he groaned, and pushed deeper into me. Even though I'd just witnessed a fireworks show to surpass all others, my body was more than happy for an encore.

I wrapped my legs around his hips, seating him further into me. I couldn't tell where I ended and he began; I only knew that it felt good. Better than good.

We rocked against each other, moaning and panting with each stroke of his cock. My body clenched around his wide length, and I called out his name combined with a groan.

The last waves of euphoria had just washed through me when Jared came. Between his guttural sound and my cries as I came, I was thankful Logan couldn't hear us. I wasn't so sure, though, if my neighbors were as lucky.

Jared left the bed and disposed of the condom, then looked back at me, uncertainty sitting square on his shoulders.

The moment of euphoria I had enjoyed became a distant memory. Shit, he was already regretting what could've easily been described as the best thing to have happened to me in a while.

27

JARED

I'd been fantasizing about sinking my cock inside of Callie since the day I first bumped into her at the grocery store. But fantasy was nothing like reality.

Not even close.

Only now that we had finally fucked, what did that mean?

We weren't in love. We were seeing where things were going between us, before I went back on tour again. Before I returned to the emptiness that had become my life on the road—even with four bandmates to keep me from being alone.

I disposed of the condom in the trash can and returned to the bed. Callie was lying on her side, bent elbow propping up her head, teeth tugging on her lower lip. The sheet was wrapped around her breasts, low enough to reveal her cleavage. My tongue and hands itched to rip the sheet off her body and explore her again.

I sat next to her and stroked her naked arm. "You all right?"

She nodded, and I gently kissed her. With the groupies I had screwed, I couldn't get away fast enough afterward. Not that they cared. They had gotten what they were after and were ready to move on. A few were looking for something more, but that didn't matter in the end. Even with Tiffany, I'd never felt the urge to hang around for long after we fucked.

Not so with Callie.

I climbed under the sheets and we quickly became a tangle of limbs, her head on my shoulder. It felt good. Great, even. Like her body had been designed for this, with me.

Her fingers traced across my chest. "How come you don't have any tattoos? Aren't rock stars supposed to have tattoos?"

"I'm not exactly a rock star. I'm a musician who plays rock music."

She smiled in the way that had always warmed me. I used to pretend that only I was the recipient of it. That I was somehow special.

"You are a rock star." She brushed her lips against mine. "You're my rock star." Her words were soft yet determined. My heart swelled at hearing them.

This time when our lips met, the passion between us almost consumed me. Letting her go was no longer an option.

But as the moment became more heated, our tongues sliding against each other in their own seductive dance, she pulled back. "You didn't answer my question."

"Which question was that?"

"Why don't you have any tattoos? The other guys in the band have them, right?"

Some more than others. "Do you have any?" I countered.

She nodded. "Just one. I got it when I moved to San Francisco, during my first week there."

I scanned the perfect, unmarked skin not hidden by the sheet. I never figured Callie to be the type to get a tattoo, but it shouldn't have surprised me. She was an artist, and the body was just another type of canvas. "Show me."

She rolled onto her stomach. The sheet shifted, revealing six small musical notes floating around her lower back, near her right hip. They were beautiful, like the woman whose body they graced. I traced my finger over them.

"That's how much I believed in you and your music," she said.

Speechless, I could only stare at the tattoo. She had done that . . . for me?

Damn if that didn't almost do me in—in a good way.

I pressed my lips against the musical notes and breathed in her lightly scented skin. Then I continued kissing her, moving up her back to her shoulder. "I haven't gotten one because I believe you should only get a design that means something to you and will always mean something to you."

"I agree," she whispered before her lips found mine again.

Our kisses grew hungrier, more intense. That wasn't the only thing to grow. My cock hardened, already missing Callie's tight heat wrapped around it.

Callie shifted from under me and nudged me onto my back. She straddled my legs and leaned over, teasing my nipples with her silky copper hair. Damn, that was hot. Then she took my nipple into her hot, pretty mouth, sucking and swirling her tongue against it. My cock responded, imagining how it would feel with her perfect lips wrapped around it.

She rocked her wet, swollen pussy against the shaft of my cock. "Oh, God," I groaned.

She chuckled. "Wow, that was fast."

"For you, babe, always." It wasn't a line. It was me realizing how much I'd missed her all these past years, despite our four-year age difference. How much I cared for her—now even more than back then.

She wrapped her fingers around the shaft and caressed the swollen head, spreading pre-cum. "Please tell me you have another condom with you."

"In my wallet."

She grabbed my wallet from the night table and handed it

to me. I removed the remaining foil square from it and tore open the package.

"I can do it." She took the condom from me and carefully unrolled it down my hard length.

Which became even harder at her touch. I swear, if it took any longer before I was buried deep inside her, I'd die from a sudden case of blue balls.

Callie repositioned her body so my cock pressed against her entrance, and slowly lowered herself. A cross between a hiss and a groan escaped my throat. Fuck, she felt amazing.

She leaned back, seating me even further inside her. Her full tits offered themselves for my pleasure. I palmed one. God's gift—for me.

Or so I would've liked to believe. I quickly pushed away the thought of someone else sampling Callie while I was on the road. We hadn't made any promises to each other, and although I had no doubt I would remain faithful to her while touring, I couldn't expect Callie to wait for me. A year was a very long time.

I pinched her pebbled nipple and was rewarded with an erotic moan. At the sound, my cock grew yet harder inside her.

Callie moved her hips, setting her own pace and rhythm, slow and teasing. She wasn't the only one who could tease. My fingers found her clit and I stroked her, relishing each oh-God-I'm-going-to-come-soon noise that she made.

"That feels so good," she moaned.

Agreed.

The pace continued, pushing me closer and closer to the edge—but not quite far enough. I removed my finger from her clit, grabbed her hips, and set a faster, rougher pace, taking care not to push myself over the edge before she was ready.

Just as I thought I couldn't last any longer, Callie's muscles clamped down on me. "Jared," she groaned.

Her husky voice, the sight of her heated pussy devouring

my length, and the strength of her muscles milking me for all their worth finally did me in. The powerful orgasm rocketed through me, intense enough to alter the trajectory of the earth around the sun. If the world suffered from a massive malfunction, I was to blame. "Fuck, Callie," I grunted.

Once I regained enough of my senses, I shifted so she was under me and kissed her. Just a light touch of the lips. "Christ, that was amazing." We were amazing together, but was it enough?

After disposing of the condom, I curled my body around hers and kissed her shoulder.

As I cuddled with her, a realization hit—I was fucked.

Purely and simply fucked.

And not necessarily in a good way, if my heart had anything to say about it.

28

JARED

Once Callie was asleep, I slipped out of her bed, careful not to wake her.

Ever since my relationship with Alexis, I'd pretty much kept my distance from the dating scene. Yes, there had been Lisa, a girl I'd dated for a month, who was responsible for Nolan and me becoming friends. And then there was Tiffany. But otherwise I hadn't bothered.

I'd thought my heart was safe. The occasional screwing of random women didn't put it at risk. Even with Tiffany, it had never been at risk. We were too different.

But somehow things felt the opposite with Callie, and I had no idea why. Sure, she was a friend. Sure, she was the one who had been looking after my son for all these years. Sure, she was sexy as hell and didn't realize it. But bit by bit, Callie had become a major part of my life and I had no idea what to do about it.

I returned to my apartment, but for the first time since Nolan moved out to live with Hailey, the space felt lonely and unwelcoming.

I needed a pet.

Maybe a nice fish.

After watching TV for a while, I finally crashed in bed. The sun was streaming through the blinds when I woke up a few hours later. At first I had no idea where I was, as dreams of a naked Callie paraded through my head. With a morning wood to rival all others, I reached out to her side of the bed to discover that not only was it empty, the sheets were cool.

I opened my eyes and disappointment greeted me at the sight of my furniture. My queen-sized bed. The bookshelf. The nightstand. The dark green armchair Mom had given me after she and Dad bought a new one. My favorite guitar in the corner. Notebooks, pencils, blank sheet music spread out on the floor, waiting for my muse to strike.

Band practice wasn't for four more hours. Even though I usually went for a run as soon as I got up in the morning, I had the sudden urge to play around with a song I'd been working on. I picked up my guitar, not bothering to take the time to shower first. I'd long since learned that when the creative urge hit, you didn't ignore it to do something else first.

But instead of the song I'd been working on, lyrics for a different one seeped into my head. I didn't doubt for a second who the inspiration was behind these words—I just didn't get why I couldn't get her out of my head.

I'd been working for two hours when the creative flow decided to pack it up for the morning, replaced by a restlessness I hadn't experienced since bumping into Callie and Logan at the grocery store. I pulled on my running shorts and T-shirt and finally hit the road. I ran long and hard, but it still wasn't enough. All I could think about was Callie, about the taste of her and how she responded to my touch. All I could think about was how much I missed her.

I returned home an hour later, panting and drenched with sweat—but with a plan. Callie and I were seeing where things were headed between us, and how we worked together when it came to Logan. There were no expectations, which I was more than fine with, but that didn't mean I couldn't cook her dinner. She and Logan had to eat. It was the least I could do.

I called Callie at work to tell her I wanted to spend the day with Logan. Sharon had returned to looking after him again while Callie was at the diner, but until I was back on tour, I wanted to spend more time with him.

"Do you want to pick him up from preschool?" she asked breathlessly. In the background, the clatter of dishes and someone calling out an order to the cook could be heard.

I told her yes, and she promised to call Sharon to tell her the new plan. "I'm sure she won't complain," she said. "Some of her friends attend a local aquacise class, and now she can join them."

I had no idea what that meant, but as long as I got to spend more time with my son, I didn't care.

"See you later" was all Callie had time for before she ended the call—and I was left missing the sound of her voice.

I arrived at Logan's preschool. Tony showed up a minute later. "Just the guy I wanted to talk to," he said. He didn't have a chance, though, to tell me what he wanted to talk to me about, as just then the kids filed out of their classroom, and Logan rushed over to me and gave me a big hug.

"Hey, big guy," I said. "You want to hang out with me until your mom gets off work?"

"Yes!"

"I have band practice, but Hailey's going to bring Rocky to visit after we're done."

His face lit up, as it always did at the mention of the puppy.

Outside, Tony and I watched the boys climb the slide ladder, huge smiles on their faces.

"I mentioned Callie to a friend of mine and he's interested in meeting her," he said. "I can vouch for him. He's a great guy.

He's widowed with a two-year-old daughter. His wife died more than a year ago from cancer."

That explained why Tony had asked the other week about my relationship with Callie. He had planned to hook her up with his friend even back then.

Jealousy and anger gnawed at my stomach. Not just because he was trying to hook them up, but because I couldn't tell the world that she was mine. We were keeping things secret for Logan's sake, but damned if I would let Tony continue to think that she was available. "She just started dating someone. Sorry."

"That's too bad."

Yeah, isn't it?

Once we were finished at the playground, I drove Logan to a nearby mall. "Maybe it's time to get you some new pajamas," I said to him as we wandered through the outdoor space. The sun shone intensely, but a cool breeze kept the air from getting too hot. "Yours are too small now that you're getting to be a big boy." Callie had already tried to buy him new ones, but he hadn't jumped at the idea. "Maybe we can find you new Spider-Man ones."

He pouted. "I like my pajamas."

"I know you do, but I bet we can find even better ones."

He shrugged, clearly not convinced that a better pair could possibly exist. But after contemplating for a few seconds, he nodded. "Okay."

A short time later, we left the kids' clothing store with two pairs of pajamas. One had Spider-Man on them. The other pair had solid green pants and a brown cartoon dog on the top.

As we continued wandering through the mall, six teenage girls approached, giggling.

"Hi," the tallest girl said. "You're with Pushing Limits, right?"

"That's right," I replied.

"We love your music. When's your next album coming out?"

I smiled because it never grew old hearing fans tell me they loved the band's music. I hoped the day never came when they said the opposite. "In just over three weeks."

"Are you playing any concerts in L.A.?"

"Concert dates will be announced soon," I said, following the script our publicist had given us. The name of the band we were opening for was still locked in a wooden box buried twelve feet under LS Records. They were keeping it a secret on purpose. Something to do with generating buzz. Even we had no idea who we were opening for.

"Can we get your autograph?" she asked.

"Sure."

The girls all magically produced the band's debut CD from their purses.

"You carry the CD everywhere you go?" I asked. Never seen that before.

"No," said a redheaded girl with freckles splattered on her nose, and my thoughts instantly went to Callie. I had always loved her freckles, even when she hated them as a kid. "We saw you walking through the mall. Joanne followed you so that we didn't lose you while the rest of us rushed to the store to buy your album. We were hoping you'd sign them for us." She removed an assortment of Sharpies from her purse.

I started signing them, chatting with the girls at the same time. At one point I glanced down to make sure Logan was still okay. He wasn't there. I scanned the area, calling out his name, only to remember that he couldn't hear me if he had wandered out of hearing range. Fuck.

Realizing I had lost Logan and he could be anywhere, fear snaked into my body and squeezed my vital organs hard. The mall was an outdoor shopping center, which meant Logan could easily leave. And if he tried to cross the street—

"What's wrong?" the redhead asked.

"My . . . the boy who was with me, he's missing." I started to walk away but then stopped. There was no way I could cover the mall on my own.

"Can you help me find him?" I showed them his picture on my phone.

"Wow, he's cute," the tall girl said. "Is he your little brother?"

"Yes." I gave them my phone number so they could text me if they found him. They ran off in different directions, including toward the mall exits.

Where the hell was mall security when you needed them? I thought.

And what kind of asshole father loses his four-year-old son in a mall?

I ducked into another kids' clothing store and searched between the racks and displays. One of Logan's favorite games was hide-and-seek.

"Can I help you find something?" a woman in her early fifties asked.

"I'm looking for my four-year-old son."

She didn't belong in the band's demographics, so chances were good she had no idea who I was. There would be no tweets going out that I had a son, nor would it go viral that I had lost said son.

I showed her the picture on my smartphone.

"Sorry, I haven't seen him. Let me call mall security for you."

"Okay, but I don't have time to wait for them." I gave her my number so they could call me, and rushed out of the store.

My phone pinged, and I read the message. Found him!!!!! He's in the toy store.

The store was across the plaza from where I was standing. I sprinted across the beige stone and entered the small store. In the corner, next to a shelf full of stuffed animals, the redhead was kneeling next to Logan and talking to him.

"Thank you," I said, working to catch my breath.

"You're welcome." She stood up.

Logan held up a stuffed dog that resembled Rocky. "Puppy."

I squatted and hugged him hard. "It's a very nice puppy. But Logan, you can't just wander off like that. Next time, you need to tell me if you want to go somewhere."

"You busy." He hugged the toy.

"No matter what, you always come first."

Because I owed the girl and her friends big-time, I asked for her address so I could send them signed posters of the band. It was the least I could do. Logan was still hugging the toy puppy by the time I had finished talking to her.

"I know he's not a real dog," I said, "but would you like him?"

He held the puppy tighter. "Yes."

"Yes what?" I even managed to sign it as I said it. Although after I almost lost Logan, I doubt my growing signing ability would impress Callie.

Logan considered that for a second. "Thank you."

We arrived at Mason's loft a short time later. "How's my little man?" Mas held up his hand to high-five Logan, who had to jump up to reach it. It had become a routine with those two. "Who's this?" Mason asked, pretending to pat Logan's toy.

"My dog," Logan said proudly, and waited for the rest of the band to do the same as Mason. I grinned at the sight of four grown men fussing over a stuffed toy as if it were a real puppy.

Four grown men, one with green dye on his hands. "You wanna explain why you have green hands?" I asked Aaron, although I already had my suspicions.

They were confirmed when he glared pointedly at Mason.

Mas snickered. "Well, you did complain that house plants die at the sight of you. I just thought I'd help you out."

Kirk snorted a laugh. "The term is 'green thumb,' drummer boy. Not 'green hands.'"

"Hi, Jared," a female voice said from the far side of the room, its owner already bored with the guys' typical antics. The husky sound of it would've left most men sporting a hard-on— but for once, it did nothing for me. I hadn't even noticed Tiffany when Logan and I entered the room.

Looking like she belonged in the sparsely yet expensively furnished loft, she sashayed her way over, wrapped her arms around my neck, and pressed her body against mine. "I've missed you, love."

"How did you know I'd be here?" I unhooked her arms from around me and walked over to Mason's fridge. Unlike mine, it wasn't covered in Logan's latest artwork. But it did have one of Logan's pictures of what could've been Mason on the drums . . . if you used your imagination.

The guys continued to discuss Mason's latest prank, much to the amusement of Logan. He was giggling so hard at Aaron's brightly colored hands, I thought he might fall over.

Tiffany joined me by the fridge. She had called last week to tell me she was in town and couldn't wait to see me, but this was the first time I'd actually seen her since our last breakup.

"I was nearby for a charity luncheon," she explained, "and I knew you'd be practicing."

"And so you just showed up?" I grabbed a can of soda and an apple juice from the fridge.

She smiled as I popped open the soda. "I was hoping to see Mason. He's always good for the latest band gossip."

That I did know. Mason had a bad habit of accidentally letting things slip. If you didn't want something to go public, you avoided mentioning it to him. It was also why he wasn't allowed on our social media sites. Aaron and I were the ones who had always done it, but at our last meeting with the label's publicist, Jennifer had recommended we hire an assistant to maintain our social media updates. Now we just needed an assistant. Preferably one that Mason didn't try to get inside of within the first five minutes of meeting her.

"And what band gossip did he tell you?" I gulped down some soda.

"That you have a son."

Soda spewed from my mouth, narrowly missing her. It hit the fridge instead.

"Classy," Mason said, laughing.

Fortunately Logan was on the couch, talking to Nolan, and didn't hear her.

"Is it true?" she asked. "Is he your son?" She jerked her head in Logan's direction.

"I haven't made that public yet"—I glared at Mason—"but yeah, he's my son." I kept my voice low, the implication behind the tone clear.

"He is?" Mason asked, taken aback. I don't think I could have shocked him more than if I had shoved an electric eel down his pants. "I was just kidding when I said he was your son the other day. But I guess that does explain why you two look so alike."

He started walking toward the couch. I grabbed his arm. "Logan doesn't know yet, so don't say anything. I'm waiting for the right time to break the news to him."

"Well, I suggest you don't wait until just before we leave on tour. And don't worry, I won't mention it to anyone." He mimed locking his mouth shut and tossing the key, then walked away to join Logan and Nolan.

"So . . . who's his mother?" Tiffany asked.

"You don't know her." True enough.

"Are you seeing her?"

I came close to saying yes, but since Callie and I had agreed to keep our relationship a secret for now, I wasn't about to break my part of the agreement. Telling Tony earlier that she was dating someone didn't count. It had been done for the greater good. "It's complicated."

She must have understood "it's complicated" to mean no because she responded, "Good. Does he live with you?"

"Nope. He still lives with his mom."

Tiffany stepped closer. Less than a foot separated us. "How come you never told me you have a son?"

"I didn't know."

She frowned. "Then how do you know he's yours?"

"You mean beyond the part where he looks a lot like me? I had a paternity test done."

"So you have joint custody?"

"Not yet. I wasn't listed on the birth certificate, but my lawyer is working on correcting that." Well, he would be as soon as I decided if I wanted to share custody with Callie or if I would seek to have full custody of my son. There were pros and cons with either choice.

"Wouldn't it be better if the mother had full custody? You're on the road a lot, and if you decide to settle down one day, it would make things easier for everyone—especially Logan—if you weren't bouncing the poor child between parents."

"Is that what happened to you?"

She laughed. "What gave you the idea my parents are divorced?"

"You just seem to know a lot about it."

She inched closer to me. I stepped back. My hip bumped against the counter.

"My parents are happily married," she said. "They just weren't around much. They were always traveling for their careers, which meant I was raised by nannies. No kid should live like that." She shrugged. "You said Logan isn't even aware that he's your son. Why tell him now? From the looks of it, his mother's doing a great job raising him. How do you know he's not better off without you—especially given your career?"

The thing was, I had no idea if he was better off not

knowing that I was his father. But I did know that he wanted me to be his dad. Otherwise he wouldn't have been so excited about the idea when he caught me kissing Callie.

"Are we practicing or what?" Kirk called out. The four guys and Logan were watching us, bored with waiting for Tiffany and me to finish our conversation.

"Sorry," I called out. "I'm ready."

"Can I stay and watch?" she asked.

"Sure. You can sit with Logan." I gave the apple juice box to Logan and introduced her to him, then removed his auditory processor from under his hair.

"What's that?" she asked.

"Logan is deaf," I said and signed. "This"—I pointed to the device in my hand—"helps him hear." Yes, I signed that too.

"But don't think for a second it means you can say 'fuck' around him," Mason said as he fished a dollar from his wallet. He handed it to Logan and winked at him.

Logan grinned, but at least this time he didn't repeat the word . . . which he had recently learned to lip-read. Mason owed me big-time for that new skill.

"I thought you said he can't hear," Tiffany said.

"He can't. But he can feel the vibrations when we play the music." I grabbed my guitar and signaled to Mason to start our first song.

The band had been practicing for two hours when we finally took a quick break. Before I had a chance to see how Logan was doing, Tiffany sashayed up to me like she was on a catwalk. She swooped in so fast to kiss me, I didn't see it coming until it was too late.

"I'll see you soon, love," she said, then quickly left before I had time to react. But what I did see was Logan looking at me, frowning. Shit. Between Callie, Tiffany, and the girl at Disneyland, he must be confused about why so many women were kissing me. And he didn't even know the half of it. How the heck did I explain this to him?

I turned around in time to catch Aaron and Kirk each hand Mason twenty dollars. Mason appeared smug behind his drums.

"What's going on?" I asked.

"The losers bet me that you wouldn't get back together with that fine piece of ass. I, on the other hand, knew you couldn't resist it. No one can."

I glared at them. "You seriously bet on my dating life?" And with Mason of all people. They should've known better, given his past gambling addiction.

"What else do you expect us to do for fun?" Aaron said, chuckling.

Any other time I would have flipped them the bird, but the last thing I needed was for Logan to learn that gesture. I could guarantee it wouldn't have impressed anyone at his school. Nor would it have scored me any points with Callie.

"You can give Aaron and Kirk back their money," I told Mason. "Tiffany and I aren't dating."

Mason laughed. "Sure. Whatever you say." He didn't give back the money. Instead, he flashed them a look that said it all: *You just wait. Jared will be fucking her in no time.*

29

CALLIE

Before Jared and I had taken our "relationship" to the next level, sitting next to him on my couch to watch a movie had been hard enough. Now it was doubly so with Logan sitting between us. No touching or kissing of Jared was allowed. I just had to channel my inner nun.

Too bad I was as close to being Catholic as I was to being a mermaid.

I glanced at the wall clock. Ten more minutes before Logan's bedtime. And then what? When I'd woken up this morning, I rather rudely discovered that the wonderful dream, in which Jared realized he loved me and always had, was nothing more than a delusion. In reality, he hadn't been able to get away fast enough during the night.

He had surprised me, though, when I returned home to discover that he and Logan had cooked dinner. I'm not talking macaroni and cheese or frozen pizza. They had cooked fettuccine Alfredo, with chicken and vegetables tossed in.

My foot bounced, counting down the seconds until the movie ended. Three. Two. One. I jumped up off the couch.

"Bedtime," I said rather hurriedly as the closing credits came on.

The corner of Jared's mouth tugged up into his sexy smirk.

After we got Logan to bed following what had become our new routine, with Jared reading Logan a bedtime story or three, we stepped into the hallway and I partially closed the bedroom door. We didn't move beyond that, staring at each other, uncertain what to do next.

Jared was the one who made the first move. One second he was staring at me; the next his lips were against mine. I didn't hesitate to open my mouth and let him in. I'd been dreaming about his kisses for the past few years—and there might've been some fantasizing while at work earlier that day. I wasn't about to waste time with chaste kisses.

My fingers knotted in his hair and I tugged the soft strands.

"Oh God, Callie," he moaned against my mouth. I took it as a good sign that he was rooting for an encore of last night.

My brain demanded that we waited until Logan fell asleep. My body outvoted it. But at least we waited until we were in my bedroom before the clothes came flying off.

The kisses suddenly went from hungry to languid. Jared wrapped his arms around me, and we swayed to the song playing in his head. His hard, thick length pressed against my stomach, leaving my girlie parts begging to get reacquainted.

But while they might've been in a rush for that to happen, Jared apparently wasn't. He traced his fingers up and down my back, an explorer on a mission. Then they changed their movements, and instead of exploring my body, I was a musical instrument and he was playing me.

"What are you doing?" I whispered.

"Creating a song."

"I don't know how it sounds, but it feels good."

The answering grin knocked my breath away.

He led me to the bed and I lay down. We continued kissing,

focused on nothing but each other. Our hands continued exploring and teasing, bringing each other to the edge, but never letting it go beyond that. Not yet, anyway.

Jared's fingers eventually slipped through my slick folds. "God, you're so wet."

I started to respond at the same time his ultra-talented fingers found my clit and circled it. Once. Twice. The words I thirsted to say came out as a moan. That was okay. It pretty much summed up what I wanted to say anyway.

He broke away from my lips long enough to reach into the drawer of my night table and pull out a box of condoms.

I laughed. "Wow, you must have magical powers. I don't remember putting those in there."

"I have many talents."

I grinned. "So I've noticed." Without asking, I took the foil package from between his fingers and tore it open.

Jared scooted back so I could sit up. I slipped it on over Jared's tip and carefully rolled it down his length.

His thumb traced circles around my nipple, his dark brown eyes locked on my gaze. "Christ, Callie, I want to be inside you. Preferably sooner rather than later."

"Sounds good to me," I whispered before his lips were on mine again. He pushed me back on the bed, spread my thighs wide, and inch by inch sank into me. My inner muscles craved to consume all of him. They clutched at him, pulled him in deeper.

Like his earlier kisses, he moved slowly at first, the strokes executed with tremendous control on his part. But after a few seconds, I didn't give a damn about his control. I hungered for him to move harder, faster, deeper.

I grabbed his ass and hinted quite clearly what I wanted.

And that's exactly what I got.

It didn't take long before the earth-shattering tremor rocked my body, sending me careening over the edge into a complete state of bliss.

Jared joined me in euphoria just as I was returning to earth, my body limp and completely satisfied. He kissed me deeply one last time, then pushed himself off the bed. After disposing of the condom, he returned to bed and gathered me against him.

I relaxed in his arms and closed my eyes. "Thank you," I whispered. The steady thump thump thump of his heart lulled me into that fuzzy zone between being awake and asleep.

Neither of us said anything. If it hadn't been for Jared drawing lazy circles on my lower back, I would've guessed he'd gone to sleep. Part of me longed to ask him what he was thinking, but the other part reasoned it was probably just as well that I didn't know. Might as well let me live with my delusions for as long as possible, before reality bitch-slapped me in the face.

I had no idea how long I'd been asleep when the warmth I was cuddling shifted. Somewhere in the depths of my foggy mind, the sound of a child crying nudged me awake.

I sat up with a start. Jared was pulling on his jeans and was out the door before I had a chance to scramble out of bed. I grabbed my yoga pants and T-shirt from the chair and shoved them on.

By the time I entered Logan's bedroom, Jared was sitting on his bed, hugging him. The bedroom light wasn't on, but there was enough light spilling in from the hallway to illuminate father and son. I turned on Logan's lamp, with a soccer ball as the base, so that he could see me when I signed.

"What's wrong?" I signed to him.

"Bad dream," he signed back. He pointed to his ear and signed, "I want to talk."

Jared watched us, clueless as to what we were saying.

"You want the processor back on?" I signed. Logan could

talk without it, but it was still hard to understand what he was saying because he couldn't hear himself speak.

"Yes. Want Jared to sing to me."

"What's he saying?" Jared asked.

"He wants you to sing to him," I replied. Then to Logan I said and signed, "Jared doesn't sing. He plays guitar."

"That's okay, I'll sing."

I flashed Jared a soft smile. The man never ceased to amaze me as to what he would do when it came to his son.

I attached the processor to Logan's cochlear implant. Once I was finished, Jared started singing. My mouth dropped open. In all the years I'd known him, I'd never heard Jared sing.

I recognized the ballad from the band's first album. While I would never admit this to Nolan Kincaid's face, Jared was just as good a singer as he was—and I'd always thought that Nolan was an amazing singer.

Jared finished the song, which was about finding your way when you were lost. Logan wouldn't understand the meaning behind the lyrics, but that was okay. The melody was soothing, and that was more important than anything else.

Logan clapped.

"Why have I never heard you sing before?" I asked. "You're amazing."

Jared's cheeks reddened. I couldn't remember the last time I'd seen him blush. "Thanks."

"No, really. You could seriously be a lead singer." Which was great if Nolan ever decided to leave the band.

"No, I couldn't. It takes more than a good voice—"

"Great voice," I corrected.

"There's more to it than just standing onstage and singing. Nolan's a born front man. He knows how to get the audience excited. He lives for being the center of attention when he's onstage."

"You don't want to ever sing lead vocals?"

Jared shook his head. "Why would I? I'm perfectly happy playing guitar and letting Nolan get all the attention." He chuckled. "And Mason, if he has his way."

That was too bad, I thought. The world had no idea what it was missing.

I removed Logan's processor and we stayed with him until he fell asleep again, cuddling the toy dog Jared had bought him this afternoon.

Jared left the room while I watched Logan sleep for another minute or two. Tears blurred my vision. Even though Logan had no idea that Jared was his father, Jared was becoming more important to him with each passing day. What Jared and I had was temporary. I could feel it in my bones. Eventually I'd lose them both—and there was nothing I could do.

30

JARED

This time when I woke up from a dream about fucking Callie, she really was with me. No waking up to an empty bed in my apartment.

Her eyes were closed, her breathing slow and even. Her shiny copper hair framed her face like a flame, but at the same time, it gave her a sweet, innocent aura. My already hard cock hardened some more.

Her dark eyelashes fanned against the faint half circles under her eyes. She'd had them since the first time I bumped into her a few weeks ago, but they were more noticeable without her makeup on. She was exhausted, and it wasn't hard to guess why. Her entire life revolved around my son: the unsatisfying job that let her get home early to be with him, the online courses she worked on in the evenings so she could eventually give him a better future, the freelance design jobs she did to earn more income. No wonder she was so tired and didn't have time for her art.

A small sound came from Logan's room. Careful not to wake Callie, I slipped out from under the covers, quickly dressed, and closed the door behind me. It clicked shut, the sound quiet enough not to wake her. It was only six-thirty, and Callie didn't have to work today.

Logan was playing with Legos, his new stuffed puppy next to him on the floor. At my movement, he looked up.

"What are you doing?" I signed, even though it was obvious what he was doing.

He signed his reply, but the gestures were well beyond my simple ASL skills. The only part I understood was when he spelled out "Lego" with his fingers.

"I help you?" I signed back. He nodded, and I reattached his audio processor.

We spent the next fifteen minutes creating some unique-looking vehicles. General Motors had nothing on us.

I signed to Logan, "Are you hungry?"

He nodded.

"Do you want to go for a drive and get some breakfast? Just you and me while Mommy sleeps?"

I left Callie a note on the floor in front of Logan's door, sent my sister a text, and grabbed my car keys and wallet. Then we headed to my favorite place for pancakes—the Pancake Cafe.

The hostess seated us next to the window, giving us a not-so-scenic view of the side street. Luckily Logan wasn't fussy about that. He was too busy studying the pictures on the menu.

I pointed to the kid-friendly selection, with the photo of a small stack of pancakes with sliced strawberries and bananas, whipped cream, and chocolate sprinkles. "These are really good. So are the ones with blueberries. And these are great too." I indicated the ones that looked as if chocolate had exploded all over the pancakes and whipped cream.

The waitress returned. Logan and I ordered the chocolate explosion pancakes. Logan also asked for chocolate milk. I ordered coffee.

While we waited, Logan colored the giraffe on the paper place mat with a red crayon. I worked on the elephant with the blue crayon. By the time we were finished, it would be a freaking masterpiece, even if we only had the three primary colors to work with.

"What's this?" Kristen said, approaching the table.

I startled. I'd been so involved in coloring the picture with Logan, I hadn't paid attention to anyone else in the restaurant. The clatter of dishes and customer chatter had faded into the background.

With Emma in her arm, my sister grinned at me. "My little bro up at the crack of dawn? Will miracles ever cease?"

I waved at my niece. She made a cute sound that I translated as "Hi, Uncle Jared!"

"You're a real comedian, sis. Besides it isn't that early."

"It's seven-thirty a.m. For you, that's early."

She had a point. For the pre-Logan me, that would have been pretty much unheard of. "Logan, do you remember Emma and Auntie Kristen?" The word "auntie" slipped out before I could stop it. I held my breath, waiting to see if he caught the mistake.

"Hi," he said brightly, waved at his cousin, who returned the wave, and went back to coloring the giraffe.

Kristen sat opposite us with Emma on her lap. The toddler leaned forward and grabbed the fork in front of her.

"Where's Callie?" my sister asked.

"She's at her apartment. It's just me and Logan for breakfast."

"So what's going on with you two? You finally dating or something?"

"No, just friends." The word tasted bitter in my mouth. There was nothing wrong with being friends, but I wanted more. I just didn't know if "more" was a good thing at this point. Not when we had to consider what was best for Logan.

"Really? I could've sworn there was something more

between you two. I've seen the way you look at her, all googly-eyed."

I snorted a laugh. "You've been watching way too many of Emma's favorite TV shows."

Kristen's gaze darted to Logan. I had no idea what Mom had told her, and I had no idea if she was aware that he was my son.

The waitress returned with our food. Logan's eyes widened at the tower of whipped cream on his plate. He grabbed his fork and dived in.

"Would you like to order now?" she asked Kristen.

Emma banged her fork against the edge of the table. Maybe I could introduce her to Mason, then her first words would be enough to distract her mom from whatever she was thinking when it came to Callie and me. Kristen was a romantic at heart and believed in happily-ever-afters. Would she even approve of us being together, given my career? She had always loved Callie like a sister. She would hate to see either of us get hurt.

As she placed her order with the waitress, Kristen removed the utensil from her daughter's chubby hand and returned it to the table.

Logan was busy eating the whipped cream off his pancakes. A white streak decorated his upper lip. The rest of the cream was brown, thanks to him stirring the chocolate syrup into it.

"I made mud," he said proudly.

I laughed. "Now you just need gummy worms and it will look like worms and dirt. Do you want me to cut your pancakes?"

Fortunately, Kristen dropped the topic of Callie and me as we ate our food, our attention mostly on the two kids at the table.

"You know, being a father suits you," she said at one point as I was helping Logan with his pancakes. My entire body froze. Fuck. This wasn't how I wanted Logan to find out the truth.

My phone pinged. I glanced at him. He was peering at his aunt, the word "father" having caught his attention. Buying time while I frantically figured out how to talk my way out of this, at least until I could explain things to Kristen, I checked the text from Callie.

> Callie: How's breakfast?

> Me: Sorry you were so tired that you had to miss out on these amazing pancakes.

She responded a moment later.

> Callie: Are you trying to make me jealous?

> Me: Absolutely. Is it working?

> Callie: Maybe.

I chuckled and typed.

> Me: While we're gone, you could work on your portfolio to illustrate kids' books. I'll take Logan to preschool once we're finished.

> Callie: You're not going to drop it about the kids' books, are you?

> Me: Nope, you're too talented to let it go to waste.

> Callie: LOL. I love you too. See you soon.

At her words, an unexpected warmth seeped in. She hadn't meant that she was in love with me, but it didn't stop me from wishing the words were real.

"It's rude to text while at the table," Kristen said, barely keeping in her laugh. Mom had reprimanded her about the same thing on more than one occasion.

I rolled my eyes and placed my phone on the table.

Fortunately, before the conversation could return to Kristen's unexpected comment about me being a father, the waitress answered my silent prayers and returned with our bill. Thank God!

After I paid it, we headed to the playground Kristen and I had practically grown up on. The equipment had long since been replaced. Now it was made from plastic in bright primary colors.

We were the only people here, other than an older couple walking their German shepherd along the path that cut past the playground.

Logan ran to the slide and scrambled up the ladder. Kristen slipped Emma into the empty baby swing.

"How much did Mom tell you?" I asked.

"About what?"

"About Logan."

Kristen pushed the giggling Emma in her swing. "He's a cute kid. I guess I'm just surprised. I hadn't realized you and Callie had hooked up. And I'm especially surprised that you would have sex with a sixteen-year-old when you were twenty-one. Wouldn't that have made her a minor?" A twinge of disappointment laced her tone.

Logan called out my name from the slide and waved. I returned the wave and watched him go down it. He ran back to the steps and climbed up again.

"I never had sex with Callie." At least not back when Logan was conceived. Never mind that she would've been seventeen, not sixteen, when it happened. That was beside the point.

Logan waved at me again and slid down the slide once more.

"Oh, God." Kristen's gaze swung to mine and her eyes widened. "He's Alexis's son, isn't he? And she's dead."

"Yes, but he doesn't know that. And he doesn't know yet that I'm his father."

Logan bounded over to us and pointed at the swing. I picked him up and hugged him, then placed him on the seat.

I could tell Kristen was itching to question me about her nephew and my relationship with Callie, but she wisely kept her million questions to herself. While the odds were good Logan wouldn't hear them, it was a risk I didn't want to take. I still had to figure out how to tell him the truth.

And I still had to figure out how this would all work out in the end. With Logan. With the band. With Callie.

31

JARED

I spent Wednesday morning on my couch, working on the song that had played in my head for the past week. Once Pushing Limits hit the road, the days of writing new material would be over. The more songs we'd written before then, the easier it would be for the third album ... if there was a third album. That depended on sales for Tangled, which was the name of both our second album and its title track.

I strummed the chord combinations I'd written so far, and made a slight adjustment from the D to the G chord. Better. My cell phone pinged a few times, but given that it was Mason, it could wait until after I picked Logan up from preschool. I'd promised to teach him how to play the guitar today. He had asked me how old I was when I'd begun playing, and when he discovered I'd been the same age as he was now, he asked me to teach him.

The kid-sized acoustic guitar sat proudly in the corner of my bedroom. Logan would feel the vibrations when he played, or at least that was the plan. Whether he could create music was anyone's guess.

I finished the lyrics I'd been polishing for the past hour and left for Logan's school. Raindrops splattered against the car windows, which made me think of Callie. Who was I kidding? Everything these days made me think of Callie.

Callie used to love jumping in puddles. The bigger the splash the better. She would say that puddle jumping made everything all right with the world, even if only for a few minutes. To her, it was worth the soaked shoes and socks. I wasn't so sure about that.

The usual group of moms was already in the waiting area when I entered. Sarina nudged the mother next to her and gave a brief nod in my direct. As a single unit, they looked over at me, and I instantly knew something was wrong. The first thought was that it had to do with Logan, but if that had been true, Callie would have called me.

"Is it true?" Sarina asked.

I shrugged. "Is what true?"

"You're Logan's father and Callie is just his aunt?" But the way she said it suggested it wasn't a question. Even if it was a lie, she had already made up her mind that it was the truth.

My body stiffened. "Where did you hear that?"

"It went viral about an hour ago." Around the same time Mason started texting me.

One mother handed me her smartphone. The picture on the screen had been taken when Logan and I were at the playground with Kristen and Emma. I was hugging Logan by the swings. Fortunately, my sister and niece had been excluded from the shot.

I scrolled down and read the article from an online tabloid. In it, my relationship with Logan was outed, and the article mentioned that a high school sweetheart, who died in a traffic accident a few years ago, was his real mother. My mouth dropped open at how much information had been revealed, along with a few bonuses that were far from the truth, but since I couldn't prove this, I'd have problems getting a retraction. Not that it mattered at this point. The truth was out there for the world to see, and it was out there before Callie and I had told Logan.

Fuck.

"Is it true you're fighting Callie for the custodial rights to your son?" Sarina asked. "I can't believe the nerve of her, thinking she has any rights to him. She's only his aunt." She made a huffing noise, like the whole idea personally wounded her.

My cell phone pinged. This time I did read Mason's text.

> Mason: Would you goddamn respond???

The song I had programmed for Nolan played. "What's up?" I answered, walking away from the group.

"Shit, man. Have you seen the story that went viral about you and Logan?" he asked.

I ripped my hand through my hair. "Yeah, I just read it."

"Does Callie know about it?"

"I have no idea. If she knows, she hasn't contacted me. I do know, though, that she had nothing to do with it." As it was, she was going to be spitting lava once she learned the truth was now out there.

"What are you going to do?"

"Fuck if I know. I mean, other than telling Logan before he finds out from someone else." I inwardly groaned. This was exactly what Callie had feared. And if one tabloid had picked up the story, it was guaranteed that others would jump on the chance to tear it wide open too. Everyone we knew would be hounded for details. As it was, I had no idea how they'd even found out that Callie was Logan's aunt and that Alexis was dead. "How the hell did you deal with it when your story was leaked to the media?"

"Not very well," Nolan admitted. "But at least I didn't have to go it alone. I had Hailey."

"I doubt Callie's going to be quite as understanding."

"You'd be surprised. She cares for you more than you give her credit for. Look, if you want to skip practice today, we understand."

"No, it's fine." The classroom door opened and the kids paraded from the room. "I have to go now. I'll talk to you soon." I ended the call and waited for Logan.

A hushed whisper fell over the room. Curious glances darted in my direction. If there was ever a moment signaling impending doom, this would be it.

A gray-haired teacher stepped through the doorway and scanned the area. Her gaze landed on me. "Mr. Leigh, if you could come with me, please?"

"Is something wrong?"

The you've-got-to-be-kidding-me expression was the only answer I needed. I followed her into the classroom. This was the first time I'd been inside it, and it was exactly what I'd expected. The tables and chairs were kid-sized, as were the shelves scattered around the room, with their colorful storage containers. A huge alphabet rug, with pictures alongside their corresponding letters, sat in the reading corner. The classroom had been designed to be bright and cheery, a place where a kid would want to come to learn.

Unfortunately, the four-year-old sitting on a chair was anything but bright or cheery. Logan's gaze was glued to the table, his arms folded tightly across his small chest. Another teacher was talking to him, but I couldn't tell if he was listening or had tuned her out.

"What's going on?" I asked, and squatted next to him. A bad feeling sliced through me, leaving a jagged edge. Sarina had mentioned that the article had gone viral an hour ago, but that didn't mean someone hadn't seen it sooner.

When Logan didn't answer, I glanced up at the teachers for help.

"Why don't we go into my office, Mr. Leigh?" the gray-haired woman said. "Rachel, can you stay with Logan for a few minutes?"

The younger woman nodded.

"Logan, are you okay if I go off with . . . ?" I glanced at the gray-haired woman.

"I'm Mrs. Mansfield. The assistant principal."

Logan didn't respond.

I followed her into her office and took the chair in front of her desk that she'd gestured at. Logan's classroom might have been bright and cheery, but it was clear that Mrs. Mansfield preferred a less upbeat, blander space to work in. It was simply furnished, with just the basic necessities—a desk, bookshelf, filing cabinet, chairs, all in black. The only artwork on the walls was a single large painting of a mountainous landscape at sunset, done in a fiery red, the harbinger of doom. It was also the only splash of real color in the room.

She walked to her seat and sat back in her chair. An urge struck me to remove my lucky guitar pick from my pocket. I fought back the impulse.

"One of the students came to class this morning," she said, "and told Logan that you're his father and Callie was only his aunt. The individual also told him that his real parents didn't want him, and that's why Logan is living with his aunt. Understandably, this upset Logan, and he hit the other child."

Shit.

I didn't know what I was supposed to say or do. If I had foreseen all of this, I could've been better prepared. As it was, I was still struggling with the idea of being a father. I knew nothing about it, other than I wanted to be like my own father, who I admired and respected.

"I suggest you take Logan home and talk to him about how

he's feeling. And I would like you and Callie to meet with our school counselor." She released a slow breath. "Is it true you're involving the courts in a custody battle?"

"I only found out a week ago that I'm a father, and I'm still coming to terms with it. Logan loves Callie and I don't want to destroy their relationship. That's all I know." It was pretty much the truth. She didn't need to know the rest. I was sure she wouldn't approve of the fact that Callie and I were just testing the waters, with no actual plans of making things permanent between us. That wasn't what Logan needed.

He needed a family.

32

CALLIE

I couldn't remember the last time I'd seen the diner this busy. My feet were ready to call a strike and I still had over an hour left of my shift.

The diner door opened. Tiffany entered with the same guy she had been with the last time. Murmured excitement stirred from the surrounding tables. If a skinny supermodel was okay with eating in a diner known for its greasy yet delicious food, then it must be okay for everyone.

They wouldn't have been as excited if they'd known that the last time Tiffany was here, she'd eaten food that would've made a rabbit jealous.

I entered the kitchen to check on my orders. While I was there, Beckie came in from the staff room. Her face was pale, a stark contrast against her black hair.

"What's wrong?" I asked.

"Have you checked any of your social media sites today?"

I laughed and shook my head. Who had time for those when you were balancing a full-time job, being a mother, part-time classes, regular meetings with your son's therapists and school, and freelance design work? Occasionally I went on it when I wasn't working, but it wasn't my priority.

"Someone's spreading a vicious rumor that Jared Leigh is Logan's father, and apparently you're dead?"

Oh God. The words became stuck in my throat, cutting off my ability to breathe. I leaned back against the counter to keep from collapsing.

Beckie's eyes widened. "Oh, shit. It's true. I mean, other than the part where you're dead. Obviously you're not."

"Callie, your order's up," Larry called out.

Beckie said something, but I didn't hear her. I was too focused on getting air in and out of my lungs.

The kitchen door swung out, and Alice poked her head in. "Callie, Tiffany Grainger specifically asked for you, but she didn't want to wait until one of your tables opened. She's sitting in Beckie's section."

Right, because I wasn't busy enough as it was. "Why the heck does she want me? It's not like Beckie can't take an order for lettuce leaves."

Alice shrugged. "Who cares what her reasons are, just as long as she doesn't bad-mouth the diner."

With a grunt that didn't begin to convey how crappy this day was turning out, I grabbed my order from under the warmer and entered the dining area. I delivered the food to the waiting table, then headed over to Tiffany.

"Hi, are you ready to order?" I gave her my best smile, plastered on with a heavy dose of superglue.

The answering smile was nothing that would ever be featured in Vogue—except maybe at Halloween. Inwardly I shuddered. "No, but I would ask you, woman to woman, to back off when it comes to my boyfriend," she said with mock sweetness. On the wall beside her was a photo of a wide, all-encompassing tornado with lightning streaking across the sky. How fitting.

"Your . . . your boyfriend?"

"Jared Leigh."

"But . . . I thought you guys weren't seeing each other anymore." At least I assumed they weren't—because he and I had been screwing for the past week. Did it mean that after he'd finished fucking me, he turned around and fucked Tiffany too?

God, I hoped not.

"Now that I'm living in L.A., we're back together."

That was news to me. Jared hadn't even mentioned her since we began hooking up.

"You love him, don't you? The boy, I mean," she said.

"Yes." I bit back the words I craved to say: I love them both.

"What if I can convince Jared to let you have full custody? I think you and I both agree his lifestyle is the worst possible one for a child."

True. "But why would you want to help me?"

"Because my parents were very much like Jared. They were always traveling. They never had time for me. I was raised by nannies. No child should have to go through that. Logan's a sweet kid. He deserves better than that. And he's better off being raised by a parent who can always be there for him. He doesn't need a parent who pops into his life whenever it fits into his busy schedule."

I could only nod, because she was right. It was what I had always feared from the beginning. It was what Alexis had feared. I was in love with Jared, but what I wanted wasn't important.

"The only thing I ask from you in return," she said, "is that you end whatever relationship it is you have with Jared. You can't be his friend or anything else you might have going on with him. It all ends now."

I frowned. "Why would I do that? Jared is Logan's father. He'll see me whenever he visits Logan."

"I don't think you have to worry about that. He'll be too busy with touring and with his life to visit."

So in the end, Jared would be nothing more to Logan than a monthly child support check. Like I feared, he would end up disappointing his son again and again and again. Plus, it was clear that Tiffany didn't want to be part of Logan's life, not in the same way I did. Maybe it was because she knew her career, like Jared's, wasn't the best when it came to being a mother. She was only interested in Jared, but unlike me, she fit in perfectly with his life.

Except where did that leave Logan?

33

JARED

Logan and I walked back to his home in silence after his assistant principal had finished speaking with me. I should've made more of an effort to talk to him, but all I could think about was what Callie would do once she found out about the article that had gone viral. All I could think about was who had leaked the information. All I could think about was what the hell was I going to do to fix it, preferably before the band's promo blitz began in two weeks. Because after that things would be crazy, and by the time life settled down again it would be too late.

At the apartment, I unlocked the door and let Logan in. Before picking him up from school, I had dropped off his new guitar in his room, propped up against the bed with his toy puppy.

"Are you really my daddy?" he asked, staring at the two gifts.

I knelt to his level. Shit, where did I start? "It's complicated, and I don't expect you to understand. But yes, Logan, I'm your daddy. I only found out about it a few weeks ago. Your mommy and I thought it was best that you and I got to know each other first before we told you the truth."

"Mommy? Hunter said my real mommy doesn't want me. He said no one wants me." Tears spilled from his eyes. The pain in his words just about gutted me.

"None of it's true. Callie is your mommy, Logan, and she loves you very much. You can't stop believing that because of what someone told you. She would do anything for you. I would do anything for you." I wiped his cheek dry with my thumb. "I love you." I wrapped my arms around him and gave him a gentle hug. "I love you very much."

At first his small body stiffened in my arms, but at my words the tension leaked from his muscles. He hugged me back. "I love you . . . Daddy."

That only made me hug him tighter, tears in my eyes.

I blinked them away and released him. "Do you still want to learn to play the guitar?"

He smiled, eyelashes and cheeks still damp with moisture. "I want to play guitar like Daddy."

This time I didn't bother blinking away the tears.

After spending time with Logan, I'd left him with Sharon while I joined the band for our daily practice session and meeting. Our first single off the new album was releasing next week. The band didn't have time for my crises. Until Callie and I discussed what to do about the situation, I didn't want to discuss it with the guys. We had other things to focus on for now. After I talked to Callie, I would talk to my lawyer and the record label's publicist to find out what needed to be done to fix the mess.

Logan and I were on the couch, watching his favorite show when the apartment door clicked open. My heart took this as a cue to pick up its pace. I wanted to break the news to Callie first about the leaked story, but one look at her face told me I was too late.

I pushed myself off the couch. Logan was faster. He sprinted across the room and threw himself at Callie. She hoisted him in her arms and kissed his cheek.

"I have a daddy," he said, coming close to puffing out his chest.

Callie smiled back at him, but the smile never made it to her eyes. Instead, they glistened with unshed tears. "I need to talk to your father. Okay?"

Logan nodded, and she returned him to the couch to finish watching his show. She then indicated for me follow her into her bedroom. Which meant she didn't want Logan to overhear us.

She walked to her window and looked out. She didn't speak at first. She just continued staring out the window, lost in thought. The bright afternoon light glared through the glass but did nothing to warm the room.

When she finally turned around, she appeared more exhausted than she had after that super-long shift three weeks earlier.

"How could you do it?" she asked, her voice calm yet slightly off. "How could you use your son for publicity like that?"

I frowned. "Whoa, what are you talking about? I had nothing to do with the information being leaked."

She laughed, the sound hard and brittle, ready to break. "Well, it certainly didn't come from me. Other than Sharon when she guessed the truth, I've never told anyone who Logan's real parents were. Only you knew about it, so the information had to come from you. I warned you that something like this would happen. Will the media now hound him every time he goes out? Am I supposed to get him a bodyguard to keep him safe? Will I have to worry about paparazzi stalking me and searching through my garbage?"

I wanted to tell her none of this would happen, but I didn't know if it was true or not. Would the leaked story in combination with the band's upcoming album mean open season on my son? And what would it mean for Callie? Would she be hounded too while Logan was with her? Or would the media quickly grow bored and move on to the next celebrity news story?

"All I can tell you is that I'm sorry. I didn't want this to happen any more than you did. I certainly didn't want Logan to find out this way."

Deep creases formed between her eyes. "What do you mean, 'find out this way'? How exactly did he find out?"

I told her everything the school had told me.

She sat down hard on her bed and dropped her head in her hands. "None of this was supposed to happen. You need to decide what you want to do when it comes to Logan, but I can't be with you anymore." She couldn't even look at me when she said it.

"What are you saying? You want to take a break?"

She laughed, the sound brittle again. "A break implies we were dating. We were never dating, Jared. We were just screwing. I was someone to entertain you while you weren't with Tiffany."

"Tiffany? I'm escorting her to a charity event Tuesday night, but that's it." Which I had failed to mention to Callie because I didn't believe it was important.

"Isn't that the same as dating?"

"No. Dating implies I'm hoping to at least kiss her. Escorting means just that. I'm taking her to the event 'cause she doesn't have a boyfriend. She would rather go with a friend than arrange a real date for the night."

"It doesn't matter what you want to call it. I still can't be with you anymore. Logan is our first priority. You need to decide what you want to do with him, especially once the band starts touring. Am I the one who's looking after him while you're away? Or will your parents being doing that?"

I opened and closed my mouth like a dying fish, incapable of making any sort of sound. I'd foolishly thought she cared about me, but she never really had. While I hated how this had all come out, maybe it was for the best.

"I don't know."

"Well, once you've figured it out, be sure to let me know." She stormed from the room. A moment later, pots banged loudly from the kitchen.

My phone played Aaron's song. "Yes?" I answered.

"The guys and I are heading over to Santiago's for a couple of drinks and to watch Burning Wire perform. Nolan's also coming."

"Sure, I'll be there." Maybe giving Callie some space was a good idea. She was angry and hurt. She needed time to let everything sink in; then we could talk again.

Logan was still watching TV when I entered the living room. "Hey, I have to go out, but I'll see you tomorrow." I raised my fist to bump his.

A heartbreaking pout formed on his lips. "You're not living with me and Mommy?"

"I'm sorry. But would you like to live with me when I'm not touring?"

"Can Mommy come too?"

Yeah, I guess I should've seen that coming. "It's up to your mommy." I hugged him. "I love you." It felt good saying that, but at the same time there was a hollowness to the words. Like it wasn't just Logan I should be saying them to.

The banging in the kitchen had stopped. Not wanting to leave things the way they were, I manned it up and entered the kitchen. Callie was staring at the covered pot on the stove. The electric ring under it burned bright. Tears stained her cheeks.

I couldn't help myself. I enveloped her in my arms. Instead

of resisting my touch as I had expected, she leaned into me. Her soft scent and her soft body in my arms reminded me how right this was.

I pulled back slightly, my arms still around her, and my lips brushed against hers. This felt right too. It also felt right when she parted her lips and let me in.

The kiss that greeted me wasn't slow and it wasn't hungry. It was filled with a longing burrowed deep—both down to her bones and mine. It was also a kiss that spoke of goodbye.

I deepened it, my hand on the back of her head, telling her I wasn't about to walk away from her like she expected. Everyone important to her had disappeared from her life. No way in hell would I be one of them.

"I'll see you tomorrow." I didn't give her a chance to respond. I said goodbye to Logan one more time and left.

34

JARED

Santiago's was nothing like the old dives I used to play in when I was first introduced to the L.A. music scene. It was the place where the up-and-coming bands wanted to be showcased. Many a musician had been discovered here by either an agent or a label. And the clientele knew this. The bar also catered to a crowd that wouldn't be caught dead in a dive.

The rest of the band was already at a table near the stage when I arrived. I dropped onto a padded leather chair next to Nolan and smirked. "Let me guess . . . Hailey's out with friends?"

"Hey, she doesn't have me whipped, if that's what you're implying." His gaze jumped to Mason, and it wasn't too hard to figure out where that had come from. Mason was positive Hailey had our lead singer whipped and that was why Nolan usually stayed home with her instead of joining us for drinks.

I laughed. "So she's not out with friends?"

"Nope. The last I saw, she was watching a girlie show with some dude in a kilt prancing around an old Scottish castle."

"Ah, so she kicked you out of the house so she could watch it without you making wiseass remarks."

Nolan grinned. "Yep, pretty much."

We didn't get a chance to talk beyond that. Burning Wire sauntered onstage, and we cheered as our friend Tomas took his place behind his drums.

It wasn't until the set was almost over that I glanced around the bar to check out the audience's reaction to the band. And that's when I spotted Tiffany at a table with a few other people. Unlike Callie, who'd been wearing a simple T-shirt and faded jeans, the women wore tight, low-cut dresses, the men high-priced suits. Callie's clothes teased you with a hint of her sexy curves. Tiffany's dress made me miss the feel of Callie's sweet-smelling body in my arms.

As if sensing me watching her, Tiffany shifted her attention from the band to me, and she flashed me the sexy smile that had graced numerous magazine covers. The sexy smile that did nothing for me. Not like it used to. It just made me miss the girl I loved even more.

I turned back to the stage.

Once the band finished their final song, hollers, screams, and whistles filled the air and left my ears ringing. The guys in Burning Wire waved to their fans, and they were barely off the stage before the fans and groupies swarmed them.

They weren't the only ones enjoying the attention. Numerous people had also spotted us and were quick to either chat with Kirk and Aaron or let Mason be his usual horndog self. Nolan was busy talking to a couple of guys. A group of girls near him watched him while giggling. I'm not even sure he noticed them. He was deep in conversation.

I checked my phone in case Callie had tried to contact me. Nothing. Needing to go to the bathroom, I pushed myself out of my seat and weaved through the crowd. Now that the live part of the evening was over, everyone had swarmed to the bar to get a refill.

A hand landed on my arm, stopping me. I turned to gently remove myself from the fan's grasp.

"Hi, Jared," Tiffany said, giving me the same smile she had given me a short while ago.

I stepped back, causing her hand to fall away. My ass brushed against the bar stool behind me. "Hey, didn't realize you were planning to be here." Not that it mattered either way, as long as Callie didn't find out that Tiffany and I had been here at the same time. That would only worsen the situation between us, even though nothing was going on between Tiffany and me.

"My friends have been gushing about the place. I thought I'd check it out." She narrowed the distance between us. "I heard about the picture of you and your son going public." She visibly cringed. "That's horrible what the paparazzi did, but you and your son will eventually get used to it."

"What do you mean we'll get used to it? Aren't there laws in California against it?" I was pretty sure there were. Whether the paparazzi obeyed them was another matter.

She shrugged. "I have no idea, but with your band's growing popularity, people will be curious about your life. They'll be curious about your son, especially since he's deaf. It's part of being a celebrity."

"I don't want him to be a part of that media circus. I want him to have the same life I had growing up."

"Then maybe you should consider allowing Callie to adopt him and have full custody. Eventually the spotlight will move from them and he can grow up having a . . . a normal life." The way she said "normal life," you'd have thought it involved moving to a cold, desolate location like Siberia.

I scowled. "Are you telling me I should give up my son?"

"I'm just saying that you need to do what's right for him. You need to do what's right for you. You're not meant to be a father, Jared. You're meant for bigger things."

"Apparently my sperm would disagree with you," I said, my tone even despite the fact that my insides were boiling at her words. Yes, I was still learning to be a good father and I had four years of catching up to do, but band or no band, I knew I was meant to be a father. I was meant to be Logan's father. I might not be a religious man, but if I were, I would've bet that God had brought Logan, Callie, and me together for a reason. And it wasn't so that Tiffany could tell me I wasn't meant to be a father.

"You and Pushing Limits are going to be big," she said. "All your hard work and sacrifices will be worth it." She traced her fingertips up my arm, her meaning clear.

I jerked my arm away. "Are you saying I can't be in the band and be a father to my son?" I had asked myself the same question a number of times in the past few days. Could I still be a good father and continue to play with the band? I had no idea, but I was willing to work hard at it and do my best for my son.

And I was willing to work harder at it with Callie.

"No," Tiffany said. "I'm just saying it's not the best way to bring up your son. You'll always be busy and will always be on the road. I told you, my parents weren't around much and I was brought up by nannies. Sure, I turned out fine, but not every kid can adjust. They feel unloved and unwanted. Is that how you want Logan to feel?"

"Look, I don't know what you're expecting, Tiffany, but I just want to be clear that there is no you and me. There hasn't been for a while now. What you and I want from life is very different."

"That's not true. I can guarantee we want the same things."

I thought about all the things that were important to her: the mansion where she lived on her own, the high-priced clothing, the trips to exotic locations, the Hollywood parties, the connections, the money, the fame.

None of those were who I was or wanted to be.

Without another word to her, I returned to my table and told the guys I was bailing. I left and drove around for an hour, trying to figure out what to do next. I loved Callie. That much I knew. I couldn't imagine anyone else being the mother of my child, and I couldn't imagine being with anyone else.

At first I drove aimlessly around the area, then the next thing I knew I was parked in front of the diner. It was late, but I had a sudden craving for a chocolate milkshake. Or maybe it was the waitress who always served it to me who I was craving.

I entered the diner and was met by Beckie, Callie's friend. "If you're looking for Callie," she said, "she's not here."

"I know. She's home. I just came in for a milkshake and fries."

The corners of her lips twitched up. "Is this for you or for Logan?"

"Me. You could say he got me addicted to them."

That made her smile more.

She led me to the same booth Logan and I usually sat in when we ate lunch here. "How . . . how's she doing? She was upset after I showed her the article about Logan, but she seemed devastated after your girlfriend talked to her."

I frowned. "Girlfriend?"

"Tiffany Grainger."

I shook my head, a bad feeling crawling over every inch of me. "She's not my girlfriend."

"Really? That's not what I heard."

"Whoever told you that was wrong."

"It was Callie."

Somehow this didn't surprise me. Not after our conversation earlier. "When exactly did she tell you this?"

"This afternoon. Right after Tiffany left."

Fuck. Well, that would explain a few things. "Do you know what else they talked about?"

Beckie shook her head. "All I know is that whatever Tiffany

told her upset her more than the news story that you're Logan's father." She studied me for a second. "I still can't believe I didn't figure it out sooner. He does look a lot like you. Do you have any idea who leaked the story?"

"No." But based on my earlier conversation with Tiffany and what Beckie had just told me, I had my suspicions. She'd sold me out. Few people were aware of my relationship with Logan. So unless Mason had gotten drunk and blurted it out, the initial information had to have come from Tiffany.

The question was, what was her involvement in Callie's decision to end our relationship? And more important, how could I show Callie how much she meant to me?

35

CALLIE

Jared's car wasn't in front of his parents' house when Logan and I arrived there Friday afternoon. Thank God. The only reason I'd agreed to visit Jared's mom when she called was because she promised he wouldn't be here. Well, two reasons. The other was that Logan was her grandson and she had every right to spend time with him.

I turned off the engine and swiveled around in my seat so Logan could hear me. "Are you ready to see your grandparents?"

"Is Daddy gonna be here?"

"Not until later. And then he'll drive you back home. Are you okay with that?" I was only staying for a short time. Being back in the house was too painful on many levels. Plus I really couldn't handle seeing Jared yet. My heart was still raw and tender. Sure, I'd have to get over it soon enough, but for now I was allowed to wallow in my grief.

Which was why Hailey and I were getting together for a couple of drinks. Just the two of us. No talk about the band allowed.

I opened the back passenger door and helped Logan out.

Logan trotted up the steps to the front door, with me following behind. It had been two days since the news story first broke, and Logan was adjusting to it better than I had expected, beyond what happened that one day at preschool.

I was a different matter. The media had tracked down my phone number and kept calling me, asking for an interview. I changed my phone number after the second day. A few more creative individuals had also discovered where I worked. As soon as I came to get their order, they bombarded me with questions about Logan and Jared, about my relationship with Jared, about Tiffany's thoughts on my home-wrecking skills when it came to her and Jared's perfect relationship. The last question made me laugh. If it was so perfect, how could I have wrecked it so easily?

I still had no idea if they had split up. One report said friends claimed the couple's relationship was stronger than ever. Another claimed Tiffany was emotionally distraught over their breakup and had recently checked into some sort of rehab. My favorite report, though, was the one claiming she was pregnant with an alien baby.

Logan rang the doorbell. The door opened a second later, and Jared's mom and the delicious aroma of chocolate chip cookies greeted us. We stepped into the house that had always felt like home, cozy with its warm colors and southwestern theme.

"I want cookie," Logan said with the level of exuberance normally reserved for his favorite ice cream.

I bit my lip to keep from laughing. "How about you at least say hi to your grandmother first?"

"Hi," he said, sheepishly.

Jared's mother bent down. "Do I get a hug?"

He threw himself at her and allowed her to hug him for fifteen seconds before he began squirming.

In the kitchen, she gave him a cookie from the cooling rack, then picked up a pitcher of what looked like strawberry lemonade. "Callie, do you mind taking this outside to the gazebo? The glasses are already out there."

"Not a problem." I took the pitcher from her and went out through the backdoor.

As I put the drink on the gazebo table, a small sound behind me, like a soft exhalation, alerted me that I wasn't alone. Thinking it was Logan, I turned around. "How's the . . ." I began.

The rest of the sentence froze at the sight of Jared standing in front of me. My heart pinched, begging me to ignore everything Tiffany had told me—but I couldn't.

I stepped away. Jared gently grabbed my arm. "Please don't go. I want to talk to you."

"I can't. I'm meeting up with Hailey."

"You still have time." When it looked like I wasn't going to run—at least not yet—he released my arm. "First, whatever Tiffany told you, it's not true. She and I aren't getting back together. We want different things in our lives.

"Second, she was the individual who leaked the information to the online tabloid. I tracked down the photographer yesterday. She'd actually paid him to do it."

"He told you that?"

He shrugged. "Let's just say my lawyer and I can be very persuasive. I'm aware that the job I signed up for isn't the most ideal one for having a family, but I promise to do my best." He fumbled for something in his jeans pocket, then took a deep breath and released it slowly. "Callie, will you marry me?" He held out his fist and opened it. I gasped at the engagement ring in his palm. It was simple, not overly flashy—at least it wouldn't have been if not for the large diamond.

I gaped at the ring. Jared had asked me to marry him. I should be throwing my arms around his neck, screaming, "Yes, of course I'll marry you," and kissing him. That's what my heart desired. But my brain was smarter. It knew what was happening wasn't real. Not for the reasons I wished it to be real. I wanted Jared to marry me because he loved me, not because he needed a mother for his son. He was leaving on tour soon and wanted to give Logan a stable home, like the home Jared had grown up in. I wished for that too, but not this way.

If I ever married, it would be to someone who loved me as much as I loved him. It wouldn't be because it was convenient.

I shook my head. "I'm sorry, but I can't. You want to marry me for the wrong reasons. I've already told you Logan can still stay with me while you're touring. You don't have to marry me for that."

My eyes teared up. I needed to escape before they gave away the pain ripping through me. "I've gotta go" was all I said before I took off running.

I didn't bother to go into the house. I already had my car keys and purse. Yes, I should've stopped to say goodbye to Logan, but I couldn't. There wasn't enough time. As it was, the tears had started falling the moment I escaped through the side gate.

"Callie," Jared called out, which prompted me to run harder.

I made it to the driveway and scrambled into my car, my breath coming hard and fast.

Guilt pounded on me for not saying goodbye to Logan. I pushed it back and twisted the key in the ignition. Without giving the house a second glance, tears streaming down my face, I drove away.

36

CALLIE

Like most girls, I had fantasized from time to time about how my future fiancé would propose to me. Some of the ideas, like asking me while we were in a hot-air balloon, were quickly discarded. I wasn't a fan of heights, and clutching the edge of the basket and hurling didn't make for a romantic picture. There were other, safer ideas too. Like the one where the girl finds the engagement ring on her dessert or in her wine glass. Okay, those might have been a little clichéd, but the main point was that nowhere in my fantasies had I envisioned being proposed to the way it actually went down.

Sure, at the end of the day it shouldn't have mattered how the guy proposed. As long as he loved me, that was all I cared about.

The lounge Hailey had suggested we meet at was not far from where I lived. I hadn't even known it existed until she mentioned it. I sank into the comfy brown leather armchair. Yep, I didn't see myself moving anytime soon. Everything about the place made me think of chocolate. The light brown carpet with beige swirls. The deep brown walls. The cream lamp shades scattered throughout. And the small dark brown tables. Or maybe it was my broken heart that made me think of chocolate. What better way to deal with a broken heart than chocolate ice cream—or chocolate-flavored booze?

Soft jazz music played in the background. According to Hailey, each night featured a different genre. Fortunately, tonight wasn't rock night. Knowing my luck, they would've featured Pushing Limits while we were here.

"You look like you could use a drink," Hailey said.

"You got that right. Can I ask you something?"

"Sure."

"How do you deal with being Nolan's girlfriend? I mean, doesn't it get hard with the groupies and with the constant media attention?"

She didn't have a chance to answer before a waiter approached our table. He was hot. If you liked blonds. And if your heart wasn't still pining over the dark-haired guy with brown eyes and heart-melting dimples. "What can I get you ladies to drink?"

"I'll have a mango margarita. Thanks," Hailey said.

"What do you have that's chocolatey?" I asked him.

"The Milky Way martini comes highly recommended," he replied, and I ordered it.

"I'll admit it isn't easy," Hailey said, answering my previous question. "It was harder at first when the media figured out who Tyler Erickson was. Then they were a major pain. The fans are great. The younger girls are especially cute with the way they get excited over the guys. It's the groupies who are hoping to score that are annoying. They don't care if Nolan has a girlfriend. They just want to tell their friends and the entire world that they slept with him. And some are more than happy to share the details in all their erotic glory." She scrunched her nose in a way that made me giggle.

"Do you ever worry about them?"

She shook her head. "I love Nolan and I trust him. Yes, it's not easy, but if I can't trust him, then none of what he and I have is worth it in the end. Do I trust the groupies? Hell no. But I have to trust that Nolan won't do anything to hurt me . . . even if I'm not there to protect him." She smirked. "So is this your way of telling me that you and Jared are finally an item?" She looked so excited about this possibility, I almost couldn't tell her the truth.

"He proposed this afternoon." You'd have thought I had announced I was going to buy a bag of stale potato chips from the lack of enthusiasm in my voice.

"And . . . you don't want to marry him?"

I finished my drink and gestured to the waiter for a refill. If I could, I would've finished that drink first, too, before answering her question. "If I ever marry, it will be because the man loves me as much as I love him. Jared only proposed because it's easy."

Hailey's eyebrows jumped up. "Easy? Sorry, you've lost me."

"Jared doesn't love me. He realized things will be a lot easier for Logan when the band is touring if his son is staying with me."

Her expression transformed into a confused frown. "He actually told you that?"

"Not in so many words. But what other reason is there for him to propose?"

"Oh, I don't know." She gave me a pointed look that said it all and then some. "Because he loves you?"

"That's just it. He doesn't love me."

The waiter placed my drink on the table. Hailey was still working on her first margarita.

"How can you say that?" she asked. "I've seen the way he looks at you."

"That doesn't mean anything. He likes me as a friend, that's all." A friend he'd been having sex with.

"I think you're wrong. But anyway, what did you tell him?"

"That I couldn't because he wanted to marry me for the wrong reason."

"What did he say?"

"Nothing."

She blinked. Twice. "He seriously said nothing?"

"Well, he might have said something, but I was too busy running to my car to hear what it was." I took a quick gulp of my drink. "Anyway, I've been giving what Jared said last week some thought. Maybe he's right. Maybe I should return to San Francisco and finish my animation degree. Maybe everything that has happened is for the best. One day Jared will fall in love with someone who will become Logan's mother, and I'll have nothing. I'll just be the aunt who's no longer needed. The question is, do I want to be the aunt who has no future other than working full-time in a diner?" At least if I moved back to San Francisco, I could begin my life over again. It was the only way my heart would have a chance to heal. I couldn't do that if I was still around Logan. It had been hard before, knowing how much he resembled his father. Things would only get worse when he was older and looked even more like Jared. Then I'd have a far tougher time moving on.

"So you won't be here for Logan while the guys are on tour?" Hailey asked.

"It depends on how long they'll be gone. I'm going to check if I can transfer back into the program for the fall. That will give me plenty of time to get Logan used to the idea of staying with his grandparents while Jared is touring." My voice cracked at the idea of losing them both, but it was for the best. For everyone concerned.

I finished my second drink and ordered a third. Since I didn't want to talk about it anymore, I switched topics. At one point Hailey went to the bathroom. I guarded the table and the drinks. No one was getting past me. No way.

She returned and we laughed, we joked, we shared. Not once did she mention Jared, Nolan, or the band, and for that I was grateful.

I continued drinking. I couldn't remember the last time I'd drunk alcohol. Probably not since I'd been living in San Francisco and partied with my friends or boyfriend. Back when the only thing I had to worry about were my assignments and exams. Back before I had to worry about being a good parent.

A glass of clear liquid was deposited in front of me, along with a plate of cheesy potato wedges. "What's this?" I asked, pointing to the glass.

"Water," the hot waiter said. "Your friend ordered them when she was on her way to the bathroom."

Hailey flashed me a smile and grabbed a wedge.

"Oh. Okay." The water did look good. I drank some of it and bit into a potato. "Mmm, these are good." Hailey sampled a bite and nodded in agreement.

"Callie?" a male voice said not far from where I was sitting.

I peered up at the blurry image of a familiar-looking guy. His voice was equally familiar. My brain sluggishly catalogued where I knew him from.

"Chris?" My ex-boyfriend.

37

JARED

From my hiding spot in the tree house, I peered through the crack between the wooden floorboards. Mom was searching for Dad, Logan, and me. All of us were well hidden around the backyard, although you couldn't miss Logan's giggles coming from behind the bush. If I could hear them, then Mom certainly could. Plus it wasn't like Mom didn't already know the prime hiding spots. Kristen, Callie, and I had played hide-and-seek all the time here when we were kids.

My phone pinged. A grin appeared on Mom's face as she looked up at the tree house. Busted. Since she already knew where I was, I checked who had texted me. Disappointment kicked me in the groin. It was Nolan, not Callie.

Nolan: Call me ASAP. It's about Callie.

I speed-dialed his number. "What about Callie?" Fortunately Logan was too far away to hear me. I didn't want him wondering what was going on. "I thought she was with Hailey."

"You wanna explain why you proposed to her?"

"Why do you think I did it, dumbass? I love her and want to

spend the rest of my life with her." Too bad she hadn't felt the same way about me.

"Does she know you love her? Or does she believe you just want to marry her to make everyone's life easier when it comes to Logan?"

I cringed. That was exactly what she believed. "I don't know why she would think that," I said.

"Did you tell her that you love her?"

I cringed again. "Not in so many words. I figured the proposal and engagement ring would show her how much I love her." Okay, maybe I was the dumbass.

"No, it has to be bigger than that."

"Says the guy who has no experience when it comes to proposing to his girlfriend. Unless there's something you haven't told me yet."

"That's because I don't feel the urge to rush out and propose to Hailey before she and I are ready. What in Christ's name possessed you to even do that?"

Logan's giggles grew louder as Mom drew closer to his hiding spot. I really needed to teach him the finer points of the game.

"I dunno. I thought it would be a good way to show her how I feel about her. I didn't expect us to rush out and get married this afternoon."

"Couldn't you have simply told her you love her and one day you could see being married to her?"

I chuckled. "It sounds so simple when you put it that way. . . . Look, I realize now I didn't exactly go about this the right way. I get it, but how am I supposed to fix it?"

"Why don't you talk to her?"

"Because that went so well last time."

This time it was Nolan who chuckled. "Yes, I guess having the girl you just proposed to run away isn't considered normal."

"You know about that?" Even my parents didn't know about

it. I had asked Mom to get Callie outside, alone, when she arrived. I hadn't explained why.

"Hailey might have mentioned it. If I were you, I'd get your ass down to where the girls are. From the sounds of it, Callie's headed for a massive hangover tomorrow."

"Where are they?"

He told me where to find them.

"I can't. I have Logan. I can't take him there." He would never be allowed into the lounge.

"Can he stay with your parents tonight?"

"I'm not sure if he's ready for that. I don't think he's ever slept anywhere besides his bedroom since Callie became his mom." Other than when he was hospitalized for meningitis, but he had been too young to remember that.

"Your call, but if I were you, I'd start dreaming up something big to let her know how you feel about her. And you should do it before we leave on the promo blitz." Which began in a week. After that, life would get crazy and who knew when she and I would have a chance to work it all out.

Nolan was right—I had to fix this mess sooner rather than later.

"Gotcha!" Mom called out from below, and hugged her grandson.

I was stuck. We had to leave now so that I could get Logan home for bedtime, but I couldn't leave Callie where she was. I needed to make sure she got home safely, preferably before she drank too much more. She didn't have to work at the diner tomorrow, but that didn't mean Logan would let her sleep in.

"We have to go home, Logan. Get your stuff." I signed the first sentence.

"Why are you learning to sign to him when he can hear?" Mom asked.

"He can't always hear. It helps if you can sign to him when he can't hear you. Like at bedtime. And Callie wants him to be familiar with ASL because he is deaf. He's part of the deaf community and she doesn't want to take that from him, but he's also part of the hearing community." It was one of those difficult decisions she'd had to make on her own about my son. Everyone had their own opinion on the topic. I didn't know how she'd done it, but she had. She'd wanted to do what was right for Logan, and that was part of the reason I loved her. But Logan wasn't the only reason I loved her. Why couldn't she see that?

While Mom helped Logan gather everything he'd brought with him, I texted Sharon, asking her if she could watch him for a short time. Fortunately she didn't ask why I required her help, although there would be no avoiding the truth once I brought Callie home.

After putting Logan to bed, I drove to the lounge where Callie and Hailey had gone. Raindrops started spitting on my car.

I entered the lounge and scanned the area for the two women. Callie had changed outfits since I'd last seen her. Now she was wearing my favorite dress. The green sundress emphasized her copper hair and hugged her curves. The thin straps revealed her soft, creamy shoulders and the spattering of freckles that I thought were adorable on her—another thing I appreciated about her over Tiffany. Tiffany would've freaked if she found a freckle on her body.

Clearly I wasn't the only man taken with Callie's skin. The douchebag she was with decided to become intimately familiar with it and rested his hand on her shoulder.

She leaned away from him. I couldn't tell from where I stood if that was because she wanted to remove his hand from her body or if she was swaying due to the amount of alcohol she'd consumed.

Her head turned in my direction and her eyes widened. "Jared, what are you doing here?" The words held a slight slur.

"I came to get you." I nodded at Hailey. She smiled softly back, the relief that I was here unmistakable.

The guy stared at me. I recognized his expression: I looked familiar to him but he couldn't place me. "Who are you? Her taxi service?" His fingers returned to her shoulder. If he didn't remove them from her soon, I would rip them off for him.

Callie shifted in her seat. "Chris, this is Jared." She gestured at me. "He's the guy who proposed to me because he needs a nanny for his son and figured this was an easier way to get one. Jared, Chris is the guy who dumped me because my sister died and left me your son to care for, and Chris didn't want . . ." She cocked her head to the side. "How did you put it? To be responsible for another man's castoffs."

The asshole's mouth dropped open. I had no idea which of Callie's assessments of the situation shocked him more. Either way, neither of us looked too hot in her view.

Hailey jumped up from her seat. "Okay, Callie, I think it's time to get you home."

Callie pouted. "What if I don't wanna go home yet?"

"You don't have to leave." Chris eyed her like he was remembering one of their fuck sessions and had every intention of reexperiencing it with her . . . tonight. "I can drive you home."

"I don't think that's a good idea," I told her, doing everything in my power not to slam my fist in his face. I could guarantee that if I hit him, the media would pick up news of the assault. I couldn't take that risk.

He glared at me. "Why don't you run along? Callie and I have a lot of catching up to do. And from the sound of it, she's not interested in being your live-in nanny with benefits."

I shoved his shoulder hard. He stumbled back a step. "It's not like that," I snapped.

"Okay. I'm ready to go home now." Callie stood up and

gestured to the waiter for their tab. "Is Logan still with your parents?"

"No, Sharon's looking after him."

"Why are you here, Jared?" she asked, voice low and soft.

"Because I care about you." I craved to tell her that I loved her, but she was drunk. The first time she would hear those three words from me would be when she was sober.

With my arm around her waist, I started to guide her to the exit. Hailey followed us.

"Wait," the douchebag said. He handed her his business card. "Call me."

I fisted my free hand but didn't say anything. Not that I had to. As soon as we were outside, she crumpled up the card and tossed it in a trash can.

"I wanna walk," she suddenly said. She broke free from me and stumbled in the opposite direction from where she lived. Then she paused and looked up at the sky. The rain had picked up since I'd arrived at the lounge and was coming down hard. She smiled and raised her hands as if in offering.

"Will you be okay with her?" Hailey asked.

"I'll be fine. As long as she doesn't trip and land on her face."

"That's not what I meant."

"I know." I placed my hand on Callie's lower back. "C'mon, let's get you to bed."

"I'm not sleeping with you, Jared." She wobbled on her feet. "This nanny with benefits is closed for business. Yep."

"Exactly how much did she have to drink?" I asked Hailey.

"About four or five martinis."

"How many did you have?"

"One. I'm driving." She gave Callie a hug and told her she would talk to her soon, then ran to her car. Callie and I walked in that direction to make sure Hailey was okay. The rain still didn't bother Callie. Her wet dress clung to her curves, revealing the outlines of her bra and pebbled nipples. My dick hardened in appreciation.

We walked in silence. I had no idea what she was thinking, and I was too nervous to ask. We needed to talk, but this wasn't the way I wanted to have the conversation, with Callie soaked and drunk, and with me sporting a hard-on.

Ahead of us, a large puddle stretched across the sidewalk. Before I could grab her hand and lead her around it, she ran the short distance and launched herself into the water.

Her sandaled feet landed in the puddle with a big splash. Dirty water splattered her bare legs, but she didn't care. She laughed like she used to when we were younger, back when she loved splashing around in puddles.

A smile tugged at my mouth. I couldn't help it. I'd forgotten how adorable she was when she jumped in puddles. Sober or drunk, she didn't care what other people thought. She splashed around in them because it made her feel good. Made her feel alive. It was something Tiffany and Alexis never would have done.

"I love this puddle," she said, and splashed again. "You don't know what you're missing out on, Jared."

And that was where she was wrong. I knew exactly what I was missing out on. This goddess of a creature in front of me was what I was missing out on. But I couldn't tell her that now, not this way. So I did the only thing I could—I joined her.

I jumped into the water, splashing both her legs and mine. She laughed harder. If anyone drove by and saw us, they would've thought we were completely insane. And maybe I was insane. I certainly had been crazy for taking forever to see what was in front of me.

I reached for her and, against my better instincts, pulled her against me. She stopped laughing and vulnerability instantly filled her eyes. I wasn't thinking—one second I was staring at those gorgeous blue eyes, and the next I was kissing her.

The kiss started out tender but quickly escalated and became more heated. Callie's breasts pushed against my chest and I had the sudden urge to find a quiet place and make love to her in the rain. To let the water wash away the pain and heartbreak she had dealt with for so long.

A voice deep inside me, where logic ruled over emotion, reminded me this was wrong. Callie wasn't in any state for me to make love to her. I needed to get her home to bed. I needed to temporarily give her space, to let her sober up.

"Sing to me," she said.

"Can we start walking again?"

She considered it for a second and nodded.

"Twinkle, twinkle little star," I began as we walked.

She giggled. "No, I want you to sing one of the band's songs like you did the other night."

"Any particular song?"

She picked "This Last Time," a song I'd written after my breakup with Alexis. It was about love and betrayal. Not exactly the song I wanted to sing to the woman I loved. I just hoped she hadn't picked it because it reminded her of everything our relationship had been about in the beginning.

I finished the song and she smiled. She didn't say anything else the rest of the way. I wasn't sure if that was a good thing or not.

My phone pinged.

Nolan: Remar called. Meeting with band tomorrow at 10 am.

Me: On a Saturday?

Ronald Remar was the president of the label. I could count the number of times on one hand that the band had met with him. We weren't a big enough act yet to warrant his attention, so what the hell did he want to talk to us about?

We entered the apartment, Callie doing her best to be quiet. Sharon didn't say anything beyond wishing us goodnight before leaving. If she was disappointed in Callie for getting drunk, she didn't show it.

Callie was wet and muddy, but she wasn't in any condition to shower alone, and I wasn't about to go there with her while she was drunk.

I escorted her to her bedroom. She sat down hard on the bed, almost slipping off the edge. Water dripped from her hair and clothes onto the bedding.

"I'll be right back." I returned with a glass of water and a couple of aspirins, both of which she swallowed without complaint. I also returned with a towel and wet washcloth.

I gently cleaned the mud from her body and dried her skin. Usually she slept naked with me, but after what her ex had insinuated about our relationship, I searched her room for clothing that resembled pajamas. I found a pair of cotton shorts and matching T-shirt, both covered with hearts and bunnies. I didn't want to leave her in her wet dress, but I also didn't want Logan to wander in tomorrow morning and find her naked.

This wasn't the first time I had stripped Callie of her clothes, but she had been fully coherent those other times. This time it felt awkward, like I was violating her privacy. It wouldn't have been so bad if she was fully awake, but she could barely keep her eyes open.

It didn't help that I missed caressing her soft skin, exploring her body, tasting her. I couldn't get enough of Callie, but none of that mattered just then. The only thing that was important was to get her changed and let her sleep off the booze.

After removing her dress and bra—my gaze on her shoulder so as to avoid looking at her breasts—I helped her with the T-shirt. I laid her on the bed and eased her cotton shorts up her legs. I was used to taking clothes off women, which was a lot easier than putting them on.

Callie murmured in her sleep, but I couldn't make out what she said. I wasn't ready to leave yet, so I watched her for a minute or two. Part of me longed to crawl under the covers and hold her to warm her up. To let her know that I loved her and that I meant everything I had said when I told her I wanted to marry her. But not because of Logan. I wanted to be with her and only her.

I leaned down and kissed her temple. She murmured again, the words still unintelligible. Even in her inebriated state, Callie looked at peace.

I kissed her again. "I love you," I whispered against her temple. "I think I've been in love with you for quite some time now, but I was too much of an idiot to realize it until recently."

She made a soft sound and shifted in her sleep.

When I returned a minute later with a bowl from the kitchen in case she was sick during the night, she hadn't moved. I placed it on the floor near her bed, so she couldn't miss it if she woke up. I set a glass of ice water next to the bottle of aspirin on her bedside table and sat in the armchair.

I spent more than an hour in her room brainstorming ways to show her how much she meant to me. Some were clichés. Others were outlandish. But when I finally snuck out of the apartment sometime after midnight, there was no question about what I had to do to prove to her that she was mine.

Now I had to hope the guys in the band would go for it.

38

CALLIE

"**M**ommy!" Logan's voice somehow broke through the hammering in my head. Whoever had invented alcohol needed to be shot. Although I guessed that by this time he was long since dead.

But that was a moot point. The sentiment was still the same.

I opened my eyes. The Sahara had more moisture than my eyes did after last night. Taking a chance that the pounding in my head wouldn't worsen if I sat up, I gave it a try. My stomach made its presence known, but it promised to behave if I promised never to drink another drop of alcohol again.

That could definitely be arranged.

Logan signed that he wanted to watch TV. Since I wasn't up for any Mother of the Year awards, especially after last night, I could get away with him watching it all day while I recovered from my hangover.

A glass of water sat on my bedside table, along with a bottle of aspirin. I was positive I wouldn't have left them there last night before falling asleep. A vague memory slipped in of Jared walking me home from the lounge, of jumping in the puddle, of Jared helping me change into my pajamas. I glanced down. Yep, it hadn't been a dream.

Unlike before, Jared hadn't stayed with me during the night. He'd helped me into bed and left. But what did I expect? He had proposed yesterday and I'd rejected him.

But it wasn't like he'd meant it. He'd done it for the wrong reasons. He would quickly get over it. I wouldn't be so lucky.

I swallowed a couple of aspirins and downed the entire glass of water. Another memory paid a visit—Jared giving me a couple of tablets and a glass of water before helping me out of my dress. He'd saved me from an even worse hangover. He could have just dumped me on the bed, still in my wet clothes, and left, but he hadn't. He might not love me, but he did care about me. Wasn't that enough? I could have married him and remained Logan's mother. I would've been able to legally adopt him, and no matter what happened between Jared and me, Logan would still be my son. Wasn't that all I desired, to still be Logan's mother?

Two months before, the answer would've been yes. Logan and I were family, the only family each of us had left. I had convinced myself that I wasn't lonely. That I was perfectly happy being a single mom. Until a few weeks ago, I'd had everything I thought I wanted.

How wrong I had been.

After Logan had finished his breakfast, I left him to watch TV while I showered. Then I emailed a couple of friends in San Francisco I hadn't spoken to in two years. At first, after I moved away, we had emailed regularly, but over time it became harder and harder to keep it up. They were all going one way with their lives, and I had gone in a different direction once I became Logan's legal guardian.

I spent the rest of the morning studying my artwork and the pictures in Logan's books. Jared's suggestion that I should illustrate kids' books sneaked into my head. But what did I know about it? It was one thing to create pictures to hang on the wall. It was something entirely different to illustrate books.

That wasn't the only thing to sneak into my head and refuse to leave. I kept thinking about Jared. About his tongue exploring mine. About his warm, callused hands skimming across my skin. About how it felt when he filled me up, both physically and emotionally.

By lunchtime, my head and my body were on speaking terms with me again. My heart, not so much. I took Logan to the local playground, but everywhere we went, I kept thinking about Jared. It wasn't just because Logan looked so much like him. It was the things he said that reminded me of Jared. It was the places we had visited with Jared.

I dribbled the soccer ball along the recently mowed grass, almost expecting Jared to steal it from me, like he had when we'd played a week earlier. The air even had the same sweet scent of freshly cut grass as back then. I had been edging closer to the goal, which Logan was guarding. Just as I was about to get into position to kick the ball, Jared had hooked his arms around me and swung me away from it. Laughing, I'd squirmed, attempting to escape, and lost my balance. That had resulted in Jared losing his balance. We'd landed on the ground with me straddling him.

I smiled at the memory. It was one of many that I had of Jared, with and without Logan. Not all involved making out or sex. I missed our talks after we'd put Logan to bed. Jared always knew how to make me smile and laugh. And even though he could have spent his evenings drinking with his bandmates or seducing groupies, he didn't. He'd spent them with me— making me fall even further in love with him.

After I settled Logan into bed, I began work on a new digital design. I'd been mulling around ideas inspired by Celtic symbols for the past three days, but I hadn't come up with the right idea. Until now. The memory of my puddle-jumping fun last night was exactly what I required.

I spent hours getting lost in the flow of the lines, the colors, the look of joy and wonder on the little girl's face as she jumped in the puddle. Her fiery copper hair fluttered gently in the breeze. Surrounding her, the woods were a peaceful green, the dirt ground fresh and alive from the recent rain. Water. Fire. Earth. Wind. She was the inner circle of the fivefold Celtic design. She was the element required to bring balance to the picture.

Noticing how late it was, I checked my phone. The smile on my face waned. Other than a text to see if I was okay after last night's drinking binge, I hadn't heard from Jared. He finally sent me another text several hours later, telling me the band would be busy for the next few days.

And after that, who knew what would happen. Pushing Limits was about to begin their promo blitz for the upcoming album, and following that came the tour.

Jared was the center ring to my own personal fivefold design and I was losing him, but there was nothing I could do about it. My parents' marriage had been solid because they'd been in love. I craved what they had, which meant I couldn't settle for anything less.

Jared cared for me, no doubt about that—but it wasn't enough.

39

JARED

After leaving Callie's apartment, I returned to mine, grabbed my notebook and pencil, and spent the next four hours scribbling down words and phrases, imagery, and symbolism. This was my usual process when writing a song. I would brainstorm, sometimes for days, trying to figure out exactly what I longed to say.

Except this time I didn't have days.

When the words stalled, I played around with the melody on my guitar. I kept going until my eyes were bleary and I had yawned for the third time in the past two minutes.

Sunlight streamed through the bedroom window. I had an hour and a half before the meeting with Remar, but before that, I wanted to discuss my idea for winning Callie over with Nolan. He'd been right when he'd said it had to be something big. Tired and clichéd wouldn't win me any awards beyond the not-so-coveted participation ribbon.

I closed my eyes, only intending to rest them for a minute or two. It wasn't until my phone pinged several times and then played Nolan's song that I opened them. I glanced at the alarm clock, and it was like I'd been poked with a burning branding iron. I flew out of bed. Fuck!

The meeting was scheduled to start in five minutes. *Fuck. Fuck. Fuckity fuck.*

Nolan had left several texts. The basic gist was "Where the hell are you?" and "You better be walking your fucking ass through the door any second now." I assumed he wasn't talking about my apartment door.

> Me: Traffic bad. Will get there as soon as I can.

Now I just had to hope I didn't actually get stuck in traffic.

Despite what I had told Nolan, traffic wasn't an issue. I showed up only fifteen minutes late. And yes, I was lucky no cops were trying to get in their month-end ticket quota.

> Me: I'm in the parking lot.

I hit Send, then raced to the main entrance.

The elevator wasn't interested in doing me any favors. I arrived at the reception area five minutes later. The receptionist, a young woman with a short skirt and long legs, led me to the conference room. "Would you like some coffee?"

Fuck yeah! "Yes, please." In my sleep-deprived state, my voice sounded like I was aiming to seduce her out of her panties. I cleared my throat. "Black, no sugar. Thanks."

"My pleasure." She blushed and quickly darted away.

I opened the conference room door and entered. Everyone else was already here, even Mason, who was notorious for being late. Remar sat at the head of the long polished table, like he was royalty and we were just the peasants. Everything about this room made me think of royalty—the expensive decor, the exotic plants, the framed platinum albums on the walls from the kings and queens of music. The only thing missing was his throne. But maybe he just saved that for his office.

"Glad you could find time in your busy schedule to join us, Mr. Leigh," Remar said, raising a gray eyebrow. Everything about this man smelled of money, including his black suit from a designer whose name I probably couldn't even pronounce. "Given this meeting was partly due to your dalliances that resulted in a child, I would've thought you could have at least been here on time."

"Sorry. Bad traffic."

Nolan shrugged an apology to me. He hadn't known about this any more than I had. We'd assumed the meeting was about the upcoming promo blitz. I should've known better. Our publicist and the marketing department were taking care of those details. Remar wouldn't have called us in for something as mundane as that.

I sat in the empty seat next to Mason. Even our drummer looked less than thrilled to be here. Remar had that effect on people. He could drain the life from you faster than a vampire could drain blood from his victim. But the man was a freaking genius when it came to running the highly successful record label, so everyone put up with it.

"Now that everyone is here," Remar said, "I wanted to share the great news with you."

Under any other circumstance, Mason would've made some sort of wisecrack. This time he wisely held back. His fingers twitched on his lap, eager to do a drum roll for Remar's announcement. He wisely held back on that too. Remar wouldn't have found it as amusing as the rest of us.

Remar's gaze scraped over each of us, gauging our reaction. "Endless Motion will be commencing the extensive US leg of their world tour April fifteenth. They've asked for Pushing Limits to open for them."

No. Fucking. Way. Endless Motion was currently the

biggest-selling rock band in the world. Opening for them was huge. Our audiences were similar, if not the same, which was a definite bonus. There was nothing worse than opening for a band whose music was such an opposite fit that fans actually threw objects, including chairs, at the stage while you performed.

"Depending on how things go, you could also be joining them for a large portion of their world tour. The early reviews of your album have been very positive, and we want to hit hard while we can. We've lined up Björn Ekstrom to direct the video for your first single. We were extremely lucky to get him on such short notice. He heard 'Tangled' and was so impressed, he insisted on directing the music video."

The conference room door opened and the receptionist entered with what I hoped was my coffee in an oversized mug. At this point, I definitely needed it. Behind her, a skinny bald-headed man with a red goatee stepped into the room. He could've easily been one of the band (minus the skinny part), with his military boots, jeans, and T-shirt. A complete contrast to Remar.

"And there he is," Remar said, beaming at the man. "We were just talking about you, Björn."

We all stood and shook hands with the director.

"Ah, so you're Jared Leigh," Björn said, after I introduced myself. "Cute kid."

"Thanks." I could feel the weight of Remar's glare directed at me. With the way he was reacting to the news that I was a father, you'd have thought Logan's existence meant the band was facing a dramatic drop in sales compared to the first album.

Once the introductions were over, we sat at the table again, with Björn at the opposite end to Remar. His gaze appraisingly swept over us. "This video will be hot, no?" he asked in a watered-down Swedish accent.

Mason and I exchanged looks. His lips stretched into a wide grin, his teeth super-white against his brown skin. You didn't have to spend a year on the road with Mason to know what he was thinking. He was that transparent when it came to women and sex.

"If we get to make out with a lot of hot babes," he said, "then I wholeheartedly agree with you. This video will be epically hot."

Aaron and I burst out laughing. "Isn't it usually the lead singer who gets to score with the hot babes in videos?" Aaron pointed out. Kirk chuckled.

"No way, man," Mason said. "Nolan already has a girlfriend. And I'm sure Hailey would rip his balls off if he even thought about kissing a girl in the video."

"So let me guess," Kirk said, smirking. "You're volunteering to take his place for the sake of preserving his balls?"

"Damn straight. And I'm sure both he and Hailey will thank me extensively for making that level of sacrifice."

The only person not laughing at that was Remar. Even Björn was chuckling. I was surprised steam wasn't whistling out of Remar's ears. The guy seriously needed to lighten up.

"Let me make this clear," Remar said. "The song has the potential to catapult to number one. This video will help it get there. So if Björn wants to shoot Nolan having sex with a woman who isn't his girlfriend, then he and his girlfriend will have to suck it up."

If what he was implying hadn't been so serious, I would've laughed at him saying "suck it up." The phrase seemed foreign coming from his mouth.

Nolan blanched, and I couldn't say I blamed him. The label had already tried to manipulate who he was romantically linked with. He didn't need them doing that again. He and Hailey had been through enough as it was.

"Does this mean we won't be playing unplugged for the

song's debut?" I held my breath. Part of my plan to win Callie's heart involved us playing unplugged on the entertainment show as originally planned.

"No," Remar said, "'Tangled' will still debut unplugged. It was what the show requested."

I needed to send whoever had made that request a bottle of wine. An expensive bottle of wine.

We spent the next ten minutes listening to Björn's vision for the video. Fortunately for Nolan's sake, his nuts weren't at risk. While "Tangled" might've been a love song, the video wouldn't be too explicit.

"It's not like you haven't kissed a girl in a video before," Mason pointed out after Björn mentioned that while there would be no sex, Nolan was expected to kiss the actress.

Nolan folded his arms across his chest. "I was single back then. I don't want to give girls the idea they can kiss me whenever they want."

None of us bothered to claim it wouldn't happen. We had long since learned that some fans confused make-believe with reality when it came to music videos. If Nolan kissed a girl in the video who wasn't his girlfriend, then some females would consider it open season when it came to kissing him.

All gazes shifted to me.

"Sorry, not happening. Nolan's the lead singer. He's the one who gets to be in the spotlight, not me." Well, most of the time. There were a few exceptions, but this wasn't one of them.

Mason opened his mouth, probably to tell Nolan and me that we were pussies. Or to once again offer his services as Nolan's replacement. We never found out which one.

"As I've already pointed out," Remar said to Nolan, "you don't have a choice. But if you want, I can always have Björn rethink the video and we'll go back to the option of making it super-sexy. Remember, over fifty percent of your demographics is female, and they buy into the sex fantasy. And that's exactly what we're selling."

And here I thought we were selling music. Silly me.

Nolan grumbled about this all being fucked up, but that was pretty much the end of it. He agreed to be the sacrificial lamb.

"All right," Björn said. "Filming starts tomorrow morning. At six a.m."

40

CALLIE

Wednesday morning, I watched Logan from the kitchen window as he and his grandfather played tag in the backyard. Even though I couldn't physically hear him through the closed window, I could hear him giggling in my head.

"He'll be fine," his grandmother said, next to me. "Enjoy yourself and let us worry about him. We're looking forward to getting to know our grandson better."

Guilt rushed me like a semi without brakes on the downward stretch of a mountainous road. "I'm sorry I never told you about him. I just…"

She redirected her smile at me. "I know. You were looking out for him and doing what your sister asked. No one blames you for that, Callie.… Jared knows he's here, right?"

I shook my head. "I haven't heard from him in almost a week." Not since he brought me home last Friday, after I got drunk, then sent me the one text four hours later.

"That's strange. He hasn't talked to Logan at all during that time?"

Not that I knew of, unless he spoke to him while I was at work. I hadn't thought to ask Sharon or Logan if that was the case.

"It's okay," I said. "He's been busy because of the entertainment show tomorrow night." Which Hailey had told me about two hours ago. The band had flown out to New York City this morning, and she'd invited me over to watch it with her. I'd told her I was driving to San Francisco for an appointment the next day and would miss the show.

I walked outside and said goodbye to Logan. "I'll see you in two days. Okay? And maybe if you're good, Grandma will let you watch Daddy on TV tomorrow night."

Logan's eyes widened. "Daddy's on TV?"

"Pushing Limits will be performing on TV live. You'll get to see Daddy play the guitar. Won't that be cool?"

Logan nodded enthusiastically. "Daddy is cool."

I laughed. I couldn't help it. "You're right. He's very cool."

I kissed him on the cheek and hugged him. This was the first time in three years I'd be away from him. Not surprisingly, the thought of that made my stomach do backflips, ending with an unimpressive belly flop.

———————

THE NEXT MORNING, I DROVE FROM THE HOTEL I'D STAYED AT last night to my old university. My appointment with the counselor wasn't for another forty minutes, so I wasted time wandering around, visiting all the familiar places.

At first I figured that I'd be plagued with memories of happier times, back when I was dating Chris. He had meant the world to me then. Funny how small that world had really been. The world with Jared was more vast and fulfilling. Chris had held me back. Jared encouraged me to not confine myself to what was sitting in front of me, which was exactly what I'd been doing with the graphic design degree. I had been doing it because I believed that was what I had to do. I'd never considered what was really important to me. I'd never considered what I loved.

Instead of memories about Chris, I revisited memories of Jared. Even on the campus grounds, where he had never been before, Jared was everywhere. A group of guys kicking a soccer ball around the green space reminded me of those times he and I had played soccer with Logan. A tree reminded me of the tree house in his parents' backyard, and that in turn reminded me of Jared's smile and his heart-melting dimples. A couple walking together nudged a memory, fuzzy until now, of Jared walking me home from the lounge and singing to me. God, I loved his voice. The voice the world was deprived of because Jared hated being in the limelight. Which was kind of ironic when you considered he was the guitarist of a rock band. A rock band that I was positive would be hitting the big-time with their new album.

No way could he avoid the limelight after that.

I walked past a guy sitting on a bench with his girlfriend. He was playing guitar, his eyes closed as he poured out his emotions through the music. He opened his eyes, and the love she clearly felt for him was mirrored back. God, what I would have done to have Jared look at me that way.

He has looked at you that way before, a voice in the back of my head whispered. You were just too blind to see it.

I rolled my eyes. I hadn't been blind. I had just been honest with myself.

I ignored the laughter echoing in my head. Then realized it wasn't coming from the voice in my head. It came from the girl with her boyfriend. And that made me miss Jared even more.

I hurried away from them.

After my appointment with the counselor, I drove to my friend's apartment. She was having a party tonight but had invited me to come over as soon as my appointment was finished. She had graduated with a degree in illustration and was prepared for my billion questions.

I knocked on her door. The familiar strains of a Pushing Limits song leaked from the apartment, and I sighed. I wasn't going to get a break, was I? I had hoped that maybe, just maybe, I could go for an hour without thinking about Jared. The universe was currently laughing at me and having a great time at my expense.

The door opened. "Callie," Samantha shrieked. She threw her arms around me and hugged me like old times. Before I could say anything, she grabbed my arm and dragged me inside. Her place was exactly as I remembered. The tables were cheap and scratched. The couch had faded to a weird shade that was best described as rusty orange, but it was more comfortable than it looked. At least it had been when I used to go to school here.

At least fifteen people were crammed in the small living room. Some were sitting on the chairs or couch. Others were sitting on the floor. The rest were standing. The only thing they had in common was the large flat-screen TV. All eyes were directed at it.

"You're just in time for the new Pushing Limits song," Samantha said.

Oh, joy.

"Oh my God, it's them," a girl on the floor squeaked as the five guys entered the TV studio and waved to the off-camera audience. "They're so hot and fuckable."

"And you know this from experience?" the guy sitting next to her said with a smirk.

She shoved his arm hard. "Of course not. But you can tell they are, and I've read the fan pages."

Ah, yes, the fan pages Hailey had warned me about. She told me not to believe anything written on them when it came to the guys and sex. Most of it was made up. I didn't ask her how she knew . . . or why she'd been reading the comments to begin with.

"I want to have Nolan's babies," a girl with a blond pixie cut said. "They'd be soooo adorable."

"He has a girlfriend," I blurted out. "And I've heard they're very much in love." *You're welcome, Hailey.*

"That's too bad."

"Jared's still available," another girl said. "He's super-hot too."

"But he's got a child," pixie cut said, "and is banging the nanny."

Nice. Now I was Logan's nanny. The girl must've been friends with my ex. And yes, I did remember his comment from the night I got drunk.

"Shhh." The volume was cranked up, preventing further conversation.

The guys walked to the black leather sectional in the middle of the TV studio. The interviewer, a guy in his late twenties sitting in a matching armchair, had each guy introduce himself to the frenzied screams of the audience. And based on the volume of the screams, the audience consisted mostly of females. Young, horny females.

If the fans' reaction was any indication, the band's new album would zoom up the charts.

"How does it feel to be preparing for the release of your new album, Tangled?"

"Exciting," Mason said. "We can't wait to get back to touring again and rock the crowds."

The guys nodded in agreement while I waited with bated breath to see what topics would have a green light and which were off-limits. My guess was that the do-not-even-go-there list included what had happened to Nolan and his family six years ago, and the recent news that Jared had a deaf four-year-old son. The interview should be about the music and not about their personal lives.

The interviewer asked a few more questions, which for the most part Nolan answered, but not without the other guys joking around and adding their own comments. The easy friendship they had in real life came through when they were interviewed together, with Kirk usually the more serious, quiet one and Mason the rambunctious joker of the group.

"You guys recently finished shooting the first video from the album, but instead of premiering it today, you're singing the title track from your new album unplugged. Correct?" The interviewer looked at the guys for confirmation.

"Actually," Jared said—and my chest squeezed so hard at his deep voice, I could barely breathe—"we're going to play a song that isn't on the album."

"Oh, so it's from the first album?"

"No," Nolan explained, "Jared recently wrote it for someone special. The record label hasn't even heard it." My heart rate picked up at his words.

For some reason, Nolan's news excited the interviewer. "Even better."

The guys walked to their instruments of choice—all except for Jared. Instead of grabbing his guitar, he stepped up to the microphone.

I stood staring at the screen as Jared started singing.

When we were young
You were always by my side
My friend, my confidante, my sun on a cold winter day
I never felt like I needed to hide away

Not a single person in the room made a sound, all mesmerized by the emotion of the song and his incredible voice.

Thought I could handle the rain

Fell for a rose all beauty, all wrong
Didn't realize until much too late
Only one real treasure was my fate
This is my song for you
The truth of my heart for you
When the clouds obscure the view
This is my song for you
You're the only one for me
That's the way it's always been
You're the air and the stars and the moon
This is my song for you

I didn't know how the record label would react to the band's sudden change in plans, especially when the song wasn't even on the upcoming album and it wasn't the new single. But in that moment, while Jared sang about his love for a woman he had known forever and who had inspired him to be everything that he was, about his love for the woman who had sacrificed everything for those she loved, I didn't care what the label thought.

I watched the stars from our old tree house
But it wasn't the same without you by my side
The sunrise at dawn is what we can have
Just give me a chance to prove we're strong
Just give me a chance to prove my love

Tears threatened to obscure my vision, and I blinked them away. He loved me? He hadn't proposed because he figured it was the right thing to do for Logan. He had proposed because he wished to spend the rest of his life with me because he loved me—Logan or no Logan.

And I had rejected him.

I sank onto the corner of the couch, my legs uninterested in holding me up anymore.

But why hadn't he told me this before? Why write a song and perform it live on TV when Nolan was supposed to be singing their debut single off the album?

I knew the answer. Because what better way to prove his love for me than doing the one thing he'd rather not do—be the one at center stage?

41

JARED

The final strains of the song faded and the entire studio broke into overwhelming cheers and applause. I had no idea how it sounded on TV, but here it was deafening.

We returned to the couch. I had done it, but was it enough to convince Callie that I loved her? I wanted to phone her, to find out if she felt the same way about me. I wanted to phone Hailey and hear about Callie's reaction when she heard the song. But I couldn't do either of those. We still had the interview to finish.

"Wow, Jared," the host said. "I had no idea of the depths of your talent. Do you sing any songs on the new album this time?"

"No, this was a one-time deal. I'm more comfortable being behind the guitar than the mic." Disappointed murmurs rose from the audience.

After the stunt I'd just pulled, I wasn't sure if I was still a member of the band. Yes, Nolan and I had created it, but I had no idea the extent of the label's rights when it came to us.

The guys had been on board with my idea to sing the song tonight. When I pointed out it could get us in trouble with the label, Mason had simply said, "Let's go fuck the hell out of the song and prove to your girl you're not some dumbass loser who fucked up proposing to her." But while the guys might've been supportive, Remar's reaction was anyone's guess.

Did I care what his reaction would be? Not really. There were some things that were just that much more important to me.

The interview continued for another fifteen minutes. The original plan for the show was to perform two songs—"Tangled" and one of our hits from our debut album. So not to entirely piss Remar off, and because we were here to promote the new album and not so I could declare my love to Callie on national TV, we performed "Tangled." Which was met with the same level of excitement as my song for Callie.

Afterward, we hung around to sign autographs for a select group of fans who had won the VIP prize. By the time we escaped the station, I had been congratulated, pawed, hugged, and kissed. The last one had taken me by surprise, when a fan unexpectedly kissed me on the lips. Out of respect for Hailey, Nolan no longer allowed fans or groupies to kiss him at all. Not even a peck on the cheek was permitted. I would have to be more vigilant in the future and adopt the same policy.

Assuming Callie felt the same way about me that I did about her.

Our newly appointed bodyguard, who looked like he could have once served in the Marines, escorted us from the building. He wasn't alone. Several members of the station's security detail were also at our side. And just as well that they were. Our appearance at the station had been well publicized. Fans were waiting for us outside, held back by a red rope on both sides of the building's entrance.

While I was sure Brian, our bodyguard, would've preferred that we hightailed it straight to our waiting limo, the band stayed back to thank fans and sign more autographs. Mason let the girls kiss him, but the rest of us kept a safe distance from the more ardent fans.

The fans were the ones who bought the albums and downloaded the singles. If it hadn't been for them, we wouldn't be where we were now. So as much as Brian wanted to get us away from the craziness, it wasn't going to happen just yet.

The downside was it delayed me contacting Hailey.

Eventually Brian successfully herded us into the vehicle, with threats that we would miss our next interview if we didn't get our asses in gear. With my heart pounding in my chest, I sent Hailey a text.

> Me: Did she see it?

> Hailey: Sorry. I don't know. She didn't come over. She said she needed to get away for a few days and dropped Logan off at your parents' house.

Shit. I dropped my head back against the limo seat. Now what?

"Sorry, man," Nolan said a moment later. Hailey must've told him what had happened. "I thought for sure your plan would work."

"Me too."

"Don't give up yet. Hailey's positive Callie loves you, and I believe it, too. Any idiot can see that she does."

I shrugged. "Doesn't matter if she has no idea how I feel about her."

"Do you know where she might've gone?"

"Not a clue." There was one way to find out.

Me: Thinking about you. How are you?

Before I began demanding to know where she went, I wanted to at least know if she was talking to me. While I waited for her to respond, I phoned Mom.

She picked up on the second ring. "That was beautiful," she said. The noise in the limo dropped to a quiet murmur.

"What was beautiful?"

"The song. You wrote it for Callie, right?"

"Yes. She didn't by any chance watch it with you, did she?"

"No, she wasn't here. But when she dropped Logan off here yesterday, she told him you were going to be on the show. Do you want to talk to him?"

Before I could answer, she passed him the phone.

"Daddy? You were inside the TV."

I chuckled. "Yes, I was on TV. So you watched?"

"Yes, but I didn't hear you sing," he said matter-of-factly.

"Is Mommy there?"

"No. I miss you."

"I miss you too." And I did. How I'd survive touring without seeing him every day was a mystery. I'd spoken to him every day, when he was with Sharon, but that wasn't the same. "But I'll see you tomorrow. Do you know where Mommy is?"

"Somewhere magical."

I considered that for a second. Something about his words sounded familiar. "Is that exactly what she said? Or did she say it was somewhere they bring magic to the screen?"

"Yes" was all he said before handing the phone back to my mom.

"Do you know where she went?" I asked.

"She didn't say. She only said that she needed a few days to think things through. Did you two have a fight?"

Good question. I had no idea. As far as I knew we hadn't.

But when it came to figuring out women, I was clueless most of the time.

After getting off the phone with my mom, I checked to see if Callie had responded to my text. She hadn't. And she still hadn't responded by the time we boarded the plane and the flight attendant announced we had to turn off our phones.

42

CALLIE

My phone pinged from my purse as I drove down the interstate from San Francisco. My heart thump-thump-thumped a fast pace the entire way, and it had nothing to do with my family dying on this same road.

My heart was racing me back to L.A. solely because of Jared.

According to their announcement three hours ago, they were opening for Endless Motion's extensive U.S. tour in just over a week. If I didn't tell him soon how I felt, it would be a while before I got to tell him face-to-face.

The sun was low in the sky when I arrived at Jared's building. I parked my car, jogged to the front door, and buzzed his apartment. No one answered. Hailey had told me the band was flying home today from New York City. I hadn't thought to ask her when exactly they were due to land.

There was no guarantee he was even coming straight home, but it was a chance I had to take.

I sat on a nearby bench. The area was well lit and the neighborhood decent, but that didn't stop my body from switching to fight-and-flight mode at the sounds sneaking up on me—every rustle of the leaves, every footstep, every car engine that hummed past.

I reached into my purse. My hand brushed against the velvet box next to my phone.

Jared had texted, Thinking about you. How are you? His words warmed me on the inside, a marshmallow in hot chocolate. By now he would know that I hadn't stuck around to see him perform. He didn't know I had actually watched him—and realized how big an idiot I'd been for not seeing it sooner. He loved me like I loved him. That thought, along with a gallon of coffee, had kept me awake on the long drive home.

I removed the velvet box from my purse and opened it. The silver glinted in the glow from the streetlight behind me. I fingered the fine chain and the silver guitar pick, a symbol of my love for him.

After the band left the TV station, I told Samantha something had come up and I needed to return to L.A. I left her place and drove straight to a nearby mall, where I bought the pendant for Jared.

I pulled my hoodie around me, and thanked God we lived in L.A. and not Chicago. Otherwise I would've been sitting there in a winter coat and still shivering.

A car door slammed shut. I glanced down the path to the road. A cab was parked there, but that wasn't what caused the air in my lungs to pause.

The dark-haired, dimpled guitarist standing there with his gaze locked on me was the one to blame for the way my lungs had temporarily ceased functioning. He walked slowly toward me, as if certain I was nothing more than an illusion that might vanish in a puff of smoke if he moved any faster.

During the drive from San Francisco, I'd been busy deciding what I would say to him. Some attempts had been witty. Others had been the equivalent of three Kleenex boxes of emotional. There was even the version where I got down on my knee and proposed to him.

But after spending hours practicing exactly what I longed to say, I forgot it all the moment he stepped out of the cab. Instead, I closed the distance between us, gazed at his heart-melting eyes for a second, then crashed my lips against his . . . and let everything I had to tell him be revealed through the kiss.

His arms wrapped around my waist and he pulled me closer. All those practiced words in my head meant nothing, truth be told. But this—the kiss, the way he held me, the love between us—was perfect. Any doubts I might have had? Evaporated.

Eventually I shifted away and rested my forehead against his. Our breaths came fast and hard, and it took a minute for me to slow my breathing enough for me to utter the words I did need to say. His arms remained around my waist. My hands stayed threaded in his hair.

"Jared Michael Leigh." My voice was soft but certain. "Will you marry me?"

A slow, sexy smile curled onto his full, kissable lips. "Yes, I would love to."

And then we were kissing again . . . until kissing wasn't enough.

How we made it upstairs with all our clothes still on was beyond me, but they certainly didn't stay on once we entered his apartment. Somewhere between the front door and his bed, my shoes, socks, jeans, and T-shirt had left my body. His clothes had suffered the same fate.

Jared kissed me again, but this time the kisses were gentle and unassuming. Which was funny given our state of undress. If anything, you'd have thought we'd be ravishing each other at this point.

That's not to say I didn't want to. Eventually.

I smiled against his lips. "I love you, Jared. I've been in love with you since I was seventeen. I don't think I ever stopped loving you." I brushed my mouth against his and continued along his jaw. The stubble there teased the tip of my tongue as I forged a path to below his ear. I gently nipped him. His answering moan stirred me. And the mere thought of what he could do to my body almost had me coming in my panties.

"God, I've missed you," he murmured against my ear. "And I'm not saying that because I'm about to make love to you."

Good thing I was holding on to him, because my knees gave way at his words. "I've missed you too. More than you can possibly imagine."

He tenderly traced his fingers down my arm. "Are we going to be okay? I mean, when I go on tour?" Hope filled his beautiful brown eyes.

I smiled and caressed his face, the movement soft but reassuring. "I know we will. I'm not saying it'll be easy, but as long as we trust each other, we'll be fine."

That gave him the measure of reassurance he needed, and with it came the kisses I craved. His mouth devoured mine, his tongue creating havoc against my own. He guided me back onto the bed. His fiery gaze consumed me, igniting the heat between my legs.

He cupped his hand against my cheek, then with a feathery touch he trailed his fingers down my neck and between my breasts, still encased in the white lace bra. Every cell in my body buzzed with energy, with desire.

His fingers continued down my stomach, pausing a moment so he could kiss the skin above my belly button. His teeth lightly grazed the place he'd kissed. I moaned at the delicious sensation.

His hands resumed their journey to my panties. Less than a minute later, I was free of them. They disappeared over the edge of his bed. Jared's boxer briefs joined them soon after.

Underwear—it was so overrated.

Jared's fingers went on to create magic between my legs. They slipped between my folds and teased the supercharged core, pushing me closer to the edge with each brush of my clit.

I wrapped my fingers around his thick length and almost moaned. Yes, I had missed this too. I swirled my thumb against the tip, spreading the small amount of pre-cum around the velvety surface.

Jared sucked in a sharp breath, then reached for a foil package from the top drawer of his nightstand. He ripped it open and rolled the condom down his length. But instead of positioning himself between my legs, he beckoned me off the bed.

He propped the pillows against the headboard and leaned back against them, then indicated for me to straddle his legs. Before I could position myself over him, he placed his hand against my waist to stop me, and reached around to undo my bra. It too joined the party on the floor.

Jared leaned forward and took my nipple into his sweet, warm mouth. His wet tongue circled it, then he sucked it to a stiff peak. Holy mother of all things amazing, this man is certainly talented with his tongue.

I moaned, the sound not even beginning to convey how I felt.

Once he was finished, a satisfied grin on his face, I slowly lowered myself until he was seated deep inside me. I didn't know where I started and where he ended—and I didn't care. All I cared about was how my soft heat hugged his hard length.

Jared rested his hand on my hips, guiding my movements and the pace. Like the kiss earlier, it was slow and sweet, as was the build-up to the peak. He kept his eyes, now dark with want, focused on me, adding to the intensity of the moment. He'd told me he wanted to make love to me, and that was exactly what he was doing.

But then came a point where I didn't crave slow anymore. I wanted to race to the peak, and I wanted to do it with Jared.

Sensing the new urgency, he increased the pace, my hips rising and plunging. It didn't take much, and before I knew it, my entire body shuddered as euphoria swept through me. Jared joined me soon after.

As the realization of what we had just done filled me with a new level of love, I cuddled up to Jared.

"When I'm on the road," Jared said, caressing my lower back, "if you start having doubts about us, I want you to remember how I just made love to you." He brushed his lips against mine in a sweet and satisfying kiss.

I kissed him back, then smiled softly. "I know we're going to make it."

And I did. Jared possessed so much love. I had seen it with his friends, his bandmates, and his family, and I had seen it with Logan. I had no doubts whatsoever that we could make this work. No, it wouldn't be easy, but if I ever doubted myself and what we had, he was right—I just had to remember tonight.

"By the way," I said, "I loved the song." I kissed him gently. "That, and how you sang it even though you don't like being the front man. That's how I know how much you love me." I lightly stroked his chest above his heart. "I don't suppose you're going to make me a copy so that whenever I miss you, I can listen to it?"

"I think that can be arranged. I'm not sure how the label will feel about it, though." He winced. "They had no clue we were going to do that."

I gave him another feather-light kiss. "It doesn't matter what they believe. You didn't write the song for them. You wrote it for the woman who believes you're the most wonderful man around. I never want you to forget that. Besides, I'm positive they'll love the song. How could they not?"

I didn't let him answer; I just kissed him long and hard. Which progressed into another round of lovemaking, only this time it was rougher and more heated—and equally satisfying, both inside and out.

"Where did you go after you left Logan at my parents'?" he asked, once we had recovered. He shifted so we were facing each other and caressed my arm.

"To San Francisco. To the university. I wanted to talk to them about transferring to the illustration department. I realized you were right. I don't want to give up on being an animator, and being a graphic designer just isn't doing it for me. I love creating pictures for kids, and I wanted to talk to a friend who had graduated from that program." Which I did before I left Samantha's party.

"So does this mean we're moving to San Francisco?" The look on his face told me he would willingly do it in a heartbeat, band be damned, if that was what I wanted.

I shook my head. "I can do it online. Although if Hailey gets accepted into the physical therapy program there, I suspect we'll be going to San Francisco anyway." I wouldn't complain if that happened. Hailey was my friend now.

He smirked. "You're probably right about that."

Talking about San Francisco suddenly reminded me of what I'd forgotten the moment I saw Jared by the cab. "I have something for you. Stay here." I climbed off the bed and walked into the hallway. I didn't bother to gather up our clothes, strewn along the beige carpet. I searched through my purse, found what I was looking for, and returned to his room.

He was still lying in bed when I climbed back under the covers, holding the velvet box with the pendant inside. I opened it and removed the silver guitar pick. On it was a small, engraved heart with the words "i'd pick you every time."

"Usually when a guy proposes, he gives a ring," I said, "but I wasn't sure what the protocol was when the person proposing is a woman. I want you to have this so that when you're touring, you'll always have a piece of me with you."

Jared took it from me and smiled. "Have I mentioned that I love you?"

"You might have mentioned it once or twice while we were making love."

"Good. Because I do." He reached under his pillow. "And I have something for you." He opened his fist, revealing the engagement ring in his palm. "Will you, Callie Louisa Talbert, be my wife?"

The smile on my face could have lit up the entire street during a power outage. "I will."

EPILOGUE
JARED

Six Months Later

I kneeled in front of Logan in the room that once had belonged to me but had since been converted into a guest room. My son was even more adorable than normal, dressed in his black tuxedo. "How do I look?" I asked.

Normally I wasn't one to dress up in a tux. None of the guys in the band were. Jeans and T-shirts were our outfit of choice. But even though Callie had told me she didn't care what I wore today, I had insisted the guys and Logan dress up.

"You look great, Daddy. What about me?"

My heart pounding from excitement, not nerves, I straightened his tie. The tuxes were black, the vests and ties bronze. "You look great too. I think Mommy's going to approve of us both."

Logan grinned, revealing the new gap where he was missing his bottom front tooth. The tooth fairy had paid him a visit last night. It was one of those milestones I'd been lucky enough to witness. Fortunately, Endless Motion had scheduled a week off due to some other obligations. It wasn't enough time for a honeymoon, but it allowed enough time for Callie and me to have one night together alone, and for me to spend more time with her and Logan as a family. Callie's adoption of Logan had gone through last week. In the eyes of the court, she was now his legal mother.

I stood up. "And you have the rings?" I asked Nolan, my best man.

He chuckled. "Yep, just like I did the last five times you asked me. Don't worry, everything is gonna be okay."

"Unless she's changed her mind," Mason not-so-helpfully added.

I scowled at him.

His hands went up in surrender. "Hey, just kidding. I might not be the settling-down type, but I can tell that what you and Callie have is solid."

Logan looked at him with a hopeful expression, waiting for Mason to accidentally curse. With us away on tour, his swear jar was woefully empty.

The bedroom door opened and my father poked his head into the room. "We're ready."

"So Callie hasn't bailed yet?" Mason said.

Kirk cuffed him on the back of his head.

"What the fuck did you do that for?" he said to Kirk, then without missing a beat, he turned to Logan. "I'll give you the money after the ceremony."

Logan grinned back at him. While the bulky drummer might've intimidated some people, Logan just saw him as Uncle Mason, the man who was bankrolling Logan's future aspirations.

My father took his grandson's hand and led him to my parents' bedroom, where the women were getting ready. I hadn't seen Callie since arriving home last night from touring. She'd stayed at her apartment. Logan and I had stayed with my parents. It took everything I had not to enter the room and kiss her, to throw away the tradition of not seeing the bride before the wedding.

Okay, knowing what the three women with Callie would've done to me might have also had something to do with my decision not to break tradition.

The guys and I headed outside to the gazebo. Two simple yet rustic flower arrangements—created from sticks, white gauze, and fall flowers—were attached to either side of the entrance. A couple dozen folding seats, covered in white fabric, faced the wooden structure. Family and friends currently occupied the chairs.

Standing in front of the gazebo entrance was a friend of Aaron's in a gray tuxedo. Richard was an ordained minister and had been happy to take part in the ceremony. I shook hands with him and took my place.

A movement at the kitchen door grabbed my attention. I looked over, as did everyone seated in the chairs. Because of Logan's cochlear implant, we had forgone the usual music. We wanted him to hear the ceremony.

Kristen stepped from the house first, holding Emma's hand and a small bouquet of red, orange, and yellow flowers. Her strapless dress was light green and simple, revealing her six-month baby bump. Emma, though, was the one who stole the show in her lacy white dress. A bronze sash had been tied around her waist, and she was carrying a small basket of flower petals.

As they drew closer, Emma let go of her mother's hand and toddled over to me. "Hi." She offered me the basket.

Soft laughter rippled through the audience. I bent down and hugged her. "You're the most beautiful flower girl I know."

She grinned.

Kristen stepped up to the gazebo, and Emma lifted her arms above her head. "Up."

"Go see Daddy," Kristen said, pointing to Craig, who was in

the front row. Emma joined him, and he hoisted her onto his lap.

Next was Hailey. She stepped out the back door, and a quick glance at Nolan told me he wouldn't be noticing any other woman, including Callie, for the rest of the day. I wouldn't be surprised if by the end of the year he and Hailey were planning for their wedding.

Hailey's dress, with two thin straps at the shoulders, ended above her knees and was a darker shade of green than Kristen's outfit. Black lace accented the body-skimming dress, and Hailey's long brown hair lay loose around her shoulders. It was easy to understand why Nolan was mesmerized.

Logan was with her and was carrying the ring-bearer's pillow Mom had sewn for the wedding. Hailey spoke to him, he nodded, and they walked hand in hand down the makeshift aisle. Hailey's gaze was locked on Nolan the entire time.

Whispering came from behind me. Aaron and Kirk were no doubt betting on when Hailey and Nolan would be getting hitched. I was sure there would be no complaints from Mason if it was sooner rather than later . . . assuming Nolan went for the stripper bachelor party I had vetoed when Mason had suggested it for me. I had a feeling Nolan would also veto the idea. No other woman would do for him, like no other woman could outshine Callie for me—but try explaining that to Mason.

Logan stepped up to the gazebo, and I hugged him. "You did great," I said, signing it at the same time. I wasn't the only one who had been learning sign language. My bandmates had also been learning it while we toured.

"You rock," Mason signed to Logan.

Logan grinned and signed the same thing back to him. My heart warmed at how supportive the guys in the band were of me being a father. I didn't know what I would have done without them.

Logan joined my mother and Sharon in the front row. Mom helped him onto his seat between the two women.

Callie appeared in the doorway . . . and I became suddenly weak in the knees—in a good way. Hailey was beautiful, but nothing compared to the goddess standing at the back door with my father. Her copper hair, shining in the late afternoon sun, like flames in a campfire, flowed in loose waves over her shoulders and down her back. Lace covered her sleeveless white dress, which skimmed the gorgeous curves I'd been craving while touring. The skirt gently flared below the hips and formed a short train behind her.

Her gaze caught mine and I imagined her inhaling sharply. Although I could tell she wanted to race down the aisle and jump into my arms, she walked slowly toward me. My lungs paused, forgetting to suck in air, but who required air anyway? Touching, holding, kissing Callie was so much more important.

After what felt like way too long, Callie stepped up to me. "Hey," she said, her voice soft. How I kept from pulling her head to mine and devouring her with kisses was beyond me. I hadn't seen her for two months, when she and Logan had joined the band for a few days on the road. Other than that, we had talked daily via Skype. But Skype was nothing like having the real flesh-and-blood woman in your arms. Every inch of me had ached to have her back there again while we were away.

"Hi," I said, finding my voice.

Callie handed her flowers to Hailey and I took her hands in mine.

"Jared Leigh and Callie Talbert, we're gathered here today in front of friends and family to celebrate the joining of your lives. In both good times and in bad, you'll stand by each other, stronger together in body and soul." Richard continued talking, but his words were a blur, my attention solely on Callie.

Nolan handed him the wedding rings.

"Jared and Callie have written their own vows." He passed me Callie's ring.

I slipped it onto her finger and gazed into her beautiful blue eyes, shiny with love. "Callie Louisa Talbert, until you stepped back into my life, I had no idea what love really meant. I loved my family, but I had never loved with the level of passion that I feel for you. You're my everything. My sun on a rainy day. The warmth in my soul. The inspiration behind every breath I take. I couldn't imagine spending a day without you by my side. And while I know it's not always easy with the distance often between us, you're constantly in my thoughts and in my heart. You're the one who keeps me grounded and keeps me real and helps me be the man I strive to be. You're the one I want to grow old with. Do you take me to be your husband?" I slid the ring into place.

She smiled. "I do." Her gaze dropped to my lips for a heartbeat, and I had to battle the urge to kiss her. She took the other ring and slipped it onto the end of my finger. "Jared Michael Leigh, we've been friends for as long as I can remember. First I loved you as a friend, and then I fell in love with you. My love for you has grown brighter with each passing day as I've watched you become the amazing, talented man that you are. You've encouraged me to follow my dreams like you followed your own. You helped me believe in myself like I believe in you. I see the love you have for your music and for your bandmates and for your family, and it makes me love you so much more. There's no one else I could imagine growing old with. Do you take me as your wife?" She slipped the ring fully onto my finger.

"You better believe I do!" I said with a grin.

"By the power vested in me," Richard announced, "I pronounce you husband and wife. You may kiss the bride."

I didn't need to be told twice. I cupped Callie's cheek and

stroked my thumb against the face I'd missed so much. Yes, Skype had nothing on this.

I kissed her, the gentle touching of lips that conveyed everything I felt in that simple gesture. Everyone cheered. My bandmates patted me on the back, and Nolan gave me a wry grin. At least he had been able to make love to Hailey last night; I still had to wait a few more hours before Callie was all mine.

I threaded my fingers with hers—and decided to screw the waiting. I had no intention of it being that long before I snuck a few stolen moments with my wife.

And God, did it feel fucking great thinking of her that way. She was my wife, my lover, my best friend, the mother of my son. We had experienced both the highs and the lows, and I wasn't naive to believe that we'd seen the end of them. Touring posed challenges that people with regular jobs never faced, but I was confident we would make it. If things became too much, for the sake of my son and my marriage, I would gladly walk away from the band if I had to. Because as much as I loved the music, I loved Callie and Logan that much more.

As soon as the last person had offered congratulations, I led Callie to the tree house. She grinned, the playful woman that I loved so much making it clear she was all for my plan. She slipped off her shoes, bunched up the hem of her dress, and climbed the ladder. I followed right behind, helping her up.

Once inside and away from prying eyes, my mouth was on hers again. This time there were no gentle kisses. No promises of what was to come. There was just this moment, this connection, this love.

"I missed you," I said in her ear once I stopped kissing her long enough to speak, my voice rough.

"I missed you too, but I wouldn't change anything." She laid her hand on my chest, where the silver guitar pick rested. "I'd pick you every time. No matter what."

"And I'd pick you every time too." I removed my jacket, vest, and tie. Then I unbuttoned my shirt.

"As much as I want to make love to you," she whispered, "I'm not sure this is the place to do it, with everyone in your parents' backyard waiting for us." She laughed, and the sweet sound almost did me in. Damn, I had missed that laugh. "Though that doesn't mean I'll complain if you remove your shirt."

And to prove it, she helped me with the rest of the buttons. Her gaze remained locked on mine as she slowly slipped each button through its hole. Her fingers caressed my exposed skin. An electrical charge hummed through my body at her touch. I was close to ripping off the offending piece of clothing just so I could feel her skin against mine that much sooner.

Once the final button was free, Callie slid the shirt off my shoulders, pushed it down my arms . . . and froze.

She let go of the shirt, and her fingers skimmed over the tattoo I'd gotten two weeks ago. The tattoo I'd managed to keep a secret . . . until now.

"It's beautiful." She caressed the brush painting a streak of green and red along my arm. Each represented the favorite color of the two most important people in my life.

A symbol of my love for both my son and my wife.

A symbol that what we had together was permanent.

Callie was my forever.

MASON

"I pronounce you husband and wife," the minister announced as the warm fall breeze tugged at the guests sitting in front of the wooden gazebo. "You may now kiss the bride."

He didn't have to tell Jared twice. Our guitarist's lips were on his new bride's mouth faster than you could say *I want to fuck you now*. And, knowing Jared, that was exactly what he wanted to do. Pushing Limits had been on the road for almost five months—the halfway mark of our tour opening for Endless Motion. With the exception of a brief visit two months earlier, when Callie and their son, Logan, joined us for a few days, Jared hadn't fucked her in a long time. How he was surviving without a bad case of blue balls at this point was beyond me. I couldn't do it.

Nor did I want to. That was one of the perks of being a rock star. I could get laid anytime I wanted. I glanced around at the prospects, sitting on the chairs in front of the gazebo. Unfortunately, the wedding was small, with about forty guests, and only a handful of the females were of legal age. When you factored in how many were here without a boyfriend, that left me with one. Not a bad option either. Pretty, petite, with long black hair. Beckie something. Callie used to work with her at the diner. I'd have gone after her . . . if Kirk, the band's bassist, hadn't already been eyeing her.

So that left me with no possibilities. Which sucked. Royally.

The happy couple unglued their lips from each other and stepped down from the gazebo, where I was standing with the other groomsmen (aka the members of the band). Nolan pulled his girlfriend, Hailey, into his arms and whispered in her ear. She laughed. If I'd been a betting man, I would've wagered those two would be married (or at least engaged) before the band hit the studio again.

At the thought of making a bet, a shiver of excitement rolled through me. I pushed it away. I couldn't go there. Not again. I had destroyed enough people with my past gambling addiction. I was a new man. A new man who wouldn't fall down that rabbit hole again.

My fingers unconsciously went to the tattoo on the inside of my forearm, hidden under the tuxedo: live. love. laugh. The words were in Sanskrit. Along with several other tattoos, I'd gotten that one after my stint in rehab several years ago. This one in particular was a motto I lived by every day. I lived and loved the music. And the laugh? Well . . .

I checked out the guests now milling around the backyard and spotted Tomas York, the drummer for the up-and-coming band Burning Wire. Perfect. I grabbed a napkin from the refreshment table. Jared and Callie's names were printed in gold on the cream-colored paper.

"Do you have a pen I can borrow for a second?" I asked the woman next to me. Her short white hair was puffy, and she had one of those oversized purses that contained everything, including two kitchen sinks.

She smiled at me. "I'm sure I have one." She rummaged through her purse and removed a silver pen. Classy. I took it and wrote, *Hi, sexy. Your place or mine?* I handed the pen back to her, thanked her, then made my way over to Tomas.

"Hey, a woman asked me to give you this." I passed him the folded napkin.

He opened it and read the note. His head shot up and his gaze searched the backyard for the note writer. I pressed my lips together to keep from laughing out loud.

His gaze settled on Beckie, who was talking to Jared and Callie. Tomas's eyes lit up with a lusting fire.

"Not her. *Her.*" I pointed at the woman who had loaned me the pen.

The heat in his gaze was instantly extinguished, and his eyes practically popped out of his head. I snickered. I couldn't help it.

Tomas's head swiveled to me and he backhanded my chest. "You jackass."

I burst out laughing. "I might be a jackass, but it was so worth it."

"For you, maybe." He looked back at Beckie. "Do you know who she is?"

I shrugged. "Not really. She used to work with Callie." I didn't get a chance to warn him that Kirk might also be interested in her. Just then Kirk sidled up to her, and it was clear she was as taken by the tall, brooding former hockey player as he was with her. At least one of us would get lucky tonight. Which left Aaron and me as the only members of Pushing Limits who weren't going to have a good fuck tonight.

Maybe he, Tomas, and I should bail on the wedding sooner rather than later and find some action elsewhere, I thought.

And I would have if Jared hadn't been like a brother to me. All the guys in the band were like brothers to me. The only brothers I had left. No, bailing so I could get laid wasn't the cool thing to do.

At the tug on my pant leg, I glanced down to find Logan

grinning up at me. Inwardly I chuckled, knowing what the hopeful expression was for. He was hoping that I'd cuss and contribute to his swear-word jar. With the band touring, he had no one to donate regularly to it. I was the only idiot unable to control his cussing around the four-year-old. It was an expensive habit when the fine was a dollar per swear word. "Hey, buddy."

"Play with me, Uncle Mason." He signed the words as he spoke. Logan was deaf, but his cochlear implant allowed him to hear most things, except for music.

I crouched to his level. "Logan, do you remember my friend Tomas? He's almost as good a drummer as I am." And with the way Tomas's band was gaining interest within the L.A. music scene, maybe one day they would be opening for us.

Tomas laughed. "Actually, I'm even better than your uncle Mason."

He wished.

"You must be good," Logan said, "because Uncle Mason is amazing." What he meant was that the vibrations through the floor when I played the drums were amazing. Logan didn't listen to the band's music. He felt it.

"What do you want to play?" I asked him.

"Soccer!" That came as no big surprise.

"Do you think your parents would mind?" I surveyed the backyard. It wasn't huge, and while under normal circumstances it would be fine, it might be problematic with so many guests milling around.

Logan tugged on my hand. "It's all good."

I somehow doubted it. I scanned the area for Jared and Callie, but they were nowhere to be found. Guess they couldn't wait until nighttime to consummate their marriage. Lucky bastard!

"Why don't we ask your grandmother first, okay?" I signed

the "okay" part. "Don't go anywhere," I told Tomas. "You might get drafted into the soccer match."

"Wouldn't miss it for anything," said Tomas, who was part Latino and had grown up on soccer.

Logan and I walked over to his grandmother, who was talking to a few guests near the refreshment table. "That should be fine," she said after I asked her if it would be okay to play a low-key game of soccer. "Just keep the ball away from the patio, okay?" She said the last part to Logan, then to me she added, "And no kicking it hard. We don't need it landing in the food."

Good point.

Logan hurried off to fetch his soccer ball. A few minutes later he and I, along with the other guys in the band, Tomas, and the cute little flower girl, were kicking the ball around the lawn. Callie cheered on her boys, who were on my team, while Hailey cheered on Nolan, who played on the opposite team.

Kirk kicked the ball past Aaron. I high-fived him. "Nice job, puck boy."

"As if you ever doubted me, drummer boy," he said with a smirk.

The phone in my tux pant pocket vibrated. I ignored it. Everyone who was likely to contact me was at the wedding. So unless my estranged family had a sudden longing to forgive me for the mess I'd dragged them into a few years ago—and I doubted they had forgiven me, or ever would—the call could wait.

Logan kicked the ball past Tomas, who was positioned between two wedding chairs, and scored a goal. He squealed with joy and jumped up and down, as did Emma, the toddler flower girl, who was on the other team. We laughed at their reaction.

Jared hugged Logan, and the memory of my father once doing the same when I was a kid almost knocked me onto my ass. I'd just scored a touchdown. It had been only flag football, but that hadn't mattered to him. He had been proud of me no matter what—as long as I gave it my all and worked hard. As long as I played fair.

I shoved away the memory and the hurt. I had moved on. No point picking at the scab again.

I high-fived Logan and got back into position. Callie tossed the ball onto the grass and the game resumed. Giggling, Emma kicked the ball, and kept on kicking it away from the rigged-up soccer field. Logan chased after her. The rest of us stood on the grass, laughing.

A bird tweeted near the tree house. Without warning, Emma stopped and pointed at where the sound had come from, the soccer game instantly forgotten. Not expecting her to stop, Logan almost careened into her. He took advantage of the distraction and kicked the ball away from her. Emma didn't even notice.

He dribbled the ball back to us but then forgot about the no-kicking rule. And wow, could the kid ever kick. The ball smacked the ass of the woman who had loaned me her pen. We all cringed as it made impact, and cringed even more at the dirty ball print it left on her beige skirt.

She turned around to find Logan staring at her backside, his mouth a perfect circle. She smiled sweetly at him. "Your daddy said you were a good player. He just failed to mention how great a player you are." She ruffled his hair and returned her attention to the elderly couple she had been talking to.

The phone vibrated in my pocket again.

I don't know what compelled me to check it, but a weird feeling warned me it was important. I removed my phone and looked to see who had texted me.

Zack: Call me ASAP! Important.

The last I'd heard, Zack was off who-knew-where on a

mission for the navy. He'd been gone for a few weeks now.

Striding to the side of the house, away from the noise, I speed-dialed his number. He answered moments later.

"Hey, McCormick, what's so important?" I asked.

"You remember my sister, Nicole?"

"Yes." She was two years younger than Zack and me, and had gone to a different high school. Whenever I had hung out with Zack at his house, she was usually there. Most fifteen-year-old little sisters loved tormenting their older brother. Not so with Nicole. You could tell she worshipped him. He was her world—and it was obvious he adored her just as much, despite how much he teased her.

But who could blame him? She did make the best chocolate chip cookies known to man.

"I've been trying to contact her for the past two days. She isn't returning my texts or messages."

"You think something's happened to her?"

"Who knows? She's a workaholic. Sometimes she gets so focused on what's she doing, she ignores the rest of the world. But if something has happened to her . . ." He couldn't say the final words.

"You want me to go to her place and check if she's okay?"

"Yes, if you can."

"What's her address?"

He told me. "It's in Desert Springs. About two and a half hours southeast of L.A."

"I'm at a wedding, but I can leave in about an hour."

"Thanks, Dell. I owe you big."

Not as much as I owed him. If it hadn't been for Zack, I would have died the night my gambling addiction caused me to hit rock bottom and I attempted suicide.

I owed him my life . . . and so much more.

I NEED YOU TONIGHT is now available.

ABOUT THE AUTHOR

Born in Brighton England, Stina Lindenblatt has lived in a number of countries, including England, the US, Finland, and Canada. This would explain her mixed up accent. She has a kinesiology degree and a MSc in sports biological sciences.

In addition to writing fiction, she loves photography, and currently lives in Calgary, Canada, with her husband and three kids.

For news about her books, social media sites, and to sign up for her newsletter, check out her website at stinalindenblattau thor.com. Newsletter subscribers will receive a bonus short story.